While Hyenas Laugh

FBI agent, James Eberle studied the two elderly women seated in front of him. "You say you witnessed a kidnapping this morning? Have you reported it to the police?"

They both answered at once. "They pushed her in a car." "No, we came straight to you."

He held up a hand. "Please, one at a time. You realize the FBI cannot become involved unless requested by the local police."

"But—"

"I will listen to you, but first, may I have your names."

The short, plump one fluttered a hand towards her friend' "You tell him, Martha."

"Martha Beeson. This is Agatha Grimes. This morning we saw a young woman kidnapped. We came straight to you because we know the FBI handles kidnappings. We thought it would save time."

"Oh, yes," Agatha said softly. "Such a nice young woman. "You really must save her, young man." A shadow flitted across her face. "Her eyes were so frightened...."

Wings

While Hyenas Laugh

by

Judith R. Parker

A Wings ePress, Inc.

General Fiction Novel

Wings ePress, Inc.

Edited by: Dianne Hamilton
Copy Edited by: Marilyn Kapp
Senior Editor: Marilyn Kapp
Managing Editor: Dianne Hamilton
Executive Editor: Lorraine Stephens
Cover Artist: Crystal Laver

Wings ePress Books
http://www.wings-press.com

Copyright © 2002 by Judith R. Parker
ISBN 1-59088-922-3

Published In the United States Of America

May 2002

Wings ePress Inc.
403 Wallace Court
Richmond, KY 40475

Dedication

For Jo Dereske

and in memory of
Kip Leslie Winsett

"The lioness stalks,
The lion watches.
The Impala dies.
The lion feeds.
The jackal and the buzzard wait
While hyenas laugh."

Guy C. Archer

Acknowledgements

My special thanks to the following for their assistance:
Howard Thomas, Public Affairs Officer,
Whidbey Naval Air Station;
Dr. Elizabeth Wise;
and members of the American and Israeli governments
who prefer not to be identified.

Prologue

Beijing

Mah Ti-Ling paused a moment, straightening his shoulders and casting a quick glance down the corridor. Only a slight tic in his right eyelid betrayed his nervousness. His grip on the black briefcase tightened, whitening his knuckles, as he strode briskly down the hall. The two soldiers standing rigidly at attention barely looked at him. His face was well known in these corridors. Without a glance at the guards, he opened the door and stepped inside.

Six pairs of eyes focused on him as he closed the door and crossed the room. The intensity of their gaze burned like an electric current as he approached the teak table, placed the briefcase on the polished surface and took a seat.

"He agreed?" the man at the head of the table asked. He was old, his skin shriveled and yellowed, reminding Mah of a piece of ancient ivory. But the eyes, the eyes still burned with the fervor of youth.

Mah allowed the corners of his mouth to curve into the slightest of smiles as his gaze met that of the oldest member, a man Mah revered above all others for this man was a true hero of the revolution. He had made the Long March, had never

wavered or deviated from his beliefs as so many had done. Mah
swallowed and nodded. "He agreed."

There was a collective hiss of indrawn breath around the
table. The tension that filled the room like an unwelcome
presence eased. The Old Man clapped his hands. An orderly,
eyes subserviently lowered, appeared from a door hidden
behind red brocade drapes in the side wall, silently served rice
wine and, as silently, withdrew.

Raising his cup, the Old Man stood. "To the final
destruction of the Imperialist Americans and the faithless
Russian bear." He sipped and the others followed suit. He
raised his cup again. "When our plan succeeds, the revisionists,
the appeasers, the money-hungry would-be capitalists will be
known for the traitors they are." The old man's eyes glittered
with hatred. "We, the true patriots, will be returned to power"
He sipped again, glaring at each of the other men over the rim
of his cup.

Seated again, his stare locked on Mah Ti-Ling. "Report,
please."

Mah opened the briefcase and took out a folder and a
glasses case. Slipping a pair of gold-rimmed glasses on his high
bridged, narrow nose, he opened the file. "The Madman will
provide the services of the terrorist group led by Mustafa
Barenji to dispense the new strain of bacteria simultaneously
into the water supplies of major cities—New York,
Washington, San Francisco, Los Angeles, Seattle, and Boston
in the United States; and Moscow, Leningrad, Minsk, Kiev,
Odessa, Murmansk and Gorkiy in Russia. In exchange we have
pledged our support in his plans to destroy Israel and
consolidate the Middle East under his rule."

"Excellent. These terrorists will be in Tirana on the
thirteenth of next month to take delivery of the bacteria as
planned?"

The tic in Mah's right eye became more pronounced. He removed his glasses and began to polish them nervously. At his hesitancy, the tension again mounted in the room. A fine film of sweat dotted his upper lip. "No. He wants proof that this new bacteria is as virulent as we say it is. He demanded a test performed by his own agents."

"He doubts our word?" The words were barked and the Old Man's eyes blazed with anger. There was a general rustle of movement, barely audible growls of anger.

Mah's lips twitched. "No. He wanted to use that excuse to obtain a supply of the bacteria. He wanted the test performed in Israel."

"Absurd. Such a test would alert all the intelligence services, especially those in the west. It would threaten the whole strategy. Didn't you inform him that we have already introduced minute amounts into the United States? The man is insane." The speaker was an Old Guard general, noted for his quick temper.

Mah ignored him and looked at the Old Man. "He is indeed mad. However, I was able to convince him that we could not agree to a first strike against Israel. But, having made his conditions, he would not back down on the test." Mah paused and glanced around the table. "Rather than risk losing his cooperation and possibly the entire conspiracy, I had to agree to a test. I was finally able to get him to agree on a very limited test in Zimbabwe. Performed, of course, under our control and supervision."

It was the general again who spoke. "It is absurd that we must pander to the whims of that megalomaniac. We still have agents in the United States. Why must we depend on this animal?"

One of the other men spoke. "We can't risk compromising our few remaining sources. Fortunately, our few tests have been thought to be natural outbreaks of new strains of old bacteria. Since the trade unions and news media exposed our army's interest in foreign trade, many of our people have been ousted from the United States and the few that remain are being closely watched." His lips curled into a sneer. "Our Leader's plans to destroy the American economy by exporting thousands of immigrants not only isn't working but has Immigration and Customs on the alert. Our country must not be seen to be involved. The Americans are no longer as naive as they once were. It is in our best interests that the blame be laid at the feet of that madman. We will deal with him later."

"He must be eliminated."

"He will be when he has served his purpose," the Old Man said. Turning back to Mah, he asked, "Can we risk this trial?"

Mah shrugged and replaced his glasses. "A minor outbreak of some new disease in such a backward country would be of immediate interest only to the local health agencies. By the time outside agencies are called in ... " He paused and risked a small smile, "The western countries are notoriously slow to respond to third world problems. Witness the famines in Africa. The news media and the decadent entertainers aggrandize themselves with great public appeals and shows of concern but the peasants are still starving."

"The Americans sent their Marines into Somalia and Bosnia," the general snapped.

"Very true but only after how many had died? Besides, the new president has his hands full with his own problems." He smiled tightly. "Americans have a puerile obsession with the sexual activities of their leaders," he shrugged, "and the United States has no national interest in Zimbabwe. No. It would not be in their interest to become involved, at least, not in time."

One of the other men spoke up. "They could call on the United Nations."

"They could, but with the European economy in trouble, Europe will not be in a mood to worry about a few natives. Look at their reaction in Bosnia. Their own backyard and they did nothing. Sanctions, pah! A few pitiful growls. Paper tigers."

"But NATO—"

The Old Man spoke. "Enough. I have decided. We will make the delivery in Zimbabwe."

"Don't you think it would be better to concentrate solely on the United States? With the Soviet Union dissolved and the squabbling among the republics, Russia is no longer a threat."

The Old Man's eyes flashed. "If you have forgotten the Bear's power, I have not. How long do you think this flirting with capitalism will last? No, it was a ploy to deceive the west, to rebuild their might with the help of the west. Admittedly, it has gotten out of hand but already the people are regretting the changes forced on them. They will come back into the fold soon enough, if the United States is brought to its knees. Already, there are grumblings among the people, a longing for the old ways. This flirtation with capitalism will not last. A strong leader will emerge and the people will flock to him.

"Despite all the arms treaties, Russia and the breakaway republics still have an arsenal of nuclear weapons. More than the Americans even suspect. Never forget that! Weapons that still threaten us. No, Russia must be destroyed."

The general nodded in agreement. "I still say we should include the major Japanese cities."

"That will not be necessary. The Japanese military is forbidden to act outside their country and their economy is in dire straits. When they are no longer able to sell their products to the Americans, it will collapse completely. They will be too busy with their own internal problems to be an immediate threat. No, once we have destroyed the United States and Russia, we will have no rivals."

He stood, a benign smile on his lips. "Gentlemen, our plan cannot fail. In three months *we* will be back in power and a new China will rule the world."

One

Washington, DC

In his office at CIA headquarters, Elwood Mayhew finished reading the report for the third time. His head lifted and he stared out the window at the trees, their leaves just beginning to unfurl like tiny pale green banners. The beauty before him failed to register; there was no room for beauty in his mind.

His attention returned to the report and he read it again. His heart began to hammer as his mind raced. This was it. The perfect situation. The chance he'd been waiting for. He just had to plan on how best to take advantage of it.

The idea had come to him the first time he read the report. It had sprung almost full blown in his mind, an epiphany. As he read and reread the report, more pieces fell into place until the broad outlines of what could be, lay spread before him. Details could be worked out later. He only needed the will to act. The corners of his mouth quirked in an unpleasant smile.

Slowly he replaced the sheets in their folder, aligning the corners neatly, before he closed the cover. For several minutes he continued to stare down at the file. Abruptly, his decision made, he picked up the phone. "Tell the director I am on my way. I have to see him immediately."

Mayhew spoke to no one as he made his way to the office of Arthur Satterfield, Director of the CIA. No hint of the impatience, of the contempt bordering on hate, he felt for the man was visible as Mayhew strode through the glass enclosed security room into the outer office and stopped in front of the director's secretary. Without greeting him, Agnes Callaghan picked up the phone. She hung up, and without making eye contact, said, "He will see you in a few minutes."

Mayhew ignored her as he took a seat, aware that she was watching him out of the corner of her eye as she returned to her typing. *The desiccated old bitch.* His eyes remained fixed on the inner door, back rigidly straight, feet aligned, the file precisely centered on his lap, as he waited. Ten minutes later, the phone on her desk buzzed.

"Mr. Saterfield will see you now," she said, cradling the receiver.

Mayhew crossed the room and opened the door. His hearing was excellent and he didn't miss her barely audible, "arrogant bastard" as he closed the door behind him. Her time would come. Maybe sooner than she thought.

Arthur Satterfield, his back to the door, was pouring a cup of coffee from the pot on the credenza behind his desk. Mayhew felt the hate blaze up in him as he studied the man. Tall and slender, with the graceful movements of a trained athlete, from the back he could have passed for a man half his sixty years.

Satterfield turned. His lined and leathery face, the sagging skin, gave him the melancholy look of a hound dog. His wise, tired eyes under bushy white brows revealed his true age.

"Coffee?" His voice was a soft rumble betraying a trace of a western twang.

"Thank you, no." Mayhew tapped the folder impatiently.

Satterfield sat down. "To business then. I assume it is of some importance. Well, sit down, man."

Mayhew sat. His grip tightened on the file. "A little background first, sir. For several years we have had a local in Beijing on our payroll. Until the recent shakeup, he's not been in a position to provide much of interest. A few months ago this changed. His new duties, though minor in nature, have placed him in a position of occasionally overhearing information from a group of hard-liners that are too fanatical even for the current government."

"Who is this agent and what is his position?"

Mayhew's lips tightened. "I would rather not say, sir. He's in a very delicate and dangerous situation."

Satterfield's eyes glittered angrily then he shrugged. If it was important, he could find out. "Why is he on our payroll? How much are we paying him and how?"

"We aren't actually paying him in money. He has relatives in Los Angeles and San Francisco. He wants us to arrange to get him out of China. Until now, the information that he's been feeding us has not been worth the effort."

"So you've been stringing him along."

"I suppose you could say that, sir. At any rate, his new position makes it important to keep him there."

"And now he's come up with something good?" Satterfield nodded towards the folder in Mayhew's lap.

"You might say that..." he parted his lips in an attempt to smile, "or you might say bad." Mayhew handed the folder to Satterfield and stared fixedly out the window as the director opened the file and began to read.

At last Satterfield closed the folder and clasped his arthritic fingers on top of it. He spoke without looking up. "Is this person really in a position to overhear such a conversation?"

"Yes."

"I assume you think what he says here to be the truth and that this scheme is indeed in operation."

"Yes, sir."

"My God!"

"Yes, sir."

Mayhew's tone jerked Satterfield's head up. Satterfield was staring as if seeing him for the first time. There was something in the look, not contempt but something… Mayhew swallowed down the bile that rose in the back of his throat. Damn the man. He knew he was barely five-nine, with sloping shoulders, pipe stem arms and legs and a tight protruding melon belly, knew that he was physically unappealing. His head sat on a long, thin neck, the skin mottled and loose. Didn't he see himself in the mirror every morning? Bastards like Satterfield thought their fine physiques made them great men. Hah! He had more brains in his little finger than all these ex-jocks had in their whole bodies. Well, their time was coming. He had made the right decision.

Satterfield leaned forward. "Go ahead. What else?"

Mayhew pulled himself together, choking back his contempt and anger. "Well, sir, it is the name Barenji that is important. A few years ago, this man and his group were responsible for much of the terrorism in the Middle East and Europe. The man is a phantom, a legend. None of the clandestine services have been able to get a line on him. No picture exists. Only one person outside his loyal cadre of fanatics has ever seen him to identify him."

He paused, his hands tightening into fists. "That person is an ex-Mossad agent called the Zephyr. Another phantom, another legend. No one outside of Mossad knows his real name. Even inside, it seems only one or two know his real identity. He was one of their ablest agents. If anyone has a chance of stopping Barenji, it is Zephyr."

"Will Mossad lend him to us?"

Mayhew's shoulders twitched. "No. Rumor has it that he broke with them and refuses ever to work again."

"Then how does that help us?"

"It is believed that Zephyr is living here in the United States, in Seattle, under the name of R. Royer."

"Do you think he will help us?"

"Apparently he has developed a hatred of all clandestine services. He wants to be left alone." The thin lips curled into a sneer. "I think he will have to be persuaded."

"And you think you can persuade him?"

"Oh, yes. I think he can be persuaded."

Satterfield stared at him a moment, a frown marring his forehead then he glanced quickly away.

Mayhew watched him closely. He obviously didn't want to know what kind of persuasion Mayhew had in mind. Wanted to keep his skirts clean, the chicken-shit bastard.

At last Satterfield said, "Make your plans but don't take any action until I get back to you. I must talk to the President."

~ * ~

The man seated in the Oval Office was not everyone's idea of a president. Wilton Gossard had drifted to the political forefront after both political conventions had deteriorated into wild and messy accusations, counter accusations, character assassination, religious fanaticism and general vileness that had shocked the nation.

The almost unknown junior senator from the state of Washington had floated to the top of the political maelstrom, captured the nation's imagination, if not its heart, and been swept into office. A former naval officer, his premature gray hair, upright carriage, and rugged good looks combined with a

11

forthright and candid manner had carried him into the chair he now occupied.

Arthur Satterfield had once served as Gossard's executive officer and the two had soon developed a mutual respect. They had been firm friends for over thirty years. Gossard's face brightened as Satterfield entered the Oval Office.

"Well, Arthur, is this a friendly visit or do you plan to add to my problems?"

"Add to them, I'm afraid," Satterfield settled into a chair. "Read this." He tossed the file onto the desk and lit a cigarette.

Minutes later, Gossard lifted his eyes from the papers. "I take it you think this threat is real."

"Yes. We've heard rumors for some time that some of the old guard had been acting independently of the government, including research in biological warfare. Obviously they believe they have come up with some new, extremely virulent strain of bacteria. One that is impervious to our current water purification process."

"But could they really introduce it into our water supply?"

Satterfield grimaced. "What's to prevent them? A chain link fence? An occasional guard? Good Lord, Will, none of our reservoirs are protected against infiltration. What few security precautions taken are for the protection of citizens. To prevent accidents, drownings. We depend entirely on our water treatment plants."

"My God. This couldn't have come at a worse time. Just when we need to concentrate all our efforts on domestic problems. If news of this threat leaks out, it could be disastrous. It could bring all our recovery efforts to a standstill. We have to stop this Barenji." The President glanced back at the file. "A terrorist whom no one can identify."

"Apparently there is someone who can recognize him. An ex-Mossad agent named Royer now living in your neck of the woods."

Gossard looked up, his eyes narrowed. "But?"

"But according to Elwood Mayhew, who will be the agent in charge of this operation, Royer will have to be coerced into cooperating." The CIA director shifted in his chair. "That doesn't bother me. At least, it doesn't in this situation. Not when the safety and security of the country is at stake. It's Mayhew that bothers me."

"Then use someone else."

Satterfield shook his head. "Mayhew is the best and we need the best for this." He paused again. "Tell me, Will, why didn't you promote Mayhew to director? He was in line for the job."

It was Gossard's turn to hesitate. "To tell you the truth, I don't know. There was just something about him that didn't gel with me. Nothing I could put my finger on." Gossard shook his head.

Satterfield nodded in agreement. "That's the feeling I get when I'm with him. I've had him checked and rechecked. The man is brilliant and there is absolutely no question as to his loyalty, but... " He shrugged and lit another cigarette. "I know that he wanted, expected my job. Although he hides it well, I also know he resents me. Even hates me. Perhaps I'm just picking up on his resentment but I get... what's the expression? Bad vibes. Probably it's my imagination."

Gossard grinned. "Then it's my imagination, too." The grin faded. "Tell you what, I'll assign one of my aides to the case. He'll accompany Royer when you find him and report directly to me. I'll make it an executive order and that will let you off the hook with Mayhew."

13

"Thanks, Will. Who will you assign? Mayhew will be flying to Seattle as soon as possible. Our best chance of stopping Barenji is during the delivery that's scheduled in four days."

Gossard picked up the phone. "Send Bergdorf in right away. Thank you." He cradled the receiver. "I'm giving you David Bergdorf. He's one of my brightest aides. I want him back in one piece."

"Jewish?"

"Yes. He ought to get on with your Mossad man. Also, he's fluent in several languages and holds a Doctorate from Harvard in International Relations."

"An egghead."

Gossard laughed. "I think you'll be surprised. His hobby is rock climbing. Rocks like Yosemite's El Capitan. And he served four years in the silent service."

Satterfield's frown lifted slightly. "A submariner. But he's never been in the field? Never been trained for field work?"

"Undercover? No. He's no spy. That's your boy's job. David will simply be there to keep an eye on things for us."

There was a knock at the door. "That will be David. I'll introduce you."

At his call, the door opened and David Bergdorf entered. Satterfield looked him over as he crossed the room. Young, probably only in his mid-thirties, of average height with dark brown curly hair. At least he wore it short, Satterfield thought with approval. Not some yuppie who couldn't miss an appointment with his hair stylist.

Then, as they were introduced and Satterfield extended his hand, he looked into Bergdorf's eyes for the first time. In their clear hazel depths, Satterfield read intelligence, honesty, and more important, courage. Bergdorf might not have any field training but he would do. The president had made a good choice.

~ * ~

At CIA headquarters in Langley, Mayhew took the elevator down a couple of floors and walked along the hall to a cubicle on the left. Sticking his head in, he snapped, "Brooks, get Whitney, Bigelow, Cowper and Watts. Bring the file on Zephyr. My office in five minutes."

He didn't wait for an answer. Over the years, Mayhew had formed a private cadre of agents. Men who shared his views on how the country should be run. Men on whose personal loyalty he could count.

Seven minutes later, the five men crowded into Mayhew's office. Only his personal assistant, Calvin Brooks, felt at ease enough to take a seat. The others formed a ragged line against the wall. Whitney pulled out a penknife and began to clean his nails as he listened.

Mayhew rapidly and succinctly outlined the problem. He watched their shock and anger grow.

"The Director has gone running to his buddy in the White House but we can't wait. Cal, I want you to unearth everything you can on Barenji, alert our agents in Europe and central and north Africa, particularly Zimbabwe."

The phone rang. Mayhew grabbed it and barked, "I told you I didn't want to be disturbed."

He listened a moment and hung up then turned back to Brooks. "Do we have anyone in Victoria Falls?"

"Only a local, Reginald Umbulu."

"Is he any good?"

Brooks shrugged. "I doubt it. He's not a trained agent. We've only slipped him a few dollars from time to time to keep us informed of local attitudes."

"Well, alert him to expect Royer and Bergdorf and give them what help he can."

"Bergdorf?"

"That call was from the director. It seems the president is sending along a watch dog." He looked at the others. "I want the rest of you ready to fly to Seattle with me this evening. Cal, you'll hold down the fort here until I get back. Now, what do we have on Zephyr?"

Brooks frowned. "It is all rumor, nothing concrete. He is believed to have taken over the identity of one R. Royer. No idea what happened to the real Royer."

"He did exist?" Mayhew asked.

"Oh, yes. Born 1956 in Boston. Parents were Samuel Royer and Deborah Rothstein. Mother originally from Paris, survived Maidenak, married Royer in France. Both parents are dead, no siblings. Royer was a child prodigy, played the violin. Thought to be something of a wimp, if not a homosexual, as a child. Joined the Marine Corps in 1978 after leaving Julliard. Served in Lebanon where he was wounded. After discharge, he visited Israel for three months." He paused. "That may have been when the switch was made. After his return, he married Rachel Klein in Boston. Nothing on the wife. Moved to Seattle in 1984. Money doesn't seem to be a problem. His income is derived primarily from investments inherited from his parents. The Royers live well within their means." Brooks upper lip curled. "He also writes music."

"Do we know where he is now?"

Brooks nodded. "Records show an address in Seattle. It was updated last year and I presume it's still good. They own the property. Do you think he'll cooperate? He's known to have an attitude problem."

"We'll persuade him. Any children?"

"No."

"Damn. It will have to be the wife. Let's hope they're not on the verge of divorce. Do we have a safe house in Seattle?"

Brooks hesitated. The CIA was forbidden to operate within the United States. He glanced at the others in the room then nodded. "Yes, one."

"Good. We'll need it for Whitney and the woman. See to it. Arrange for a Company jet to take us to Seattle in…" he glanced at his watch, "two hours. We'll land at Boeing Field. Arrange for a rental car to meet us. Also contact the Navy. Do we have a carrier in the South Atlantic? We'll need a place to rendezvous with Bergdorf and to brief Royer. This is top security. The Chinese and those ragheads must not learn that we are on to them." He glanced at the others. "The rest of you get your gear together and get back here as soon as possible. I've got to go see our sailor boy upstairs."

He looked at each of them, his voice taking on a pedantic solemnity. "Men, this may be just the opportunity we've been waiting for. A chance to save this country and confound its enemies for all time. I know that each and every one of you shares my concern for this country. That's why I picked you for this assignment. I hope you won't let me and our country down."

He motioned Brooks to stay as the others filed out. "We'll need a cover for Royer and Bergdorf. We can send Carter. He can brief them. Also, call in Spears. Get him booked out of here immediately. I want him in Victoria Falls ahead of Royer."

Brooks nodded. "Boss, are you sure you want Whitney to handle the woman?"

Mayhew lifted an eyebrow. "Why not?"

Brooks swallowed. "Whitney has an unsavory reputation with women. He's beaten a couple of them half to death."

"Then I'd say he'd be perfect to keep Royer's wife in line."

"But what if Royer demands to talk with her?"

"Force her to make a couple of tapes. You know it will be necessary to eliminate her when she's served her purposes. We'll have no choice if our own plans are to succeed."

Brooks frowned. "Our plans?"

"Yes, Cal, our plans. I'll explain when the time is right." He laid a hand on the younger man's shoulder. "I think this is our chance, Cal. Together we're going to save this country. We're going to save it from those Chinese bastards and from itself. Trust me in this."

Two

Seattle

The pearl gray light of breaking dawn filtered through the white nylon curtains. Rachel Royer blinked away the last vestiges of sleep and slipped out of the king-size bed. The thin lawn nightshirt outlined full but firm breasts as she arched her back and stretched, running a hand through sleep-tousled hair.

A smile softened the harsh planes of her face as she glanced down at her husband. She knew hers was not a pretty face, at least not in the conventional sense. There were too many angles and planes, too much character for mere prettiness. But, according to Roger, it was an arresting face, even beautiful when the lines were softened and brown eyes warmed by love, as she felt it now.

A rush of tenderness swept over Rachel as the man turned in his sleep, the blanket slipping down to expose his muscular chest. She tiptoed around the bed and gently pulled it up, tucking it around his shoulders. How happy he made her! A tiny frisson of superstitious dread danced up her spine. Perhaps too happy. Mythological gods would have resented, envied such happiness. She shrugged the thought away.

Resisting the urge to wake him, she dropped a feather-light kiss on his forehead and headed for the bathroom. Richard needed his sleep.

She spent a long time in the shower, taking sensuous pleasure in the abundance of hot water, luxuriating in the scent and feel of the expensive French milled soap as she lathered her body. So much hot water. It was one of the joys of living in the United States that she never ceased to appreciate and enjoy. Before stepping out of the shower stall, she rubbed herself liberally with aloe lotion.

She towel-dried her shoulder length auburn hair and rubbed her body briskly, even roughly, until her skin glowed then paused to study herself critically in the full-length mirror. At thirty-four, she still had the firm body of a teenager. She smiled, knowing that her slenderness was deceptive. Under the fragile, feminine exterior every muscle, every nerve was as finely tuned as a racecar.

Richard had remodeled the basement into a fully equipped gym and they had worked out together three hours a day, every day. At least they had until… She forced her thoughts away from Richard's failing kidneys and moved into the dressing room.

Passing over the lacy lingerie that Richard liked, she pulled on a pair of cotton briefs and a sports bra then donned a light blue Adidas jogging suit. Picking up her Reebok running shoes, she tiptoed back into the bedroom.

"I'm awake. Come and give me a kiss," Richard whispered, his hazel eyes still dull and heavy with sleep.

She crossed the room and dropped to her knees beside the bed. "Go back to sleep, darling." She brushed a brown curl off his forehead and dropped a light kiss on his forehead. "I'm going for my run. I'll wake you when I get back. We'll go down to The Brasserie for breakfast."

need to be in perfect condition belonged to her old life, didn't it?

The track was curving north now. Why not go home? She suddenly longed to feel Richard's arms around her, hear his voice whispering in her ear.

Mentally, she shook herself. She had only six more laps. Do it. Don't quit now. She'd never been a quitter and she wouldn't start now. Richard would still be asleep and he needed his rest.

Without breaking her stride, she pulled the orange from her pocket and rolled it, for a minute, between her palms. Then she worked the knife out of her pocket, opened it and cut out a small core. Squeezing and sucking, she swallowed the juice.

At the picnic area, she jogged over and deposited the skin in a litter barrel then, jogging in place, she rinsed the knife at the drinking fountain and replaced it in her change pocket. She rinsed her mouth, spitting out rather than swallowing the water and continued her run. She passed the two elderly women again, marching determinedly, their arms swinging in unison. Both nodded and Rachel returned their smile. They had to be in their late sixties at least and they were out walking every day, rain or shine. She admired their dedication.

Her thoughts turned inward again. She and Richard were luckier than many. At least they had the money to buy the small but highly sophisticated portable dialysis machine. A machine so advanced that it was contained in a case no bigger than a small suitcase, and could be handled as carry-on luggage whenever they traveled.

As long as he had dialysis regularly, he was able to function almost normally and would probably be able to do so until a donor was found. His doctors were not unduly concerned, why should she be?

Because they didn't love him as she did. Because just the thought of life without him left her feeling achingly empty and desolate. If it hadn't been for Richard...

She jogged on, no longer seeing the beauty around her. Instead, she saw the sere hills of Lebanon, the smoke and flames rising to blot out the cerulean sky. Her ears rang again with the whine of ricocheting bullets, the wails of fear, the cries of pain from the wounded. Her nostrils flared as if smelling again the odor of cordite, of blood, of bloated bodies decaying under the burning sun. It seemed she could even taste the dust and smoke. She saw herself as Richard had seen her, crouching in the rubble of a building, clutching a dead child to her breast.

But that wasn't the real me, her mind whispered. Would he still love me if he knew what had gone before? Perhaps, but if he learned the truth now, would he ever trust her again? Lies by omission were just as bad as outright lies, weren't they?

She pictured the way his eyes had looked as he gently took the child's body from her. The sadness and compassion so at variance with the Marine uniform he wore.

It was only later that she learned how much a part of his character the seeming incongruity was. Richard was a gentle man, sensitive and compassionate. His hitch in the Marine Corps, his service in Lebanon had given him a hatred of war. Only his highly developed sense of responsibility, his belief that every man had a duty to his country had caused him to enlist. And, as he had once told her with a rueful grin, joining the Corps had put an end to the teasing he had been subjected to all his life because of his musical gift. He'd forever dispelled, at least in his own mind, the wimp image that had made his teen years a misery.

Her pace slowed as her mind wandered. Richard, so gentle by nature. A gentleman in the truest sense of the word but a

24

strong man nevertheless. She suspected he was much stronger than even he realized.

Richard and his violin. What feelings he could still coax from it, even now. What heights he could have reached if a piece of shrapnel hadn't shattered two bones in his left hand and damaged the nerves. Wonderful, talented Richard.

In the years they had been together, she had never ceased to be amazed by the fact that he loved her. She had no illusions about herself. She was not a lovable person. There was a hard, self reliant, pragmatic core within her that only Richard had been able to penetrate. He was her antithesis. Richard was not a killer, either by instinct or training.

A fierce longing to be with him seized her. She lifted her head and focused on her surroundings. How many laps had she run? It no longer mattered, all that mattered was that she go home. She rounded the south end of the lake and cut across the grass.

Traffic had picked up on Green Lake Drive. She jogged in place, waiting for a break to cross the street. She noticed the man jogging towards her from the south and a tiny frisson of alarm raced up her spine. Her eyes sharpened, noting his leather shoes. Instinctively she turned towards him, her muscles tensing. Her senses sharpened. A man in a business suit approached at a brisk walk from the north. A warning jangled through her.

A gray sedan slid to a stop on her left as the jogger lunged towards her. Automatically she dropped into a fighting stance. The businessman swerved and slammed into her and she felt a stinging in her thigh.

She whirled, jabbing an extended knuckle into the man's throat. As he stumbled back gagging, Rachel whirled aiming a kick at the jogger's stomach that he avoided with practiced skill. Something was very wrong. Her reactions were too slow.

Her mouth was too dry, her perception vaguely distorted. She knew she was in trouble as he countered with a karate chop she was only partially able to avoid. The ground swam and she felt herself falling, spiraling down. She heard a voice snap, "Get her in the car."

Blackness, thick as molasses oozed through her brain, trapping her, as she was shoved into the car. She struggled against its viscous tentacles. Her hand clutched the back of the front seat and she tried to pull herself up. As the door slammed, she saw the startled eyes and open mouths of the two elderly ladies as they strode by. Then the forward surge of the car broke her grip and she fell back. A sweaty hand clamped over her mouth, mashing her lips painfully against her teeth as she screamed. Fingers bent like talons, she clawed at the hand and heard her captor swear. Then she was in a vortex, being sucked deeper and deeper into darkness.

~ * ~

Richard rolled over lazily letting the light breeze from the open window cool his sweaty skin. The bedroom door burst open, slamming back against the wall, jarring a Donna Payne Miller painting. It swayed crazily, its wire sliding on the hook until it was dangling sideways.

Richard's eyes shot open, lighting first on the painting. Earthquake? The big one? For a second his shocked eyes were held by the painted horsemen galloping up the wall then they focused on the two men in the doorway. At last his eyes focused on their hands and the two Spectre 9 mm automatic pistols aimed at him.

He froze, mouth half open. His gaze flashed away from the guns and fixed on the faces. Disbelief followed by fear washed over him.

The two men ignored him, scanning the room. The one on the left moved swiftly across the carpet and jerked open the dressing room door. He moved into the bathroom. Moments later he returned and nodded to the man still covering Richard from the hall door. Then he cautiously approached the bed from the side, staying well out of his partner's range of fire.

"You breathe wrong, buddy and you're dead. Get your hands out where I can see them and do it slow."

Stunned and bewildered, Richard complied. The man gripped the bottom on the blanket and whipped it off the bed. The sheet followed. Warily, he pulled Rachel's pillow to the floor then circled the bed and jerked the pillow from under Richard's head. Richard watched, too amazed to collect his scattered wits. The man ran his free hand over Richard's pajama bottoms then backed away and his lips curled. "He's clean, Big. Get Mayhew."

The man called Big stepped to the side and called, "It's clear."

Moments later Elwood Mayhew entered the room. "Bigelow, take Watts and search the house. Cowper, wait outside. I don't want to be disturbed."

As the two gun-toting men left the room, Richard transferred his attention to the ugly man in front of him. His fear began to be replaced with anger and he sat up.

"Just what in the hell is going on?" He swung his feet to the floor.

"Stay where you are. We're just going to have a little talk."

"Who the hell are you?"

Mayhew glanced around the room, picked up a blue velvet Victorian chair, carried it to the bed and sat down. He pulled out a slim leather wallet and showed it to Richard.

Richard read the identity card, blinked and read it again. "CIA? You've got to be kidding. Why is the CIA breaking into my house?"

"You are Richard Royer?" Mayhew asked, pocketing the wallet.

"Yes."

"We have a little job for you."

"What is this? Some kind of joke? I can tell you right now, I don't think it's a damned bit funny."

"It's no joke. We need you."

"Hey, come on. You don't really expect me to believe this? Since when did the CIA break into people's homes to recruit? I know your outfit isn't very popular any more but you can't be that hard up for recruits."

"We're not. Let's just say we need your particular expertise."

"Now I know you're crazy. Get out of here before the little men in white coats haul you back to whatever loony bin you escaped from."

Mayhew sighed. His face took on a disappointed look but Richard noticed that his eyes glittered with suppressed enjoyment. His guts tightened. The man really was mad.

Mayhew slowly shook his head. "Zephyr, Zephyr. Why make this any more difficult than it has to be? We really do need your help. We need you to stop Mustafa Barenji. You're the only one who knows him by sight and therefore has a chance of stopping him in time. We know that he will be in Zimbabwe on the thirteenth to pick up a new strain of bacteria from a group of Chinese. If he isn't stopped, he and his terrorist group will wipe out half of the United States and Russia."

"Look, I don't know what you're talking about. I never heard of this Mustafa whatever. You've got the wrong man."

"You may not have any loyalty to this country but I think you should know that Barenji's payoff is China's promise to destroy Israel. Surely you have some loyalty left to your own country even if you have turned your back on Mossad."

Richard felt like he was in the middle of a nightmare. Nothing made any sense. He shrugged helplessly. "I don't know what to say. Nothing you tell me makes any sense. I don't know this terrorist you're talking about. I'm a violinist and composer, not a spy."

Mayhew's face hardened. He stood up and replaced the chair. "Okay, Royer. If that's the way you want to play." He opened the door and called Cowper inside. Turning back to Richard, his voice slashed like a whip. "Get up and get dressed. You're leaving for Victoria Falls in ten minutes." Mayhew's voice softened but each word was uttered with pedantic clarity. "You are going to find Barenji and you are going to get that bacteria for us. If you don't, your wife dies."

Panic flared in Richard's eyes and his heart raced. "Rachel?"

"That's right. We picked up your wife this morning on the jogging path at Green Lake. Either cooperate or she dies."

He turned to Cowper. "See that he's dressed and ready to leave in ten minutes. Watch him, he's a tricky son of a bitch."

"Wait. This is crazy. Wait. What have you done with my wife?" he called as Mayhew disappeared into the hall. He scrambled out of bed and dashed for the door.

He never saw Cowper's hand as it smashed him back on the bed. His head swam as he struggled to get up.

"Just do what you're told, buddy boy, if you ever want to see that redheaded cunt again. The guy that's with her is a real misog... woman hater. You don't behave yourself, he'll enjoy making her die real slow."

Cowper jerked him up and shoved him towards the bathroom. "Get cleaned up and dressed, you smell worse than a rutting goat. You got a plane to catch, Mr. not-so-great Mossad agent. I heard you were a real mean ass but you don't look so tough to me."

Richard staggered into the bathroom, his mind whirling. Rachel. They had Rachel. They were crazy, crazy as bedbugs. Crazies were dangerous. The crazies had Rachel. He'd have to play along with them until Rachel was safe. Jesus, this couldn't be happening. It had to be a nightmare. Only why didn't he wake up?

Three

A persistent buzzing roused Rachel. The fly lit on her cheek and she tried to brush it away but something was holding her arm. Her head ached abominably and her mouth was as dry as the Negev desert, her tongue thick and swollen.

Reluctantly she opened her eyes. The light sent splinters of pain shooting through her head, leaving her weak and dizzy. She closed her eyes and some of the pain eased. Where was she? Why was she here? It was hard to concentrate.

Memory began to return. Green Lake. The two men. The car. The pinprick on her thigh. She'd been drugged and kidnapped. Terrorists? For a moment panic threatened but she fought it. Concentrating, she brought the faces of the two men she'd seen clearly into focus. Americans or possibly European. No, their voices had been pure American. The last vestige of panic melted away. Americans could be dealt with, not like...

The fly crept up over her forehead and down her nose, distracting her. She rolled her head to the side and it buzzed angrily away.

The movement made her stomach heave. While she waited for it to stop roiling, she concentrated on listening. Somewhere in the distance she heard the muted sound of traffic. Closer she heard the intermittent growl of a small engine. A familiar sound. A motorcycle? Lawn mower? No, a chain saw. She waited for the whoosh and thud of a falling tree. It didn't come. Someone cutting up firewood then.

She focused on closer sounds. The fly continued to buzz somewhere in the room. She could hear the faint murmur of a radio or television, but not in the room. She could detect no sound of breathing.

Next she concentrated on feeling. She tried to move her hand again. Fabric bit into her wrist. Tied. She wiggled her feet. Tied, too. She centered on the rest of her body. She was lying on something relatively soft, probably a bed. She concentrated again on listening. No movement, no breathing.

Through barely open eyes, she glanced quickly around confirming that she was alone. Ignoring the first swift pain, she cautiously raised her head and studied the room. It was an ordinary bedroom furnished with a dresser against one wall and sporting a cracked mirror. In front of the one window were a straight-backed chair and round wooden table. The draperies were open but she noticed with interest that they extended well beyond the window frame and were made of a heavy material that would block out all light when closed.

There was only the one door, in the wall opposite the bed, and it was closed. What lay behind the door? And who?

She turned her attention to the bed. It was twin size, with an old fashioned metal head and foot railings. Her hands were tied securely, to the center rung of the headboard, with thin strips of cloth. Her ankles were firmly tied to the footboard. The stench of stale sweat and urine wafted up from the bare mattress.

Pulling against the cloth bindings chafed her wrists and only tightened the knots. There was no give in the material that bound her. Panic swept over her like a tidal wave so fast, so overwhelming, she couldn't stop it. The springs screeched as she arched her body, twisting, straining with all her strength. The door opened as she fell back, panting.

He was tall, wide-shouldered and looked solid. Rachel's gaze settled on his hands and watched as he finished cleaning a fingernail, closed the penknife and dropped it in his pocket. His voice was surprisingly high for a man his size, as he said in thick southern drawl, "Relax, bitch. You aren't going anywhere."

"Who are you? Why am I here? What do you want with me?"

The man moved out of the shadow of the door and grinned down at her. She felt a momentary rush of relief as she studied his face. At least he wasn't an Arab.

"Let's just say you're going to be our guest for a while. Sort of an insurance policy." He grinned. "Yeah, an insurance policy. And your husband is going to pay the premium." He laughed but there was no humor in it.

"You're holding me for ransom?" she asked, incredulously. She choked down an almost hysterical urge to laugh. It wasn't political. Just an ordinary criminal act.

He moved closer to the bed. "Yeah." He laughed, spraying her face with spittle. "You could say that. Now you're going to make a nice little tape recording for your husband."

He held a small tape recorder in front of her face. "Just tell him you're okay, being treated real nice. You tell him to cooperate and everything will be just fine."

"But we don't have that kind of money."

"Money is all you damn women think about, isn't it? Well, your husband can't buy his way out this time. We've got a little job for him and he's going to do it if he ever wants to see you again."

Fear choked her and she barely heard his words. Kidnapped! How many kidnap victims were ever returned alive? Not many. Not when they had seen their captors, when they could identify them. This man had deliberately let her see his face!

She choked back the urge to scream. To have survived all that she had in the past, only to be killed by a gang of ordinary criminals. It was ludicrous.

She didn't want to die. *Think. Don't panic. Think. Use your brain.* Her body began to relax as she fought down the fear. Could she talk her way out of this? She glanced into his eyes and shivered. Hate. Contempt. And satisfaction. He was enjoying her fear. Nothing to be gained by being cooperative. She swallowed convulsively.

"Go to hell."

Slowly, almost casually, he raised a hand and slapped her a stinging blow across the face. "That ain't no way to talk."

He laid the recorder on the floor and checked her bindings.

Could she trick him? He couldn't know about her, about her past. Play on his contempt. Make him think she was weaker, more frightened than she was, although, God knows, she was frightened enough. Buy time. "Please. Do I have to stay tied like this? My arms hurt."

"Now isn't that too bad." He bent over, leering down at her. "What would you do if I untied you? Would you be nice to me?" His hand roamed lightly over her stomach and breasts.

His foul breath and dirty teeth repelled her. She pressed back against the mattress. He grasped a nipple, pinching and twisting. She gasped in pain. He straightened and the grin widened. "Sure you don't want to make this tape?"

She shook her head.

"You will." He unzipped her jacket and forced his hand inside her bra squeezing her breast. She gritted her teeth against the pain. He bent over, crushing her mouth with his, forcing his tongue between her lips.

34

She let her teeth part. His tongue invaded her mouth. Bile rose in the back of her throat, threatening to choke her. She snapped her teeth shut, biting with all her strength.

He screamed then slammed a fist into the side of her face. It was a short, desperate punch without a lot of force behind it, but it stunned her, relaxing her jaw muscles. He jerked back. Blood stained spittle ran out of the corner of his mouth. "Bitch. I'm going to enjoy killing you. Slowly. And I hope your husband gets his goddamned head blown off."

Her head snapped sideways as he slapped her, bounced back as he backhanded her. She could feel warm blood trickling down her upper lip. He turned and stalked out of the room, slamming the door behind him.

~ * ~

As he shaved under Cowper's unwavering stare, Roger's mind churned like a millrace. Who were these people? He wished he'd taken a closer look at the identification Mayhew— that was the name wasn't it?—had shown him. It had to be fake. The CIA didn't go around breaking into people's homes. Rachel. Did they really have Rachel?

He pushed his fears aside and tried to concentrate on some kind of action. His heart refused to believe these men really had Rachel. He had to leave her some kind of message. In the clutter of Rachel's cosmetics, he spotted an eyebrow pencil. Shifting his stance, he palmed it and opened the door to the toilet cubicle.

Cowper took a step forward. Richard forced himself to meet the man's eyes and smile sardonically. "It'll be a tight fit but do you care to join me and hold my hand?"

"Smart ass. Just hurry it up."

When Richard came out, he hurriedly washed his hands and strode into the dressing room, praying that Cowper would follow without checking the cubicle.

He grabbed a sports bag from the shelf and hastily stuffed in a change of clothes. He opened the closet and reached for the dialysis machine.

"Cool it. This isn't any vacation. Leave the big bag."

Richard opened his mouth to explain then silently closed it and the door. If these crazies thought he wouldn't be able to do whatever it was they wanted, they might kill Rachel out of spite. His heart skipped. Did they really have Rachel? He grabbed his watch off the dresser. Seven o'clock. Rachel would have been back from her run by now. It lent credence to their story. Too much credence. If this was a nightmare, why didn't he wake up? Why the hell had the CIA kidnapped Rachel? What could they possibly want from him? What the hell was happening?

Cowper hustled him down the stairs. The sight of Mayhew calmly sitting on his couch in his living room, leafing through one of Rachel's magazines added a further touch of the bizarre to his nightmare. Bigelow was standing by the front door.

Mayhew tossed aside the magazine and rose. "Cowper, bring up the car. Okay, Royer, let's go."

"But…"

"No buts." He turned, calling to Bigelow, "Get Watts and let's go."

Bigelow disappeared into the kitchen, returning moments later with another man. Mayhew hurried them out of the house and down the front steps as a gray sedan pulled to a stop.

"Watts, keep the house under surveillance. Let me know immediately if there is any undue interest."

Bigelow climbed into the back seat first, his hand in his pocket. Richard could see the outline of the gun and gave up the momentary idea of making a break. Mayhew shoved Royer's shoulder and he climbed in. Mayhew settled himself in the front seat as the car moved down the street.

No one spoke as they threaded through the early morning traffic on Aurora Avenue heading north. He wondered where they were taking him, but decided against asking. He'd find out soon enough. Perhaps Rachel would be there.

They pulled into the slowly moving line for the Mukilteo ferry. Richard felt his pulse quicken as he watched the line of cars loading. When they got out of the car, perhaps he could make a break as the ferry pulled away. Jump into Puget Sound, if nothing else. He was a strong swimmer. They wouldn't dare shoot at him in broad daylight with plenty of witnesses around. The captain would hardly reverse the ferry, CIA or no CIA. He would swim to shore and find Rachel.

The line was short and the bored deck hand waved them to the front of the ferry. His muscles tensed as the driver set his brake and turned off the engine. His hopes dropped as no one made a move to get out of the car.

He sank into a fog of depression, hardly aware of the twenty-minute ferry ride or the race north up Whidbey Island. His interest wasn't caught until the car swung into the Naval Air station at Oak Harbor.

Four

Whidbey Island Naval Station

Cowper showed his identification and was waved onto the base. A jeep pulled in front of them and motioned Cowper to follow. Minutes later the car swung onto the flight line and pulled to a stop beside an F-14 Tomcat.

Mayhew got out and joined the pilot and another officer. Minutes later he returned to the car and motioned for Richard to get out. Bigelow slid out and stepped back, his hand on his gun.

The feeling that he was trapped in a bizarre nightmare increased as the pilot handed him a flight suit and helmet and turned away to the plane. Mayhew took the helmet from his shaking hand.

"Get into that suit. The pilot has been instructed not to talk to you so don't get any ideas."

"But where am I going?"

"You'll be briefed when you arrive. In the meantime, I suggest that you keep in mind what will happen to your wife if you fail to cooperate. Now, get dressed. The Navy doesn't like to be kept waiting."

"I'm not going anywhere until you listen to me."

"Royer, you are getting in that plane if we have to knock you out and hog-tie you."

"Where's my wife?"

"Safe. As long as you cooperate." Mayhew leaned close, glaring into Richard's eyes. "You get on that plane or you'll never see your wife again."

Mayhew's eyes were glittering. Richard backed away. The man was just mad enough to do as he threatened. Perhaps whoever was supposed to "brief" him, would be reasonable. Or at least rational. He'd have to play for time. He climbed into the flight suit.

~ * ~

For Rachel the hours passed slowly. Shadows on the wall slowly shifted. The sun rose higher in the sky. Her fear grew as the effects of the drug wore off. She tried to remember what he had said about Richard. What could they possibly want from her husband? It didn't make sense. They had to kill her, she'd seen them, but why Richard?

She dozed and awoke. The mattress seemed to have sprouted lumps like mushrooms. Mushrooms. Food. How long had it been since she'd eaten? Hunger knotted her stomach. Pictures of food floated through her mind: a heaping plate of scrambled eggs with toast dripping with butter; a beautifully broiled steak with a big baked potato crammed with sour cream and topped with chives.

Her bladder became uncomfortable, forcing out the thought of food. An old riddle ran through her head. If a carrot is a carrot and a cabbage a cabbage, what is a pea? A great relief. She caught herself on the verge of giggling. It snapped her back to reality.

Where was Richard? No, don't think about Richard now. He couldn't help her. No one could help her. She would have to depend solely on her own wits, her own training.

Her hands were numb. She had to get her circulation going. Slowly, she began opening and closing her fingers then fingers pressed together, applied isometric pressure. She worked her way down her body, flexing each muscle group as much as her position would let her. When she finally relaxed, she was wet with sweat. The next thing was to get out of this room.

She called out, called again, louder. The door opened and her captor glared at her. "Shut up or I'll gag you."

"I have to go to the bathroom."

He smirked. "Now ain't that just too bad. You ready to make that tape?"

She hesitated. As soon as he had the tape, he would probably kill her. Still, if she could get loose, she would at least have a chance. Better to die fighting than trussed up like a goat.

She nodded, letting him see her reluctance.

"I'll get the recorder."

"First I have to use the bathroom."

"No way. You make the tape then I'll let you up."

She shook her head. "Bathroom first."

"No."

She shrugged and turned her face away, letting a tear escape from under one closed eyelid. "Then I'll just have to wet the bed," she whispered.

He glared down at her for a moment then approached the head of the bed. "Shit. This better not be a trick," he said as he untied her hands. He moved down and unfastened her feet. "You make one wrong move and you're dead. You understand?"

She nodded and sat up, trying to rub the circulation back into her hands. A million pins and needles shot through her feet as she tried to stand. Clinging to the bedframe, she shook one foot then the other, trying to increase circulation.

"Stop fooling around. Get going."

On wooden legs, she staggered towards the door. He followed, a gun pointed at her back. His fetid breath floated over her shoulder and her nostrils flared in revulsion.

Goose bumps popped out on her arms as she entered the cold bathroom. She glanced around ,searching frantically for anything to use as a weapon. A pocket comb, half the teeth missing, lay next to the lavatory basin. Useless. There was a showerhead above the tub but the curtain rod and curtain were missing. Her heart sank. There was nothing.

She studied the window. It was double hung with opaque glass in the lower half. It was small; still, given time, she was sure she could wiggle through it. Would he give her the time?

He nudged her with the gun. The dusty vinyl tile squeaked as she stepped farther inside and reached for the door. He shoved it out of her hand as she tried to close it.

"Not on your life, sister. You got to go, go, but the door stays open."

So much for that idea. She drew herself up. "You could at least turn your back."

He smirked. "No way. Now are you going to use the john or you want to go back to bed?"

She shrugged. There were things more important than modesty. Like her life. He wouldn't break her this easily.

Feigning embarrassment, she turned sideways to the door and slid the pants over her hips. Her heart leapt as her fingers encountered the penknife in her waistband pocket. Good Lord, the bastard hadn't searched her. It was all the edge she needed.

She delayed on the toilet until the man became restless. The paper holder was empty and she grimaced in disgust. As she stood and pulled up her pants, she worked the knife out and palmed it.

"Come on, come on."

"May I wash my hands and face?"

"I suppose so. Just hurry it up."

She turned on the water and reached for the one dirty towel hanging on the rack. Keep it natural. Don't let him suspect. Open the knife under the towel. Now. Easy. Careful. The knife blade opened. Good. She laid them together on the edge of the lavatory. Stall. Buy time. Rinse your face. Okay.

Keeping the knife hidden in its folds, she dried her face and hands. Still carrying the towel, she moved towards the door. Were her reflexes still sharp enough? They'd better be. She'd never get another chance.

"Leave the towel."

She widened her eyes as she moved closer. "But it's so dirty." Two more steps. One more step. "Don't you want to put it in the laundry?"

"Hell, I ain't doing no laundry. Throw it down."

Another step. "If you say so." Now.

She flicked the towel into his face with her left hand and with all her strength stabbed the penknife into his gun hand. The blade sliced between two bones, the point penetrating through the palm and slammed against the gun butt.

The gun exploded, deafening in the small room. The bullet ricocheted off the tub, gouged a furrow through the paint on the wall and shattered the window.

Ears ringing, Rachel slammed the heel of her left hand under his chin, bouncing his head back against the doorjamb. Releasing the knife, she rammed a knuckle into his belly and brought a knee slamming into his groin.

She danced back, lifting her leg for a finishing kick but it wasn't needed. He slid down the door, unconscious. She wrenched the gun from his bloody hand and tucked it in her waistband. She hesitated only a moment then knelt, quickly searched him, amazed that her old instincts had rushed back so swiftly.

Bills in a money clip, small change, the knife, a dirty handkerchief but no keys. She found a wallet and opened it. The CIA identification rocked her. Why would the CIA kidnap her? Not for ransom, that was for sure. And what had this man, Homer Whitney, meant about Richard being needed?

A sick fear lay like a lead weight in her stomach as she stood. She had to get to Richard. She ran through the house and out the front door and looked frantically around. There was no car in the driveway. She pulled the garage door up, dashed to the brown sedan and wrenched open the door. There were no keys in the ignition. Hastily she searched behind the visor, under the floor mat, felt along under the car. Nothing.

Where were the damned keys? Somewhere in the house. No time to make a search. Whitney wouldn't be unconscious long. She had to get away.

The quiet residential neighborhood was unfamiliar. The houses were moderately affluent, set back on large lots. The street was empty, not even a parked car.

The chain saw she had heard earlier started up again and Rachel followed the sound. She began to run. In the driveway of the third house, she saw a pickup. She moved up the drive, hugging the hedge of rhododendrons.

The truck was parked pointed towards the street, its tailgate down. The noise of the chain saw stopped. Rachel crouched in the shrubs, waiting. Minutes that seemed like hours passed before she heard the heavy thunk of an ax hitting wood.

She crept out of the bushes and peered over the door to the cab. The keys dangled in the ignition. She climbed in, eased the door shut without latching it and hunched down, waiting for the chain saw to start again. When it did, she sat up and turned the key. The engine roared to life.

"Hey! That's my truck! Stop!"

Rachel caught only a glimpse of the angry red face as she threw the truck in gear, stomped on the gas and raced out of the driveway. Right or left? It didn't matter, just get away fast. The closest corner was left and she swung the truck in that direction. She raced around the corner, praying it wouldn't be a dead end. Unfamiliar with the neighborhood, she wasted several minutes of driving through a profusion of residential streets before she found Bothell Way and headed south, relieved.

She drove as fast as the law allowed, obeying all traffic laws. She couldn't risk being stopped for a traffic violation, driving a stolen vehicle.

Questions flooded her mind. Questions without answers. Why had she been kidnapped? Was Whitney really with the CIA? The identification had looked authentic but that didn't mean anything. What had Whitney meant about Richard paying? Obviously he hadn't meant money. What had he meant about being shot? Who would be shooting at Richard? A suspicion entered her mind, a suspicion too ludicrous to be considered. Or was it? Her gut tightened.

Parking on the street above their house, she slipped through the yard that abutted theirs. Old skills, old ways were returning. She studied the house for a long time before making her way across the back yard approaching the rear door.

It was unlatched. She took a moment to study the lock. Tiny scratches showed where it had been forced. She eased it open. With Whitney's gun ready, she made a rolling dive into the corner between the freezer and the kitchen door.

When there was no sound, she scrambled up, silently crossed the kitchen and peered down the hall. Nothing. Quickly she checked the living and dining rooms. Empty.

Her pulse began to race. The house had the too quiet emptiness of an abandoned building. Where was Richard?

Nerves taut, she climbed the stairs, stepping over the fourth tread that tended to squeak. She checked the two guest bedrooms and hall bath. All the time her mind screaming—no—no—no.

With trepidation she approached the master bedroom. As she threw open the door she realized she had been holding her breath, praying. She was prepared for almost anything except what she found. Nothing. Absolutely nothing. The room was empty.

Her quick glance swept over the disheveled bed, the crooked picture. She inched her way to the dressing room then into the bathroom.

She felt the tension drain out of her, leaving her weak and empty. She slumped against the wall. Richard was gone. No, not gone, taken. What she had been dreading. But where? Why?

Fear and tension loosened her bladder and bowels and she rushed into the toilet cubicle. From the corner of her eye, she caught a glimpse of white toilet paper sticking out of the inset magazine rack. She reached for it.

Her pulse quickened as she saw the brown marks. She relieved herself, jerked up her pants, carried the note to the window and unrolled it. Her eyebrow pencil fell to the floor.

Kidnap Vic. Falls Zimbabwe CIA Zephyr?

The words were crudely printed and barely legible but one word leapt out, Zephyr.

Rachel crumpled the paper, carried it back and flushed it down the toilet. The bastards. Why had they taken Richard? Did they think he was Zephyr? By what right had they dared invade her home? Stolen her husband? Involved Richard in their dirty little games?

She noted absently that her hands were shaking. She took several deep breaths to control the anger building inside her. They wouldn't get away with it this time. No, not this time.

In the dressing room, she opened a closet door. Her heart plummeted as she pulled out Richard's dialysis machine. The rage in her belly exploded in a white hot flame. A killing rage.

~ * ~

Washington, DC

The president waved a hand toward a chair in front of the fireplace and picked up the phone. "Dewars on the rocks and bring me a Heineken." He replaced the phone and joined Satterfield. "Well, Arthur?"

"Mayhew will be putting Royer on a Navy plane at Whidbey Island. He needs a secure place for his man to brief Royer. If either the Arabs or the Chinese get wind of our interest, they'll abort the test in Zimbabwe and we may not get another handle on them until it's too late. He suggested a carrier but we don't have anything in that part of the Atlantic. The only thing in that area is a British carrier."

The president nodded. "I'll make the arrangements."

"Your man will need to be at Andrews Air Force Base at 0600. He'll travel with one of our agents who will brief him on their cover and provide them with documents. I've arranged for them to fly on a cargo plane leaving at 0630 for the NATO base in the Azores. From there, they will helicopter to rendezvous with Royer. After the briefing, the helicopter will bring them back to the base."

"And then?"

Satterfield smiled. "Then they join a charter flight that will be making a refueling stop in the Azores. A film crew on their way to Kenya. It will fit in nicely with their cover. A private plane, belonging to a very prominent entertainer who is already in Kenya, will take them from Nairobi to Victoria Falls."

"You don't mean—"

"Yes. What did some of the newspapers call her after her trip to North Viet Nam—Hanoi Hannah, wasn't it?"

"Does she know she'll be providing transportation for our agents?"

"Definitely not. She's been given their cover story, led to believe she's doing a kindness for a couple of poor persecuted sympathizers and giving the good old US of A a poke in the eye. She grabbed at the chance. That's one sleek little leopard that will never change her spots, for all she's remarried and sucking up from the good old capitalist trough."

The president chuckled for the first time since Satterfield had briefed him on the Chinese bacteria.

~ * ~

Rachel rapidly packed a small bag then carried it and the dialysis machine down to the garage and put them in the trunk of Richard's BMW. A moment later she was in the basement, opening a safe hidden in the paneling of the remodeled gym. She removed her passport, hesitated then added Richard's to her purse. She grabbed a thick envelope of currency without bothering to count it. She knew it contained twenty-five thousand dollars in used, unmarked hundred dollar bills.

Rachel froze as a car screeched to a stop in front of the house. She slammed shut the door of the safe and closed the paneling then ran back into the garage and jumped into the BMW as she heard the front door bang open. Locking the car doors, she started the motor and pressed the automatic door opener.

Slamming the gearshift into reverse, she waited impatiently for the door to open. Whitney dashed into the garage and grabbed for her door. She floored the accelerator, barely squeaking under the still rising door.

Whitney jumped on the hood, but as she sloughed around into the street, he slid off. She jammed into first gear and roared down the hill. As she turned the corner, she saw Whitney scramble up and dash for his car. Another man ran across the street towards him. Then she was around the corner and racing towards Interstate 5.

The sun was hovering over the Olympics behind her as she turned onto Interstate 90 and headed into the Cascades. Using the car phone, she called for reservations on a night flight to New York. Calling another airline, she booked a flight from New York to London. A third call and she was booked on to Johannesburg. She would barely have time for what she had to do.

She left Interstate 90 and began to climb on a narrow secondary road. Rounding a switchback, high on the mountain, she saw Whitney's blue sedan a couple of miles behind her. Either he had been able to follow her or he knew about the cabin. Her only hope was to get there ahead of him. She increased her speed to the limit and raced through the afternoon shadows.

Braking only enough to slide into the side road, throwing a spray of gravel, she geared down and charged up the narrow private road then slid into the driveway and braked to a halt in front of the cabin. Without bothering to shut the car door, she raced for the porch, digging out her keys as she ran.

She didn't need to turn on the lights to maneuver past the furniture and reach the gun cabinet. A moment later, she had it unlocked and grabbed the Winchester 30.06 from its rack. Seconds later, with a box of ammunition in her other hand, she dashed out the back door and into the trees.

The wall she had built inside herself so many years before began to crack. The anger and hatred she had kept locked away since Lebanon began to seep into her blood, her mind. Her gut trembled with rage. Damn them. Why couldn't they leave her alone? She'd opted out of their nasty little games a long time ago. Her anger was a throbbing malignancy within her. Now they wanted her back. So be it. But by God, they'd play by *her* rules this time.

She dropped behind a boulder as Whitney pulled up behind the BMW. She watched him slide out of his car and creep over to hers as her fingers unerringly loaded the rifle. *Come on, you bastard.*

He closed her car door, shutting off the dome light and began to inch along the front fender, his gaze fixed on the cabin door. As he made a dash for the porch, she saw the gun in his hand and smiled. She'd never liked killing an unarmed man. And she was going to kill this bastard. Kill him because he was giving her no choice; kill him before he could kill her. Only by killing him would she be able to buy the time she needed to find Richard. The lines of a poem she had learned in childhood ran through her mind—

She is wedded to convictions in default of grosser ties;

Her contentions are her children, Heaven help him who denies!

He will meet no suave discussion, but instant white-hot, wild

Wakened female of the species warring as for spouse and child.

Rachel's lips curled in a tight smile as she watched Whitney. Kipling had known what he was talking about—the female of the species *is* and always has been, more deadly than the male.

Whitney bounded onto the porch and made a rolling dive through the open door. She eased farther back into the trees then froze as he came out the back door. He spotted the path to the outhouse and started to move warily down it.

Rachel dropped to a crouch and began to work her way in behind him. All the lessons she'd learned so long ago surfaced, lessons drilled into her until her muscles responded automatically. She walked toe first, feeling the ground before putting her weight on the foot. She would risk no snapping branch, no rolling pebble. She ghosted through the underbrush, stalking. Excitement coursed through her veins, the primordial thrill of the hunter closing in on the prey. No jungle cat could have moved more silently or been more deadly.

Whitney obviously wasn't used to maneuvering in the woods. He made more noise than a rutting buck.

By the time he reached the clearing in front of the outhouse, Rachel was only a few feet behind him. All of her past seemed centered in this one moment, all of the fear, the hate. She snapped off the safety and smiled sardonically as he froze. He was making it almost too easy. "Throw that gun to your right."

He hesitated and she could almost read his mind. "Go ahead, if you feel lucky." Her voice was steady and ice cold. Almost, she wished he would make his move. Almost.

He threw the gun.

"Now turn around, slowly."

He turned. There was nothing in her face or in the way she held the rifle to encourage him but she read the scorn in his face—the disdain, not of her personally but, of all women. Well, he wasn't the first man to underestimate her.

He eyed the rifle in her hands. "Look, lady, I was only following orders."

"Yeah. So were Bormann and Mengele. What were your orders?"

"To grab you and hold you."

"Why?"

"To force your husband to work for us."

"What would the CIA need with a crippled violinist?"

"Come off it, Mrs. Royer. You have to know that your husband was one of Israel's top agents until he retired. Or didn't you know?" He leaned towards her, searching her face, obviously reading the shock and dismay before she could conceal it. So her suspicions weren't so preposterous after all.

Some of his wariness eased. "Yeah, you knew. What did he do with the real Royer? Kill him?" He took a step towards her, the leer back in his eyes. "You better put that gun down before you hurt yourself. You put it down and just maybe I won't beat the shit out of you for causing me all this trouble."

Rachel took a step backwards, leading him on. "Tell me why you took my husband."

"I just told you."

"So, tell me again. Tell me everything and maybe, just maybe, I won't kill you." His eyes told her he didn't believe her. Didn't think she'd pull the trigger.

He waved his handkerchief-wrapped hand at her. "See what you did to me, you bitch. You're going to pay. Now just put that rifle down before I take it away and beat your brains out with it."

He lunged at her, a hand out to knock the rifle away. Coolly she took another step back and squeezed the trigger. The bullet slammed into his chest, jerking him up on his toes. His eyes widened in shock. He teetered for a moment then fell on his side.

Rachel circled warily until she could look down into his face. There was no softening in her as she watched him struggle to get up then fall back on his side.

"Fucking bitch."

"You made a mistake." She smiled. "You took the wrong Royer. My husband is exactly what he seems to be. A gentle, rather wonderful man."

He stared up at her blankly then comprehension dawned. He tried to sit up. "You? You're Zephyr?"

"Yes. And your stupidity is likely to kill a good man."

He fell back. His voice dropped to a whisper and his eyes began to glaze. She had to bend over to hear his words. "More than that... the whole country. You've got to stop them ... Chinese ... new bacteria... transfer in Zimbabwe... needed Zephyr... only one who knows... Barenji... "

Barenji. The name cut through her like a knife. She stood, transfixed with dread, as Whitney coughed once and died. Barenji. She shuddered.

Pulling herself together, she carried the rifle back to the house, unloaded it and ran an oiled rag through the barrel before replacing it in the gun cabinet. She found a crowbar and hammer in the storage shed and carried them to the outhouse where she carefully pried up the seat boards.

She dragged Whitney's body into the building and tipped him into the pit. Shit to shit. A fitting crypt. Sliding the nails back into their holes, she pounded the boards back in place and refitted the seats. As an afterthought, she dumped in a ten-pound sack of lime.

By the time she was back in the cabin, she had forced all thought of Whitney from her mind. All of her attention was fixed on saving Richard.

In the bathroom, she removed the medicine cabinet from the wall and took an oversized cosmetics case from its hiding place. She replaced the medicine cabinet and carried the case into the bedroom.

Placing it on the bed, she removed the contents. Several wigs in various lengths and colors, a case containing several sets of contact lens in different colors, an elaborate nail kit that also contained a very efficient set of disguised lock picks, a variety of cosmetics, a small radio fitted with a listening device, two lighters, and a compact.

Setting these aside on the bed, she pushed a hidden lock and lifted out one side of the case. Inside were a half a dozen passports and documents. She took out one set and replaced the others. Selecting the wig and cosmetics that matched the picture in the passport, she repacked the rest.

Returning to the bathroom, she began to cut her hair.

Five

Seattle

FBI agent James Eberle hung up the receiver and grimaced. With all the work piled on his desk, the last thing he needed was to have to listen to the fantasies of a couple of lonely geriatrics. Still the Bureau had to maintain its image and these ladies had refused to be put off with anything less than a "real" FBI agent.

He looked up, as his office door opened, and forced a welcoming smile. The two elderly ladies entered hesitantly and paused as his secretary closed the door behind them. They glanced around the room, awe plainly written on the faces then turned their attention to him as he stood up. He wondered if he met their expectations of a "real" FBI agent. Of course, he wasn't as handsome as Robert Stack or as urbane as Robert Loggia, just your average clean cut features, blue eyes and sandy brown hair. He smiled inwardly. But he was something Stack and Loggia weren't, a "real" agent. Sometimes even he found it hard to believe he'd accomplished his boyhood dream.

Inviting them to have a seat, he studied them as they had studied him while they settled timidly into chairs facing the desk. Beneath their obvious nervousness, he noted a quiet determination. No, they didn't look like a couple of cranks. Still...

"You say you witnessed a kidnapping this morning? Have you reported it to the police?"

They both answered at once.

"They pushed her in a car."

"No, we came straight to you."

He held up a hand. "Please, one at a time. You realize the FBI cannot become involved unless requested by the local authorities or until after forty-eight hours."

"But—"

"I will listen to you, but first may I have your names?"

The short, plump one fluttered a hand towards her friend. "You tell him, Martha."

Eberle studied the cool, refined features of the older woman as she spoke. A retired teacher, he guessed.

"Martha Beeson. This is Agatha Grimes. Agatha and I always take a brisk walk, ten times around Green Lake, every morning. Regular as clockwork, rain or shine. Early, before the crowds. We have been doing so for the last three years. This morning we saw a young woman kidnapped. We came straight to you because we know the FBI handles kidnappings. We thought it would save time."

"Oh, yes," Agatha breathed. "Just like in *The Untouchables*. You must hurry and save her. Such a nice young woman."

"You know her?"

"Well, not exactly. I mean we don't know her name. But she runs every morning and she always smiles and waves to us."

Martha nodded slowly. "As Agatha says, a nice young woman. Manners. Not like so many young people today. You really must save her, young man." A shadow flitted over her face. "Her eyes were so frightened..."

He let them tell their story in their own words then led them through it again several times, posing questions, making notes.

Finally he closed his notebook. He wrote a name on the back of one of his business cards. He hesitated a moment then scribbled CALL ME underneath. He handed the card to Martha Grimes. "As I said earlier, you will need to notify the Seattle Police Department. I would suggest that you ask for this man. Give him my card."

After he ushered them out of his office, he sat for a moment frowning down at the notes he had taken. The women had given him a remarkable amount of information, including excellent descriptions of two of the men and even the license number of the car.

He leafed through his notes again until he found a statement by Agatha. "I'm sure she lives on Fourth Avenue. Anna Hughes's sister was giving a shower for her niece, Rosalie, and I was hunting for the house. Driving slowly, you understand. That's how I happened to see her. It was the third house from the corner. She was backing out of the garage. I waved but I guess she didn't see me."

Either the two women had actually witnessed a kidnapping or they had remarkably good imaginations. If it was a hoax, they had certainly made up a lot of details. Details that were both unnecessary and easily checked. The FBI didn't enter the picture until notified by the local authorities. Still. The hairs at the back of his neck lifted, crawled. It was a feeling he'd learned not to disregard.

Eberle's frown deepened as he reached for the phone.

~ * ~

Richard's mind whirled. Cramped in the fighter as it flew east into the rising sun, he struggled to make some sense out of what was happening. But nothing, absolutely nothing made sense. He searched the cockpit for the intercom but couldn't make heads nor tails out of the instruments in front of him. He beat his fist against the panel in frustration. A calm voice spoke in his ears. "Sir. Please do not touch anything. This flight will last several hours. I suggest you relax and enjoy it."

Richard rubbed a hand against his knee. Sure. Relax. Enjoy the flight. Nothing to it. Forget that your wife has been kidnapped. By the CIA, for God's sake. The government ... the U.S. government... *my* government has kidnapped my wife. Relax. Enjoy a free vacation courtesy of the CIA and the U.S. Navy. Jesus H. Christ. I'm going crazy. Not going, gone. This isn't happening. He closed his eyes, willing himself to sleep. Surely when he woke up, it would be in his own bed.

He awoke a couple of hours later as the plane banked into a steep turn. Richard studied the terrain as they swept in for a landing. The rolling hills, the neat fields indicated they were somewhere in the Midwest.

The plane rolled to a stop and the canopy popped open. Stiff and shaky, he climbed out of the plane with the aid of the pilot. A fuel truck, accompanied by a jeep with two Marines raced up. Two Marine guards marched him a few feet away while the plane was refueled.

"I've got to take a leak," he said, addressing the remark to no one in particular. One of the Marines walked over to the jeep, conferred with the driver and came back. "This way, sir."

He was motioned into the front seat, while two armed guards rode in back. The jeep sprinted across the tarmac and pulled up beside a concrete block building. The two guards led him inside, pointing to the latrine. Hope flared as they took up positions on either side of the door. It died just as rapidly as he entered and looked around. There was no window, no other door, no escape.

When he came out, they marched him back to the jeep, which whisked him back across the runway. They stood, rifles at the ready, as he climbed back into the plane. No one spoke.

~ * ~

Washington, DC

David Bergdorf arrived at Andrews Air Force Base, sweating and rushed, his mind still reeling from his briefing by the president. The whole scenario seemed unbelievable, particularly his assigned role. He was both excited and a little frightened. The idea of going along on a clandestine mission was the stuff of movies and books. He was no James Bond or Mel Gibson. And this wasn't a novel or a movie. If he made a mistake, there was no one to re-write the script or yell cut.

He felt dwarfed by the huge transport as he walked beneath the wing and stopped to stare up at the two giant turbofans. He climbed the personnel steps aft of the wing. An airman met him at the door and motioned him forward, slamming the door behind him. A row of fold-down seat lined the bulkhead. The CIA man, Carter, looked up as David was escorted to an adjoining seat, nodded then returned to his contemplation of the files in his lap.

David glanced out of the porthole as he fastened his seat belt. The plane was already beginning to taxi. He closed his eyes and willed his stomach to stop roiling. He took several deep breaths, determined not to let the CIA man see his nervousness. The big plane lumbered down the runway and into the air. Perhaps distraction would help. He tried to ask Carter a question but the noise defeated him. A few minutes later, an airman brought them Styrofoam cups of black coffee. David took his gratefully and used it to wash down a mild sleeping pill. It was the only sure way to control his fear of flying.

While he waited for the pill to take effect, he replayed in his mind his briefing by President Gossard. The Chinese were intent on destroying the western world with the use of some new bacteria. They were using Moslem terrorists to dispense the bacteria, led by a man everyone feared but only one person knew. Unbelievable. Fantastic. Only he and some unwilling Israeli could save the free world. More than fantastic, something out of a Grade B movie. Totally unreal. A script at which Mel Gibson would turn up his nose.

He glanced out the porthole, shivered and closed his eyes. It was all a nightmare. It had to be. As he drifted off, he thought Mel Gibson at least wouldn't be afraid to fly.

~ * ~

The F-14 taxied to a stop. The pilot popped the canopy and climbed out, motioning Richard to follow. Sweating in the humid air, Richard stared groggily around. Was this the second or third stop they had made to refuel? He'd stopped caring; accepting the fact there was no escape. Not now, not yet.

A tanker truck was already refueling the plane. Two jeeps pulled up and the pilot headed for one of them as another pilot climbed out. Two marines, automatic weapons at the ready, moved in on him. A civilian stepped around them and handed Richard a brown paper bag.

He took it wordlessly and glanced inside. It contained a plastic wrapped sandwich and a Coca Cola, the sides of the can wet with condensation. He stared at the man, who grinned and shrugged.

"Lunch. Better eat it in a hurry. You're off again as soon as the plane is fueled."

Richard started to hand the sack back then changed his mind. He was hungry. Starving himself wasn't going to help Rachel. Why make it easier for them? Silently he popped the top of the Coke and drank half of it. The sandwich was bologna, soggy with mayonnaise. He hated mayonnaise. He only managed half of the sandwich before his stomach rebelled. He stuffed it back in the sack, drank the rest of the coke and added the can before handing the sack to the waiting man.

The man started to turn away and Richard asked quickly, "Where are you taking me? And why? What's this all about?"

The man shrugged. "That's not for me to say. Time to get back in the plane."

"I've got to take a leak."

The man looked uncomfortably around. They were at the end of a taxiway, surrounded by nothing but sand and a few low palmettos. He gestured towards the edge of the tarmac. Richard walked to the sand, the marines a step behind him, their faces impassive. He studied the color of his urine and tried to estimate the output as he urinated. No problem yet but he would need more fluids. Without dialysis, his body would need all the fluids it could get. He walked back onto the tarmac.

"I've got to have water, at least a pint."

The civilian shrugged. "Sorry."

Richard felt the anger that lay curled in his belly begin to expand. "Hey, don't give that sorry shit. I need fluids and I need then now. Get me something more to drink or I don't get back on that plane."

The civilian looked at him uncertainly. Richard folded his arms and stared back. Finally the man shrugged and walked over to one of the jeeps. It took off across the runway.

Richard slipped his arms out of the flight suit, tying the sleeves around his waist, and walked toward the plane, planning to stand in the shade of the wing. The pilot motioned him away. The kerosene fumes were so strong, he didn't argue.

A few minutes later, the jeep reappeared out of the heat waves and screeched to a stop. The civilian got out carrying a quart thermos. Richard took it, poured a top full of the water and drank it. It was ice cold. He shot a look of gratitude towards the man. He drank the whole quart and handed it back with a quiet thank you.

When he climbed back on board, the pilot showed him the relief tube. In less than half an hour, they were back in the air, still heading east.

Hours later, Richard awoke to a sight that brought beads of terror to his brow. Above, blotting out the night sky, was a huge plane and his pilot seemed to be climbing right into it. He wasn't aware of his cry of panic until the pilot's voice erupted in his ears.

"Relax, buddy. We're just refueling. Do it all the time. No big deal. We'll be on our way again before you know it."

Relax. No Big deal. God. Was this nightmare never going to end?

Six

Rachel glanced at the wristwatch with its bright orange plastic strap, checked in the mirror to see if the ankle length orange flowered caftan hung straight and sighed. God! She looked like an aging flower child. Not even Richard would recognize her in this get up. She glanced at her feet, clad in rough leather huaraches they'd picked up in Mexico. Her feet were too white, too clean; she'd have to remember to rub dirt on them when she got outside. She frowned at the press-on nails, in bright orange, that decorated her fingers and toes. Were they a little too much?

She leaned towards the mirror and adjusted the brown wig then slipped on a pair of huge tortoise-shell glasses, which did nothing to hide her green eyes but did change the outline of her face.

Satisfied with her appearance, she picked up a large straw purse with MEXICO woven on the side in bright straw letters. Most of the twenty five thousand dollars was hidden in a lead-lined film holder. She stuffed it on the bottom. A cheap Polaroid camera, hung from her shoulder, completed her disguise.

She locked the cabin, remembered to rub dirt on her feet and climbed into the BMW. It was full dark by the time she pulled into a long-term parking lot a mile from Sea-Tac airport. Paying a month's rental, she took the shuttle bus to the terminal.

A glance at her watch told her she was running late. At the counter, she paid cash for her ticket. She checked the dialysis machine then her heart twisted as she watched it disappear with the other luggage. What if it didn't make her flight? What if the airline lost it? What if it ended up in New Zealand instead of New York? But she couldn't take it through security, not here. It was too unusual an item. It was sure to cause comment, be remembered. But, oh God, what if it was lost?

These thoughts occupied her all the way to the gate. From her window seat, she craned her neck, trying to see the baggage carts. Finally she gave up. It would make it or it wouldn't, there was nothing she could do now.

As the plane reached cruising altitude, Rachel settled back in her seat to plan her next move. Someone would be looking for Whitney. And they would find him. That she knew. The question was, how soon? She was too experienced to have any illusions about the CIA. Like all clandestine agencies, they had their screw-ups like Whitney, but on the whole they were an efficient organization.

They would find the cabin, find Whitney and their anger would drive them. No agency took lightly the killing of one of their own. They would find the car and know she had flown somewhere. She didn't doubt they would track her to New York. If she'd had more time, she could have covered her tracks more effectively, but time was the one thing she didn't have to spare. At least her disguise should slow them down.

Finding Richard quickly had to be her top priority. How long could he go without dialysis, how long before the poison spread through his body?

She forced her thoughts away from Richard to concentrate on the CIA This whole operation was a screw-up. Rushed. If they'd had the time for an adequate investigation, they would never have grabbed Richard. So, they hadn't done their homework. Chances were good they didn't know everything, yet. If so, they wouldn't be able to track her before she landed in New York. If they didn't pick her up getting off this plane, she was home free.

She turned down the drinks offered by the stewardess, but ate everything on the dinner plate and was even able to cadge an extra dinner roll. Plans made, hunger appeased, she turned off the reading lamp, let back her seat and closed her eyes. She had done all she could. The next few hours were in the hands of the gods. She remembered her premonition of the morning. Perhaps there *were* old gods, jealous gods. Eventually she drifted off into a restless sleep.

She awoke stiff but partially refreshed as the plane began its approach to Kennedy Airport. She waited until the passengers started filing off before rising and joining the thickest part of the crowd. If they had found her car, had traced her onto this flight, they would be waiting.

As she stepped off the ramp, her gaze swept the waiting area, searching for watchers. They were either very good or they weren't there. She forced down the urge to run as the group began spreading out inside the terminal and walked unhurriedly instead to the nearest Ladies Room.

It was relatively uncrowded. She strolled to the last cubicle and stepped inside. Weak with relief, she leaned against the locked door for a second. She'd made it. They'd never catch her now.

Time for a whole new personality. She pulled off the brown wig and hung in on the door hook. A moment later, the caftan joined it. Sitting on the toilet, she took off the huaraches, pulled the orange nails from her toes and slipped her feet into Indian moccasins taken from the straw purse. Wiggling her toes, she sighed with relief. Wearing sandals was too near being barefoot. She liked the comforting feel of shoes protecting her feet.

Time was slipping away. Standing up, she rolled down the legs of the faded jeans she had been wearing under the caftan and adjusted the pale blue tube top. From the bag, she took a tightly rolled white Mexican cotton blouse and slipped it on, leaving it unbuttoned and tying the tails at the waist.

Also from the straw bag, she took a smaller cotton purse, a blue plastic watchband and a long blond wig. She transferred the remaining contents: an over-sized compact; new passport and documents; cigarette lighter; an unopened package of Marlboro cigarettes; change purse; billfold; contact case; comb; baggage claim check; and the money.

Her hands began to tremble as she popped the orange nails from her fingers and tossed them in the straw bag. Take it easy. Too much hurry could be disastrous. A few seconds later she had replaced the watchband and the orange one disappeared into the bag. She settled the blonde wig, adjusting it with the help of the compact mirror. The brown wig, caftan and huaraches disappeared into the straw bag.

Relief washed over her as she stepped out of the cubicle, deposited the straw bag in a wastepaper basket and walked to the row of lavatories. With the speed of long practice, she added blue contact lenses. After washing her face and hands, she combed the wig, fluffing it around her face. So far, so good. She took a deep breath and opened the door. *Your walk! Change your walk!*

When she left the rest room, she moved with the awkward gait of a teenager. Only one more period of danger lay ahead. If they knew about the dialysis machine, if they were watching it...

She looked at her watch and breathed a sigh of relief. The transformation had taken only ten minutes. There would still be a crowd around the carousel. She trotted clumsily toward the baggage claim area, the cosmetic case in one hand, camera and purse flopping from her shoulder.

The carousel area was crowded, the baggage just beginning to appear. She shoved her way to the front and waited. Would the dialysis case come before the crowd thinned out? Would it come at all? A hundred pairs of eyes seemed to bore into her back.

It came and she swung it down in front of her, her nerves taut. The hand clamping hard on her should that she half expected did not come. Her shoulders, tightened by tension, began to ache as she wormed her way out of the crowd.

She hesitated outside the baggage area, peering around and tapping her foot impatiently, giving every impression of impatiently waiting, expecting to be met.

When she was certain no one was paying her any undue attention, she found a cart, loaded the dialysis and cosmetic cases on it and headed for the British Airways ticket counter.

She waited patiently in line then in a true Swedish accent, said, "Marta Jorgenson. I believe you have a reservation for me." She handed the ticket agent a Swedish passport and cash for the ticket.

In the lounge area, she decided she could risk one drink and ordered a gin and tonic. She rarely drank but occasionally enjoyed the astringent taste of gin. She was amused when the waitress asked for I.D.

Leaning back, sipping the drink, the tension began to drain away, her jangled nerves calmed. An hour later, relaxed and confident, she boarded the plane to London.

London. In London she would find help. Much as she hated to, she would contact Mossad.

Watching the early morning sun wash over the skyscrapers of New York as the plane circled northeast, she felt in her bones that she was only hours behind Richard.

I'm coming, darling. Hold on. I'm coming.

Seven

Victoria Falls, Zimbabwe

Reginald Umbulu hung up the phone with a shaking hand. Had he heard right? He could feel his heart racing with the hard, swift beats of a talking drum. He replayed the words in his mind. Yes, the code words meant that he was being upgraded to active status.

Active status! Excitement coursed through him. He jumped up and began to pace the small closet he called an office. His broad, black face split into a grin. A real spy! At last *they* had realized his worth. He wasn't sure who *they* were, but he always thought of *THEM* in capital letters. Since that first funny little man had recruited him, he'd never seen any of *THEM*. A muffled voice called him once a month for his report and the money always arrived in a plain brown envelope with no return address and a Bulawayo postmark.

Now, this unexpected call. It wasn't even the proper day of the month. And the message, oh, the message. He stopped pacing and stared out of the small window. Two agents would be arriving the next day and he was to assist them in their mission! He, Reginald Umbulu. An international spy! Conscious of his new status, he buttoned his jacket and tightened his tie. He straightened his shoulders, puffing out his chest.

Forgetting the damaged leg on his chair, he dropped his three hundred-plus pound frame onto it. The leg split toppling him onto the floor. Chagrinned, he heaved himself up and crossed the room, cracking the door and peering out. The hall was empty. He shut the door, unsure what he had expected to see. Peter Lorre? Sidney Greenstreet?

Sighing, he perched on the edge of the table he used for a desk, his forehead tightening in concentration. What would Agent 007 do in this circumstance? Reginald had read all of the Bond books, some a half a dozen times, and he'd seen all of the James Bond films. He just wished they wouldn't keep changing the actors. His favorite was Sean Connery. But even Connery couldn't compare to Humphrey Bogart and Robert Mitchum, whose movies he'd watched as a child, squatting in the dirt, the flickering images projected on a wrinkled sheet strung along the side of the itinerant projectionist's beat-up old Ford truck.

He jerked his mind back to the present. It was all well and good to dream of being an international spy, but this wasn't a dream. This was real. He was expected to take action, but what? How?

A *plan*. He needed a *plan*. His mission was to locate all Chinese and Arabs in the area before the agents arrived then give the agents all of the assistance they required. He'd be working with *real* agents, trained professionals.

Well, the first part wouldn't be too hard. His brother worked at the airport. He'd call him first. Then he'd call his wife's nephew who was employed at the Elephant Hills Hotel. As head bellman, he'd have no problem checking on the guests here at the Victoria Falls Hotel.

His eyes swept the room. Secrecy. Wasn't that important? And files. Didn't spies keep files? Of course. He could filch some file folders from the accounting office.

He opened the door and glanced cautiously up and down the hall before slipping out. After all, now that he was on a mission, he couldn't be too careful. Who knew what other agents might be watching. He sidled a few steps down the corridor then paused. Would James Bond sneak down a hall? Humphrey Bogart? Of course not. Besides, he had every right to be here. This was his hotel. Squaring his shoulders, he strode past the front desk and into the accounting office. Giving his wife's youngest sister a patronizing smile, he opened the supply cabinet and helped himself to half a dozen folders, a tablet and a hand full of pencils.

"Reginald Umbulu, what you think you doin'?"

"You just hush, Malia. I got important business to take care of. Secret business, so you just don't ask no questions. Sharpen these pencils while I find a new chair. That one in my office broke."

Carrying his pilfered supplies and a chair from the dining room, he retired to his office, locking the door behind him. He shoved the remains of the broken chair under the table. He'd carry them out later. Now he had work to do.

He stared for a moment at the file folders then sat down and began carefully lettering the tabs: SECRET; MORE SECRET; MOST SECRET; MOST UTTERLY SECRET. He paused then labeled the last two PARTLY SECRET and NOT SECRET.

Smiling he stacked the folders to the side and picked up the tablet. If he were going to do a good job, he would need help. To be a master spy, he needed his own network of sub-spies. He began to list his relatives then his wife's relatives then friends. When he had finished, the list covered two pages. For once, having a large family would be an asset.

He picked up the phone and dialed. While it was ringing, he glanced back over his lists. He and his network would have all of the information the agents wanted long before they arrived tomorrow. *THEY* would be pleased. Perhaps pleased enough to send him to the United States, to spy school, train him to be a real spy, send him to exotic places. He would fly on a big jet plane like the ones the tourists arrived on, meet beautiful girls in romantic bars, drive racing speedboats across tropical lagoons. He'd finally be able to see cities larger than Bulawayo. Paris. London. New York. Maybe even Las Vegas. His brother's voice broke into the dreams.

~ * ~

Azores

From the large window overlooking the NATO base, Timothy Bottoms watched the big transport plane taxi to a stop with bored eyes. Coralita was pissed. As if, for God's sake, he'd preferred spending the night staring out the window instead of in her bed. Effing Yanks. Always up to something. Screw them. Dreamily, he began to catalog Coralita's charms.

He snapped awake and grabbed his binoculars as two civilians exited the plane. He leaned forward, studying them, memorizing their features, noted the briefcase the shorter man carried. They climbed into a waiting sedan and were driven rapidly across the tarmac.

Bottoms cursed as the car disappeared behind a building then let out a breath of relief as the sedan reappeared, heading towards an idling Sikorsky SH-3H helicopter. He flipped through his memory file for statistics as he watched the two men board. The statistic that most interested him was the helicopter's range, over 600 miles. He was even more puzzled when it headed east over the Atlantic. There was nothing but water, miles of water in that direction…unless the helicopter was rendezvousing with a ship. He watched until it became only a small dot and finally disappeared over the horizon, still heading east.

~ * ~

The Sikorsky hovered over the pad then gently settled onto the rolling deck of the HMS Farango. David Bergdorf watched with interest as the whirlybird was quickly lashed down. He didn't recognize the rank of the officer that greeted them, but followed as he and Carter were led through a maze of passageways and finally into a comfortable cabin.

"Captain Maccauley's compliments. This is his cabin and at your disposal while you are on board. He regrets that he is not able to greet you himself but he is engaged on the bridge." The young officer waved a hand towards a credenza. "Hot coffee, tea and a selection of cold sandwiches and deserts. Please feel free to help yourselves. I will escort our other guest here as soon as he arrives."

It was Carter who spoke. "Do you have any idea how long that will be?"

"We are in radio contact with the pilot. His ETA is less than ten minutes."

Seventeen minutes later, a green-faced and shaky Richard Royer was escorted into the cabin. He gaped at the occupants with the blank stare of a shell-shocked soldier.

Bergdorf led him to a chair and gently shoved him into it. "How do you take your coffee?"

Richard continued to stare at him. His wife had been kidnapped, he'd been flown half way around the world, landed on what was obviously a British carrier somewhere in the Atlantic and now some idiot was asking him how he took his coffee. Sweet Jesus. Had the whole world gone crazy?

"I said, how do you take your coffee?"

Richard licked his dry lips and croaked, "Black. I take my coffee black."

A thick mug was thrust into his hands and he sipped it gratefully. It seemed to bring the room and the men more fully into focus. Bergdorf had taken his seat beside Carter. He was watching Richard intently.

"My name is David Bergdorf. I am a special representative of the president. I will be accompanying you. This is Agent Carter of the CIA. He has prepared our cover."

Carter cleared his throat and shuffled the papers on his lap. "We'd better get started. Royer, your name will be Richard Rossiter. Your cover will be a representative for Talent Universal. You are going to Victoria Falls to see a group of native dancers. If they are good, your agency may be interested in booking them on a tour of the United States sometime next year. You are not a negotiator. You are only there to judge the quality of their performance."

He smiled good-naturedly. "That lets you off the hook for any negotiations. If you get any pressure, you will be able to say that isn't in your bailiwick."

He opened the briefcase and pulled out a folder. "Here's your background. I suggest you start memorizing. I'll need these back before we leave."

Carter turned to Bergdorf. "I understand that you are to stick close to Rossiter so you will be traveling as his 'assistant'." He grimaced at David's look of distaste. "Sorry. It's the only thing we could come up with in such short notice. And, let's face it, your... ah... sexual preferences will make you seem the more innocuous. Your new identity is David Rubinski"

Richard stared down at the folder in his hand. He shook his head, trying to clear it. Incredible. This spy stuff was real. Somebody was actually sending him to the middle of Africa to find other spies and collect some kind of deadly germs. Sweet Jesus. He had to make them understand they had the wrong man.

He looked at Bergdorf, whose head was bent over his own file of papers. He cleared his throat. "Look, Bergdorf, I don't know what this is all about but you've got the wrong man."

He felt himself flushing at the faintly contemptuous look of surprise on Carter's face. Roger glared back belligerently. "It's crazy. The whole thing is crazy."

Bergdorf studied Richard's face for a moment then turned to Carter. "Would you mind leaving us for a few minutes. They probably have a pot of coffee in the ward room."

Carter closed the briefcase with a snap and stood up, looking at Richard in disgust. "You're an asshole even by Mossad standards." He stalked out of the room. Richard expected him to slam the door but he didn't. He closed it quietly but with a firmness that underlined his contempt more than slamming would have done.

Richard glared at Bergdorf. "There it is again. Mossad. What the hell is he talking about?"

David sighed and folded his hands over the file in his lap. "Look, Royer, I can't say that I approve of the way this has been handled. I don't blame you for being angry. But you're not making things any easier."

"For God's sake, will you tell me what this is all about? My wife is kidnapped, my home broken into by a bunch of goons, I'm shanghaied and flown half way around the world, landed on a carrier somewhere in the middle of an ocean and you want *me* to make things easier. Jesus H. Christ, what the hell is going on?"

"I was skeptical when Satterfield said this was the only way we could get you, but I understand what he meant now." Bergdorf slammed an angry hand against his knee, his voice rising. "Damn it, man, our countries are facing the worst threat in history. We need you. We need Zephyr's knowledge and expertise."

"There it is again. Zephyr. Who or what is this Zephyr."

"Damn you, Royer. Will you stop playing games. We know. Do you understand? We know!" he shouted.

"Then you know a hell of a lot more than I do," Richard shouted back. He fought down his anger and struggled to speak calmly. "Look, please believe me. I don't know what you're talking about. Please, start at the beginning and tell me just what is going on."

Bergdorf's knuckles whitened as he struggled to contain his temper. "You are a bastard, aren't you? You want it from the top? Okay, if it means you'll cooperate, I'll play your stupid little game."

He explained in detail on the reports that had been received from China. Richard listened in growing horror.

When Bergdorf had finished, Richard stared at him for a moment then said, "This is real? It's not some kind joke?"

"Joke? Do you think the president has time to play jokes? For God's sake, Royer, this is as real as it gets."

"Okay. Now tell me about the Zephyr."

"For Pete's sake," Bergdorf sprang to his feet and glared down at Richard and said through gritted teeth. "You really are a bastard."

Richard raised his hand. His voice quiet, "Never mind. Just humor me in this. Pretend I know nothing. Tell me."

Bergdorf turned away and began to pace. "Everything I know is hearsay. In the late 80's and early 90's, Zephyr was one of Mossad's top covert agents. He is credited with any number of intelligence coups, an extraordinarily skilled agent." Bergdorf paused and gave him a sarcastic look. "He's supposed to be daring, courageous and deadly."

"But who is he?"

"No one knows. Supposedly only two men high in Mossad know his real identity. However, there are leaks in every organization. He is supposed to have retired in the early 90's and gone to ground in the United States. Retired. Wants to be let alone." Bergdorf squinted at Richard. "Supposedly he has a hate on for all clandestine services. I can't tell you any more than that."

"And why is this Zephyr so important now? Surely the CIA has agents just as capable." He smiled bitterly. "Although after what I've just seen, I wonder."

"Because Barenji, like Zephyr, is a legend. Zephyr is critical because he is the only person that knows Barenji by sight."

"So you send legend to catch a legend."

Bergdorf smiled for the first time. "Yes."

Richard did not smile. "You have one very big problem." He stared at Bergdorf and said quietly, "I am not Zephyr."

Bergdorf made a motion of disgust, denial.

"Please. Listen to me. I really am not this super spy. I am Richard Royer, ex-violinist and so-so composer." He shrugged his shoulders helplessly. "I can't help you. Believe me, if what you say is true, I truly wish I could."

Bergdorf's face tightened in anger. "They told me you were a real low-life bastard. Now I believe them. Just cut the crap. I don't want to hear any more of it."

"Listen—"

"Shut up. Just shut up." He dropped back down on the sofa, shifted away from Richard and opened the file in front of him.

Reluctantly, Richard opened his own file and stared blankly at the typewritten pages. He began to feel suffocated. He loosened his tie and unbuttoned the top button of his shirt, but it didn't help. He began to pant, sucking in great gulps of air. He remembered, as a child, catching a moth in a jar. It had flown frantically around and around, beating its wings helplessly against the jar, until his mother had made him turn it loose. Was this how the moth had felt?

He was in as much a trap as the moth had been. Only there was no one to make them let him out. He would have to get out on his own. Should he tell them about his need for dialysis? Explain that he couldn't do what they wanted. Would they let Rachel go? With all that he now knew, would they consider him a security risk? He began to massage his temples. The thoughts pounding into his brain sent cold chills racing up and down his spine. He'd seen too many movies, read too many thrillers. They were fun to read, but he'd never believed such things really happened. But this wasn't a book or a movie. This was real. Wasn't it? If not, it was the longest nightmare he'd ever experienced. The longest and the worst.

He shook his head. He couldn't risk Rachel's life. He would have to play their game until he found his chance. He had no choice. Rachel's life depended on him.

He glanced at Bergdorf. Okay. He'd play their game. He didn't believe this Chinese scenario. It was simply too incredible. For some reason, the CIA wanted this Zephyr. And by some absurd reasoning, they had decided he was this spy, Zephyr. Another thought occurred to him, equally ridiculous. Perhaps they did know he wasn't Zephyr but thought he could lead them to Zephyr. Was that why they wouldn't listen to him?

In the end, he supposed it didn't matter. He was here and Rachel was... where? He really had no choice. He'd have to play along, at least for now. Play along and watch for a chance to get away. And if he couldn't? Don't think about that. Play along for now. But in the end, he'd make them pay. Oh, yes, they'd pay. And if they had hurt Rachel, he'd hunt them down. Hunt them down and kill them.

His breathing eased. He picked up the file and began to read.

Eight

Rachel tossed fitfully in her sleep as the 747 droned through the sky. Barenji. The PLO terrorist whose orders had nearly killed her in Beirut. The man she had been sent to find. No, that wasn't true. They had never expected her to find him. Oh, no, he was meant to find *her*.

She was back in Beirut. Crawling through the rubble, choking on the dust and smoke. He and his men were there, behind her somewhere, hunting. She knew he'd find her. He had to. She'd seen his face.

She crawled into the basement of a bombed-out building. Slithering behind a tottering slab of broken concrete her hand touched warm flesh. Rachel choked back a scream as an injured Lebanese woman shoved a dead baby into her hands, begging her to save him. She tried to tell the woman that the child was dead, but the woman was too far gone to understand.

Minutes later the woman died. Rachel had cowered beside the dead bodies through the long night. Starting in terror at each sound. By morning she was half-crazed with hunger, thirst and fear. It was pure panic, a subliminal instinct for survival, rather than conscious thought that drove Rachel to strip the woman's body and don the black garments. In her confused state, abandoning the baby never occurred to her. The woman had pressed the child on her and she clung to it.

As pale fingers of light from the new day penetrated the darkness outside, the hole in which she was hiding took on the aspects of a tomb. She didn't want to die cowering in the dark. She wanted to die in the sunlight! That she was going to die she accepted. Clasping the body of the child to her breast, she crept out of the basement, back into the fighting.

Hours later, exhausted mentally and physically, she huddled in the ruins, waiting for death. Barenji's assassin was close. She could sense him. The man with the knife. The man who liked to cut, slowly, with the expertise of a butcher. Soon he would find her and it would all be over. Only it hadn't been the assassin who had found her, it had been Richard.

She awoke, sweating and exhausted, as the plane landed at London's Heathrow airport. She collected her luggage, passed without hitch through immigration and wheeled her luggage through one of the NOTHING TO DECLARE lanes at customs. After reconfirming her South African Airways flight to Johannesburg, she stowed the dialysis machine and the overnight case in a locker and caught a shuttle bus into London. She had eleven hours to complete her plans. For Richard's sake, it was time to put hate behind her and contact Mossad. She would need help. The kind of help that only they could give her.

~ * ~

HMS Farango, Atlantic Ocean

Carter stretched and began to gather the files into his briefcase. "That's all I can do for you. Your papers should pass any normal inspection. You will be met at the base in the Azores and escorted to the charter flight. Don't forget that those passports will have to be turned in when you get back to the States."

"If we get back," Richard muttered.

Carter gave him a sharp look then manifestly ignored him.

David opened the door, motioned to the guard and told him that the F-14 passenger was ready to leave. "You can inform the Captain and the helicopter pilot that we will be leaving in about two hours. Please knock on the door," he glanced at his watch, "at 0500 hours."

Carter paused in the doorway to wish them good luck. His glance at Royer indicated he thought they would need it.

David crossed the room to the head. At the door, he looked back at Richard. "I'd suggest you get some sleep. You can use the couch. Toss down one of those back cushions, I'll sack out on the floor."

In the gray dawn, chilled and still exhausted, Richard scurried across the deck to the helicopter pad and followed David into the waiting machine. He had no appreciation of the spectacular sunrise as the Sikorsky raced towards the islands. He forced all thoughts of Rachel out of his mind and concentrated on perfecting his new identity.

The car that met them was a nondescript Simca driven by a man in civilian clothes. The man drove sedately across the base in silence. Pulling up beside a 727, he jumped out, opened the trunk and pulled out two suitcases.

David made a production of tipping the man then handed one suitcase to Richard and picked up the other. Somewhere during the long trip from Seattle Richard's own bag had disappeared.

They had no trouble spotting the film crew they were joining. They stood out like a parrot among a flock of sparrows and were just as raucous.

"Hey, Richard, baby." A rotund little man detached himself from the group and trotted up to seize Richard's hand. He peered myopically up at Richard. "You are Rossiter, aren't you? Someone said you were joining us here. Max. Max Zylkocec. Didn't we meet at Cannes last year?"

"'Fraid not. I missed last year." Richard managed to retrieve his hand from Zylkocec's sweaty clasp and resisted the urge to wipe his palm. He glanced to where the group was beginning to straggle up the steps and into the plane. "Looks like we made it just in time."

Zylkocec glanced over his shoulder. "Yeah, about time, too. Come on. I'll introduce you to everyone when we get on the plane. You gonna be in Kenya long? Wait till you meet Kiley Mann. When this picture comes out, she's gonna be one hot property." He giggled and nudged Richard in the ribs. "Hot in every way, know what I mean. Just don't forget who introduced her, okay? One of the script girls is a cute little number but cold, man, you know what I mean? But she'll warm up. Africa does that to broads, know what I mean?"

He kept up a running commentary on the cast and crew as they straggled into the plane. Finally distracted, Zylkocec bounded ahead to yell something to someone.

David punched Richard on the arm. "Loosen up, man, and get with it or you'll stand out like a sore thumb." He winked. "Know what I mean?"

Richard forced a laugh, the sound grating from his throat like the rasp of a rusty gate. God, how could he laugh at a time like this? He didn't belong here. It was stupid. The whole thing was stupid. He'd never be able to carry it off. His gut tightened in panic.

"Easy. Look, we're supposed to be lovers. We'll grab seats in the back and pretend we're in our own little world." He grabbed Richard's hand and pushed through the crowd to the back of the plane. He stuffed his bag in the overhead rack, took Richard's and stuffed it under the seat. "You take the window seat and pretend to sleep."

Richard slipped into the seat and closed his eyes in relief. By the time the plane had leveled out, he was no longer pretending. But it was no refreshing rest. The nightmares that plagued him left him even more enervated and disoriented.

The hot, humid air hit them in the face like a sauna, heavy with the fetid stench of rotting vegetation, when they left the plane in Nairobi. A black clad man, his white teeth gleaming in his chocolate face, holding a hand printed sign with the name Rossiter, approached. Carrying their luggage, they slipped away from the group and met him a few feet away.

"I'm Rossiter."

"If you will come this way, sirs, your plane is waiting. If you will give me you baggage checks, I will see that your luggage is brought to the plane."

"This is all we have."

"Fine, sir." He snapped his fingers and two scantily clad boys leaped forward and took their suitcases. "Come with me."

"Don't we have to clear customs?"

"No, sir, since you are not staying in Kenya. But you must go directly to your plane." He rolled his eyes towards a soldier who was approaching. There was no missing the automatic weapon in his hands. "Come. You must go directly to the plane."

They followed the courier across the tarmac to a large private jet. An attractive attendant stood waiting at the bottom of the steps. She smiled as they approached.

"Mr. Rossiter. It is a pleasure to have you aboard. We can leave as soon as you are settled."

The two boys dashed up the steps with the luggage, dropped it and took a hasty look around before bouncing back down at a harsh word from their military escort. Their eyes were dancing as they held out their hands. Richard handed them each a couple of dollars as the courier berated them. He subsided and backed away when David handed him a ten.

"Shall we board, gentlemen?"

They preceded the attendant into the plane and settled themselves in two comfortable easy chairs. The attendant shut and locked the door then disappeared into the cockpit. Moments later the plane began to taxi.

The attendant reappeared. "I am Miss Stevens. I will be serving you a champagne brunch as soon as we are airborne. If you will fasten your seat belts, we will be taking off momentarily." She flashed another toothpaste smile as they buckled up and then took her own seat.

Richard and David exchanged glances. David settled back with a sigh. "Now this is the only way to travel."

~ * ~

Reginald Umbulu grabbed the phone on the second ring. His pulse quickened as he recognized the voice. "They will be arriving by private plane in two hours. Do you have their room booked?"

"Yes, sir. One deluxe room with two beds."

"Good. Have them met. Do not go yourself. You will make contact with them after they are checked in. Do you have the information they require?"

"Yes, sir. There is a—"

"Not on the phone, you idiot. Tell them when they arrive."

"Yes, sir. I'm sorry—" He was talking into an empty line.

Reginald slowly replaced the receiver. A moment later he picked it up again and dialed his second cousin who operated a small tour company.

~ * ~

Richard felt his pulse quicken as he stared at the sheet of mist that spewed into the air. He craned his neck seeking his first view of Victoria Falls. He could see nothing through the mist. He settled back and tightened his seat belt as the plane circled and began its descent.

Miss Stevens gave them her toothy smile as they thanked her and headed for the terminal. They had landed briefly in Bulawayo to clear customs and immigration and now headed directly into the terminal.

A black man in a neat but too small chauffeur's uniform approached them. "Mr. Rossiter? Mr. Rubinski? I am Matthew. I am to take you to your hotel. It is twenty miles into Victoria Falls." He took their cases with a wide grin. "This way please."

Richard stared out of the van window, intrigued in spite of his confusion and anger. Somehow the sight of an elephant ambling beside the road seemed more natural than anything that had happened to him in the last twenty-four hours. In the rabbit-hole world he had been thrust into, the abnormal had become normal, the irrational, rational. Somehow, he had to adjust, to cope. More than cope, conquer.

The Victoria Falls Hotel was a monument to English Colonial architecture, but Richard was in no state to enjoy its beauty. He wanted nothing more than a cold shower and clean sheets. He could smell the stink of his sweat; his body trying to cope with the toxins that his kidneys could no longer process. How much longer could he go without dialysis?

He was hardly aware of the huge bellman who led them to the large, airy bedroom. His tired brain barely took in the twelve-foot ceilings, the tall windows, the slowly revolving ceiling fan. His gaze fastened on the nearest of the two queen-sized beds and he stumbled towards it. God, if he could just have eight hours in a comfortable bed, maybe, just maybe, he could come to grips with this nightmare.

Somewhere behind him, the bellman was chattering. Would the man never leave so he could sleep? A phrase caught his ear. He turned and stared at the man.

"What did you say?"

"I said you might hear the hyenas laughing tonight."

Richard stared at the expectant look on the man's face. He blinked, trying to concentrate. The sentence meant something. What was it? Of course, this was their contact. What was he supposed to answer? It came to him. "Only if something dies tonight."

The bellman's smile broadened and he nodded. He stepped back into the hall and glanced quickly in both directions before closing the door and moving closer to Richard. "My network has made many inquiries and I have much information for you. There are three suspicious men here in this very hotel. One is traveling on an Israeli passport but my agents believe that he is of the Muslim faith. There are also two gentlemen traveling with Egyptian passports. There is also a Greek couple, but who is to say that they are really from Greece. They, too, could be Arabs in disguise. Also, there is a Mr. Whitehead with a British passport staying at the Elephant Hills Hotel but my agents feel sure that he is really an Arab. At least he is unlike most English that have stayed here. Too dark and his manner is not quite that of an Englishman, a least not the type of Englishman we are used to seeing. Also, there is a Chinese gentleman, Mr. Ho Lee, and two gentlemen who claim to be Japanese at Elephant Hills."

Richard stared at the man. What was he supposed to do now?

David stepped into the breach. "Thank you, Mr.—?"

"Umbulu. Reginald Umbulu."

"Thank you, Mr. Umbulu. You have done an excellent job."

"What do you wish me to do now? It is a pleasure to work with such esteemed agents." He addressed this to Richard.

"Uh, is there any way you can have them followed? Without their knowing, of course. We need to discuss what you have told us. We'll get back to you later."

"Of course, sirs. I have arranged to work both night shifts so I will be available if you need me. You have only to ring the desk and ask for me."

David quietly maneuvered the bellman to the door. "Well, thank you, Reginald. We'll be in touch with you later this evening. You've done an excellent job."

As soon as David closed the door, Richard headed for the bathroom. He paused in the doorway and looked at David. "I am going to take a shower. Then I am going to crawl in that bed and I am going to sleep for eight hours."

David stared at Richard's grim face, taking in for the first time the sunken eyes and lines of exhaustion. Some of his resentment died away. He cracked a crooked smile. "Go ahead. We can both use a shower and a little sleep. But I can't promise a full eight hours."

Nine

London

Rachel caught an airport bus to Victoria Station then a taxi to Beauchamps Street. After quick stops in a couple of boutiques, she took a bus to Portabello Road. Stopping at a telephone kiosk, she dialed a number, let it ring four times, hung up and re-dialed. This time the phone was answered on the first ring with a guttural, "Yes."

She gave a code that in the past had identified her as a Mossad agent and one which indicated extreme emergency. The old codes were probably no longer in effect, but someone was sure to recognize the emergency code. "I need an immediate meeting with the Chief of Station." She named a time that would give them time to check her personal code and named a busy restaurant near Marble Arch. "I shall be wearing a black suit and carrying a paperback copy of Paradise Lost." She hung up before the other party could respond.

She strolled up Portabello Road, making a number of purchases then took the bus to Charing Cross Station. She headed for the ladies lounge where she transferred her Portabello purchases to a large cotton shopping bag, which she then stuffed in a paper shopping bag with the name of a famous store prominently displayed. This she checked then flagged a taxi to Marble Arch and checked in at the Cumberland Hotel.

When she left the hotel, she was wearing a designer suit, her hair attractively arranged, her face carefully made up. Her movements were restrained and graceful, her manner cool but pleasant. English aristocracy at its best.

As she had expected, the restaurant was crowded, mostly with women. She had very little trouble spotting her contact. She was only surprised to recognize him. So Dani Urazi was now the London Chief of Station. Well, even when he was a young recruit going through training with her, he had been ambitious.

She moved slowly into his line of vision, the book carefully displayed and watched his reaction out of the corner of her eye. She saw his glance light on the book then swiftly move to an older man seated near the door.

She had expected him to have a backup nearby. She felt a moment of consternation when his glance swept on to light on a middle-aged woman. She shrugged mentally. A woman made things a little more difficult but not impossible.

As he approached, she turned and looked at him, letting her face register polite inquiry then incredulity and finally pleasure.

"Dani! I certainly never expected to run into you like this. You are even more handsome now than you were at Ein Geddi."

"Ellia. Ellia Davidian. My God! I had no idea."

"Do you think you can find us a table?"

He looked around the room. "Perhaps we should go somewhere more private for our reunion."

"I think not. This will do very well. How about that table in the corner?"

When they were seated, she smiled and said, "I think we should speak in Hebrew, although I doubt we will be overheard here. So, are you married?"

They talked inconsequentials until they had ordered and been served. When the waitress was gone, Rachel rapidly reported the events leading up to her arrival in London, deleting only the location where the transfer of the bacteria was to take place.

"My God. If the person you mention is really involved, you can be sure that it bodes ill for Israel. You must come to Jerusalem with me."

"No. I will cooperate with Mossad and pass on any information but my first responsibility is to my husband."

"Ellia, your first duty is to Israel. You are Mossad."

"No. Never again. Not after what you did to me. Forget it. Now, this is what I will require…"

~ * ~

Victoria Falls

"Up and at 'em, Lover Boy."

Richard groaned and clutched the sheet tighter under his chin. David grabbed a corner and jerked it off the bed.

"Damn. Is that all they teach in CIA school? Okay, I'm getting up." Richard rubbed his sleep-matted eyes, looked at David, blinked and looked again. "What the hell? Are we going to a masquerade?"

"Don't you like it?" David looked down at his dark red, skin-tight pants, ran a caressing hand over the hot pink silk shirt and fingered the heavy gold chain at his throat. "It's the very latest Carnaby Street look." He struck a pose. "Really, darling, you've hurt my feelings. I think I look simply scrumptious."

"Knock it off, asshole. You'll never convince anyone with that insulting caricature. For God's sake, that stereotype is as old as it is wrong. I'm going to take a shower."

"Be my guest, but don't knock my clothes until you've seen what they've provided for you."

Richard groaned and disappeared into the bathroom.

"Don't take too long. Umbulu will be here in fifteen minutes," David reminded him.

When Reginald Umbulu slipped into the room, his mouth dropped open as he stared from one man to the other taking in their colorful raiment with obvious admiration. Embarrassed, Richard snapped, "Let's get to work," and sat down at the table.

"Yes, sir. I have lots of information for you."

Reginald, after a quick look around the room, moved to close the drapes before approaching the table. With the flourish of a stage magician, he whipped a file folder from inside his coat and placed it on the table before seating himself.

David turned a chuckle into a cough as he read the heading: MOST UTTERLY SECRET.

With great dignity, Reginald opened the folder. "First, the three gentlemen who are staying at this hotel. Avram Adoni is traveling on an Israeli passport, which lists his home as Jerusalem. He states he is taking a little vacation before continuing on to South Africa for business reasons. He is fifty-six years old and walks with a slight limp. But ..." he paused, giving them each a conspiratorial look, "in his baggage is a Muslim prayer rug!"

Richard and David exchanged glances. Richard nodded to Umbulu. "Most interesting. Please continue."

"The two gentlemen traveling on Egyptian passports are Hassad Habbab, age twenty four and Nussa Abjhan, age twenty three. They claim to be students traveling for pleasure. They have inquired about boat trips down the river. I consider them most suspicious. After all, our Sundowner Cruise above the Falls is quite renowned but downstream ..."

He rolled his eyes and shrugged, shifted his notes and continued. "The Greek couple are Mr. and Mrs. Theodore Andopoulos from Athens. They are in their middle thirties. They have been here for three days and have been constantly sightseeing. Yesterday they made a trip to a couple of villages down river. Mrs. Andopoulos has made several inquiries concerning health care for the villages. Why, I ask myself, is a Greek housewife interested in our health care?" He shrugged, and turned a page.

"A German gentlemen, Herr Doctor Herman Bach, checked in this afternoon. He has a suspiciously dark visage. Also, he retired to his room immediately upon arrival and has remained there. I was therefore unable to make any search of his luggage."

He folded his hands on the file and looked from one to the other. "The rest of the guests in this hotel are all either Scandinavian, African or of English extraction, with fair skin and light eyes. I have made it a personal objective to view each guest and to note their passports."

"Excellent work. Now, I believe you mentioned some oriental guests?"

"Yes. At the Elephant Hills Hotel." He shifted through the file.

"Mr. Ho Lee, age sixty one, of Hong Kong. The gentleman checked in yesterday and has taken only one tour."

Richard leaned forward. "Where did he go?"

Umbulu frowned. "To the crocodile farm. Most unusual for a first day trip. Indeed, guests usually stroll the many paths above the Falls or visit the native village attraction first."

He pulled another page from the file. "The two Japanese gentlemen also arrived yesterday. They met today with the manager of the Elephant Hills Hotel. From what my wife's nephew overheard, they have come to demonstrate a new computer system for the hotel. However, their computers were misdirected by the airline, but they expect them to arrive in the next day or two. They are Mr. Yamaguchi and Mr. Morita, aged fifty nine and thirty three respectively."

He turned another page. "Mr. Adrian Whitehead of Manchester, England arrived today. On the flight before yours, in fact. Not at all the type of Englishman we are accustomed to seeing. At least according to my brother at the airport or my brother-in-law's sister who works in the office at Elephant Hills."

Umbulu paused and stroked his upper lip. "There is only one other suspicious party. Mr. and Mrs. Raoul Bellegrazia from Italy. They arrived yesterday, went immediately to their room and have not as yet emerged. Large meals have been delivered to the room but always the bellman, who is my wife's second cousin, has been instructed to leave the cart outside the door. Later, the cart with the empty dishes is left in the hall. No one has seen them since their arrival."

Richard caught David's eyes and smothered a smile. "How old are these invisible Italians?"

"How old? Let me see. The gentleman is thirty two and the lady, twenty five." He closed the file. "I assumed that you would want to see these people for yourselves. The Japanese gentlemen, as well as all of the guests staying here will be in the dining room this evening. I have taken the liberty of booking you a table," he removed a large turnip watch from his pocket and glanced at it, "in fifteen minutes. The table I have reserved commands a clear look at the door and gives a good view of all of the other tables."

"Excellent work, Reginald. You have certainly been diligent." Richard started to rise.

Reginald held up his hand. "Also, there is a performance of our dance troupe in the kraal tonight. Mr. Ho has made reservations. Also Mr. Whitehead and the Greek couple. I have made reservations for you also."

"Well, it seems you have been very efficient. We'd best get along to the dining room."

~ * ~

London

Sir Edmund Mortimer removed a cigar from the humidor and rolled it between his palms as he gazed absentmindedly at the portrait of the queen. Merton Chadwick was used to Sir Mortimer's seeming inattention and continued with his report.

"To sum up, sir, our CIA contact reports some kind of flap, all very hush-hush even in the agency. The president contacted the prime minister direct for the use of one of our carriers for a secret meeting. Captain Maccauley reports that all three parties at the meeting were Americans. One arrived from the Seattle area by Navy jet, the other two arrived from the Azores by helicopter. The meeting lasted a total of seven hours. The man who arrived by the Navy fighter, left on the helicopter with one of the men. Our agent in the Azores reports that two men arrived from the Washington, DC area on an Air Force transport and left immediately by helicopter. The helicopter returned a few hours later with two men, however one was not the same man that arrived on the transport. The two men then joined a charter flight for Nairobi. Our man in Nairobi learned that two men from the charter never cleared customs in Nairobi but were met by a private jet with a flight plan filed for Bulawayo, Zimbabwe then on to Victoria Falls."

"And we have no one in Bulawayo or Vic Falls?"

"No, sir. However, we have sent an agent up from Johannesburg. We haven't received a report from him as yet."

"Well, keep me posted. It must be something important if the president and the prime minister are directly involved. We mustn't be caught napping."

"Yes, sir."

~ * ~

Seattle

FBI Agent James Eberle opened the file on his lap. "Walter, I think we have something sticky here. The woman that was reported kidnapped from Green Lake is Rachel Royer. We located the house. Both the back door and the garage door were standing open. Also the front door was unlocked. MacGregor and Howe took a cursory look through the house. In the master bedroom, they found the bedclothes thrown on the floor, a picture hanging lopsided on one wall and a dent in the plaster where the doorknob could have hit it. There were forced entry marks on the back door.

"They then canvassed the neighbors. A woman across the street saw the husband," he paused to look at his notes, "Richard Royer, enter a car with three men at about seven-thirty in the morning. The neighbor thought it was unusual because Mr. Royer is generally a late sleeper. She described the car as a late model gray sedan. She thinks it was a Chevrolet. Also, Mr. Royer's BMW is missing. She also confirmed that Mrs. Royer jogs every morning."

Eberle shifted uncomfortably and looked at his boss. "The woman told them that a stranger had been hanging around the neighborhood all day. She pointed him out and MacGregor thinks he recognized the man. He's sure that the watcher's name is Otis Watts." Eberle rubbed a hand over his neck. "If it is Watts, he's CIA."

Walter McPherson leaned forward. "Is MacGregor sure?"

"Yes. Seems he ran into him when he was in Washington a couple of years ago."

"What the hell is the CIA doing kidnapping people off the streets in Seattle? What's the story on the Royers?"

"All above board from what we've been able to discover so far. Royer was on his way to becoming a distinguished concert violinist until he injured his hand. Apparently he is now beginning to make a name for himself as a composer. Also, the neighbor says he has been ill. The wife seems to be just that, a housewife. How deep do you want us to dig on this thing?"

Walter slapped an angry hand on the desk. "As deep as you can. I want to know why the CIA thinks it can come into this town and grab citizens off the street. Find out everything. I'll call Washington. If the CIA is running a covert operation in my area, I want to know why I wasn't informed."

Ten

Victoria Falls

Richard and David found the dining room, gave their names and were escorted to their table. Reginald Umbulu had been right when he said their table commanded a complete view of both the door and the room as a whole.

Moments after they were seated, a busboy appeared with water and glasses. He positioned himself with his back to the room. As he filled Richard's glass, he whispered, "Mr. and Mrs. Andopoulos are seated at the third table on the far wall. The lady is wearing a brown and orange dress. Mr. Adoni is the gentleman seated alone to the left of the door."

He moved around the table and set a glass in front of David. "The Egyptians have not arrived as yet." He finished pouring the water and straightened. "Sirs, my name is Luke. Your waiter will be Joseph." He grinned and winked. "Joseph is the second cousin of my wife's brother. Mr. Umbulu is my great-uncle, of my mother's family."

When Luke was out of hearing, Richard raised his water glass. "I think a toast is in order to Reginald and his 'network'."

"To Reginald and may he never run out of relatives," David replied with a rueful smile.

While they were studying the menu, an oriental man appeared and was seated, followed shortly by another single gentlemen. Their waiter confirmed that the new arrivals were Mr. Ho and Mr. Whitehead from the Elephant Hills Hotel.

Richard studied Whitehead, noting his darkly tanned face and hands and his dark, curly hair. Mentally he agreed with Umbulu. There was something distinctly un-English about his mannerisms. But then what did he know?

The trapped feeling returned. What in the hell was he doing in the middle of Africa looking for spies? He didn't want to be here, he wanted to be home in Seattle, in his own house, with his wife by his side. He wanted Rachel, wanted to watch the expressions flitting across her face when she didn't know he was watching, wanted to hear her voice, to hold her in his arms, feel the warmth of her body pressed against him.

But Rachel was in some unknown place, being held against her will by agents of his own government. Being held to guarantee his cooperation. He'd been playing along, waiting for a chance to escape. But what if he did manage to elude David, even Umbulu and his *network* of relatives? Carter had taken his wallet. He had only the twenty dollars they had given him, no credit cards and only the false passport. How could he even get back to the States? Suppose he clobbered David, took the money he was carrying and managed to get a flight? One phone call and Rachel could be dead before he was halfway across the water.

Very well, he was trapped. Accept that fact and go from there. How to get out of the trap? Suppose he told David that he couldn't do whatever it was they wanted. Not wouldn't but couldn't. Tell them about his medical problem. Try to convince them he was simply too sick. Would they believe him? Suppose they did. He would no longer be of use to them. Would they send him home? Free Rachel?

98

His gut told him no. The thought chilled him. Of course, they wouldn't. If he were no longer of any use to them, they wouldn't hesitate to kill him and probably Rachel, too. He had no choice. He would have to do what they wanted.

He picked up his fork and attacked the salad in front of him. He'd need all of the strength he could muster. The best way to save himself and Rachel was to get this... this faradiddle over with. Thank God the Marines had toned his body and Rachel had insisted on the home gym.

Was what he had been told the truth? If so, he was expected to outwit trained terrorists. Outwit, that was the key. He sure as hell couldn't outfight them. He'd have to think, concentrate. He cast his mind back to his Marine training, to Officer's Candidate School, to tactics classes, searching his memory for any scrap of information that might help.

They had just finished their salads when the two Egyptians came in and were seated only a few tables away. Richard studied them covertly while he worked his way through the bland, overcooked food. His appetite was soon satisfied but he forced himself to eat everything put before him and drink glass after glass of water. As he ate, he watched the two Egyptians out of the corner of his eye. There was something about their obvious nervousness that set a warning bell ringing in Richard's brain.

He stirred his coffee absentmindedly, straining to recall every detail of those long ago classes, while he studied the room and its occupants.

David leaned over the table. "It looks like this is going to be easier than anyone could have anticipated. One of us can follow these fellows and the other, Mr. Ho. We can grab them when they make the transfer."

Richard shook his head. Some of the things he'd learned in a talk by one of the "spooks" who had come to talk about infiltration flicked through his mind. The old man had gotten off the subject and started telling stories from the old OSS. Perhaps that buried memory had started the bell ringing. Without thinking, he said, "Too easy. I don't like it."

Richard signaled the waiter and ordered a dessert he didn't want. While Joseph was writing the order, Richard whispered, "Tell Mr. Umbulu we want everyone followed when they leave the dining room. Also put all of the others under immediate surveillance. He will know what I mean."

Joseph grinned broadly. "Yes, sir." Raising his voice slightly, he said, "I assure you the trifle is very fresh and very good."

A half moon, assisted by discreet lighting, held the darkness at bay as Richard and David joined the other guests strolling towards the kraal. They stopped outside the gate and lit cigarettes, keeping up a dilatory conversation, watching the last arrivals. Only as the gates were closing, did they slip inside. They found seats on the top bench and Richard studied the enclosure. In the center was a dirt-packed arena with a fifty-foot pole in the center. The kraal was enclosed by a twelve-foot wooden wall. The bleachers extended around about one third of the wall. Richard could spot only three doors; the one through which they had entered, a smaller door to the right of the bleachers and a third directly across the arena.

Richard located Mr. Ho prominently seated in the second row immediately behind the two Egyptians. He frowned inwardly and began searching the crowd. He found it interesting that Whitehead had also taken a seat on the top row and seemed more interested in the audience than in the preparations taking place in the ring below.

Moments later he spotted the two Japanese gentlemen seated in the front row and Avram Adoni in the middle of the packed bleachers. The Greek couple were on the far side of the stands in the third row. Richard leaned back and withdrew the brochure he had picked up as they passed the desk and studied it while they waited for the show to start. He read that the Zambezi River was nearly a mile wide where it fell into the narrow crevasse created eons ago by some cataclysmic event and varied in height from two-hundred-fifty-six feet to three-hundred-forty-three feet. The grounds of the Victoria Falls Hotel ran down to the very edge of the rift and presented a spectacular view of the Falls pouring into the chasm only a few feet away. Across the river was Zambia.

He stuck the brochure back in his pocket, as the lights dimmed, and stared at the spectacle taking place in the dirt ring, his mind busy. Why was the transfer taking place in this out of the way spot? How much bacteria would it take to contaminate the reported cities? What kind of containers would be required? How big? How could it pass through customs without causing comment?

The chanting finally broke into his thoughts and he found himself intrigued by the aboriginal rhythm and melody. Without conscious thought, he began mentally composing.

Later, the only thing he was able to recall of the show was the man diving from the top of a tall pole and swinging by a foot, his head only inches from the dirt. That and the beginning of a piece of music.

The exit was through a small souvenir shop. Richard and David strolled leisurely about the shop, occasionally fingering a trinket or a carving. When the Japanese gentlemen left, Richard signaled David and moved to the door. He smothered a grin as a group of young blacks began scattering in the various directions taken by some members of the audience.

Richard strolled in the direction taken by the Japanese. David soon caught up with him and asked impatiently, "Shouldn't one of us be following Mr. Ho?"

"I think Reginald has Mr. Ho covered. I'm more interested in our Japanese friends. Did you notice anything after the show?"

"Only that I think we can forget about Mr. Adoni. I overheard him asking about one of these animal skin rugs. He has a daughter in Johannesburg who collects small unusual rugs. He's taking her a fine Muslim prayer rug. Did you see something I missed?"

"Mrs. Andopoulos dropped her program."

"So?"

"One of the fellows ahead picked it up and returned it to her."

"Well, the Japanese are known for their courtesy."

"Ummm. Any idea where this path leads?"

"To the Falls, I believe."

"I thought it might. Let's step up the pace a little. Our friends have disappeared around those trees. Oh shit."

As they rounded the group of trees and bushes, the trail split. Their quarry had vanished.

Richard dropped his voice to a whisper. "Take the right. If you find them, stay with them, if not come back here."

Richard crushed down the urge to run. The sound of pounding footsteps would surely alert them and blow his cover. Instead, he assumed the posture and brisk stride of a man out for an evening constitutional. After several hundred yards the path swerved again and ran along the very lip of the gorge. Fifty feet ahead stood one of the men.

Richard didn't break stride as his glance took in the man's too relaxed posture, the feigned look of surprise as he turned to stare at Richard. Richard nodded briefly as he strode on by, heart racing. This was it. Somewhere in the bushes was at least one terrorist. He could feel him.

What the hell was he supposed to do now? There was no time to circle back and get David. He had to do something, but what? A rush of adrenaline flowed through his body.

The path swerved again around a clump of vegetation. Out of sight, Richard turned around and dropped to his knees. Carefully he began inching his way back, creeping along the edge of the path, staying in the shadows. He heard the murmur of voices and dropped flat. His Marine Corps training took over. He slithered through the undergrowth on his belly until he had them in view.

Three men stood at the edge of the gorge. Richard couldn't distinguish words but the tone of their voices indicated they were arguing. He rubbed a handful of dirt over his face and hands then worked his way within a few yards of the trio.

The third man took a step toward the two Japanese, his hand raised in a threatening gesture. Richard sucked in his breath. It was one of the Egyptian students.

The smaller Japanese shrugged his shoulders and opened the camera case hanging at his side. He removed a small box and opened it. Richard caught the refection of moonlight on glass.

The terrorist lifted something from the box and Richard saw it was a glass ampoule. Before Richard could move, the terrorist snapped the top and threw the ampoule into the river below. He was reaching for a second one when Richard exploded off the ground in a running tackle. He slammed into the Japanese holding the box, knocking him into the Egyptian.

Richard rolled away, grasping for the box that had tumbled to the ground, when the second Japanese leaped on his back. He twisted away, jamming the box inside his shirt and scrambled to his feet.

From somewhere behind him, Richard heard voices and a woman's soft laugh. He swung around but before he could move, the man was on him again, grappling for the box. Richard slammed a heavy fist into the man's belly and stepped back. Dirt crumbled under his foot. He felt himself falling, tumbling through the dark toward the river below. A millisecond of incredulity was washed away in shocked horror. Three-hundred and forty-three feet. The words from the brochure flashed before his eyes. His scream of pure terror echoed over the roar of the falls. Then his head struck an outcropping of rock. As he pitched into even greater darkness, he heard the macabre laughter of a hyena.

Eleven

London

Rachel was aware of the two people following her after she left the restaurant. She had time. Losing them would be no problem. She strolled towards Marks and Spencer, window-shopping as she went, pausing now and then, checking, until she was sure there were only the two tails.

Inside the store she wandered through the various departments, stopping to purchase a pair of sunglasses, a brown wig, and a pair of inexpensive brown shoes. In the dress department, she took her time in selecting a cheap lime green nylon dress.

She retired to the changing room and shrugged out of the black suit and into the dress and shoes. She was adjusting the wig when the privacy curtain was suddenly jerked back. The little gray-haired lady from the restaurant looked at her in flustered surprise. "Oh dear. I'm so sorry. I didn't realize this room was occupied. I'm sure the girl told me ... oh, I am sorry." She backed out, letting the curtain fall.

Rachel smiled. Dani had lost none of his cunning, his agents were well-trained, but perhaps not well enough. She'd soon know. Within seconds, Rachel had ripped off the green dress, pulled a tightly rolled yellow skirt and matching sweater from her purse and slipped them on. She jammed her feet back into her black pumps, stuffed the brown shoes out of sight on the shelf. The green dress was hung back on its hanger with the black skirt and jacket underneath. She pulled the blond wig from her purse and quickly adjusted it. The brown wig and sunglasses disappeared into the bag.

Moments later she sauntered casually out of the dressing area and headed towards the door. From the corner of her eye, she saw the woman idly browsing through a rack of dresses, her gaze fixed on the dressing room door. Rachel paused a moment at a table of brassieres and surreptitiously surveyed the aisles until she located the man. He looked more than a little uncomfortable as he perused a table of women's purses while he watched the other woman.

Rachel walked through the door and up the street. After a series of moves designed to allow her to spot any tail, she knew she was clear and returned to her hotel. In her room, she picked up the phone and requested a wake-up call, stripped and crawled into bed for her first real sleep in over twenty-four hours.

When the phone awakened her several hours later, she showered and dressed in the yellow outfit. She checked out of the hotel and took the underground to Green Park. Moments later she found the package cached by the Israelis. Without bothering to check the contents, she moved rapidly out of the park, flagged a cruising taxi and was driven to Charing Cross Station.

She assumed she was being followed. If they weren't any sharper than the two this afternoon, she would soon be home free. She collected the package she had left in the locker and headed for the ladies lounge. No one followed her in. She hoped the agent she had fooled at Marks and Spencer hadn't gotten too bad a chewing out.

Fifteen minutes later an elderly, gray-haired woman clad in cotton stockings, rundown shoes and a cotton wash dress covered with a ragged sweater and carrying a shopping bag emerged from the lounge, stretching and yawning. She peered around myopically through a pair of wire spectacles and then limped slowly out of the station and up the street to a bus stop. She changed busses several times, stopped in two coffee bars, and walked a number of deserted residential streets before deciding she had lost any tail, and headed for Victoria Station.

In the ladies room, she changed back into her own clothes, donned the blond wig, added blue contact lens and repaired her makeup. Discarding all of her Portabello purchases except for the gray wig, she caught the shuttle to Heathrow.

Two hours later, Rachel was seated in the first class section of the South African Airways flight to Johannesburg, munching caviar and sipping champagne as she tried to tune out the boring conversation of the Capetown banker seated next to her.

Where was Richard? Would she find him in time? Each beat of her heart seemed like the tick of a clock counting away the seconds, the minutes, the hours. How long could Richard survive without dialysis? Anger began to build again in her gut.

Why was this happening to her, to Richard? Why couldn't they have been left in peace? They had been so happy. They were even considering having a child. Richard wanted to wait until a kidney had been found but she wanted a child now. Her biological clock was ticking away, too. She wanted a child. Not just a child, Richard's child.

Glancing out the window into the darkness it seemed they were suspended in the sky like a toy plane hanging from a wire. She closed her eyes, willing the plane to fly faster...faster.

Twelve

Somewhere in the black fog that surrounded him, Richard heard his name called. Through the haze of semi-consciousness, instinct warned him of danger, warned him not to move. Something was pressing painfully into his belly and side. He opened his eyes then quickly shut them and waited for the wave of vertigo to pass. He opened them again, more slowly this time and sucked in his breath as he stared into the abyss. A wave of mindless terror swamped him.

The mist, glowing in the moonlight like a gossamer shroud, could not hide the sheer wall. Hundreds of feet below, the Zambezi River glistened like a silver thread.

He held his breath, fearing even the slight rise and fall of his chest might send him hurtling down. He pressed his body into the rock, willing the stone to part, to make him a part of it.

The moment of blind terror passed. Cautiously, he raised his head a fraction of an inch then another. He grasped convulsively at a tiny outcropping. The surface was wet, slippery. His fingers slithered off. Slimy moss clung to them. Panic flashed through him again.

Instinctively, his muscles recoiled, dislodged an accumulation of detritus and sent it cascading off the narrow ledge. Paralyzed with horror, he watched a stone plummet unchecked into the yawning void. He felt his left foot slipping over the lip. A scream of pure terror began to build in his chest. He choked it down as a voice called from above.

"Mr. Rossiter. Can you hear me? Please do not move. We shall have you up in a few minutes. My son has gone for ropes."

Richard supposed it was really minutes but it felt more like hours before he heard someone scrambling over the rock above him. A shower of dirt and pebbles plummeted on him and strong hands lifted his chest. Panic gripped him again as his leg slid off the ledge. He clawed at the rock.

"Be still."

At the sharp command, Richard stopped struggling. He felt a rope being tied under his arms then pulled up to where he could reach it. He could feel warm breath on his ear and smelled the rank odor of male sweat.

"Grip the rope, sir!"

Ignoring the pain in his scraped fingers, Richard grasped the rope. He tried to speak but could only croak, "Yeah."

"Very good, sir. Please hold on tightly. I am going to lift you. Can you use your legs?"

He flexed his leg muscles then nodded weakly.

The rope tightened as the boy pulled him to his feet. His head swam. He leaned against the face of the rock. Opening his eyes, he glanced down at the ledge. It was barely eight inches wide. Panic swelled again, choking him. Suddenly the rope seemed too thin, too weak to support his weight. He pressed his body closer to the rough rock, hugging it. Letting go of the rope, his fingers scrambled over the surface, found minute cracks and clutched at them.

Arms came around him. The boy grasped the rope in front of him and shouted, "Okay, pull."

The rope went taut, cutting into Richard's back and armpits as he was yanked off his feet. He cried out, wanting to cling to the spurious security of the rock. Frantically, he grasped the rope, fingers sliding over the smooth nylon. It wouldn't hold them. They were going to plunge to their death. His heart pumped so hard he could hardly breath.

The boy's legs came up, straddling him. Planting his feet against the rock the boy began to walk up the face of the cliff, cradling Richard against his body, and Richard realized, keeping them from swinging out of control.

Agonizing minutes later, hands grasped him from above, dragged him over the edge and lifted him onto the grass. When his senses cleared, Richard found himself looking up into the grinning face of Reginald Umbulu and the ashen face of David Bergdorf.

Voice unsteady, David asked, "Are you okay? Any broken bones?"

"No." Richard's throat was so dry he had trouble getting the word out. He swallowed and tried again. "No, I don't think so." Then his memory kicked in and he was swept with a wave of anger. "They got away."

"Oh, no, Mr. Rossiter." Umbulu's grin stretched even wider. "We have them tied up nice and tight in the trees."

"All three?"

"Three?" Umbulu and David exchanged glances. "There were only two. The Egyptians."

Richard sat up. His head whirled. He put out a hand to steady himself and fought down a twinge of nausea. "The bacteria!" He groped in his shirt and pulled out the box.

David took it out of his shaking hands and opened it. Two ampoules were still nestled safely in their foam packing.

David helped him to his feet and kept a hand on his arm. "Let's get you back to the hotel."

"I saw one ampoule thrown in the river."

"We can talk about it back at the hotel." He turned to Umbulu. "Can your boys keep these bastards out of sight for a while?"

"Certainly. I will give them instructions and join you in a few minutes." He placed a huge paw on Richard's shoulder. "Would you like a couple of these fellows to carry you back to your room?"

"No. No. I'll be fine. A couple of Tylenol and I'll be good as new." As if a couple of pills could cure him! It was time to end this charade. He would have to get on dialysis soon. His body could only take so much. As he followed David up the path, he cast a quick look at the gorge and shuddered.

In their room, Richard collapsed onto the bed. His muscles trembled like jelly.

"Are you okay?" David asked.

"I will be. I need a drink."

"I'll order something."

"Not liquor, water. Bring the pitcher."

He emptied the whole pitcher then struggled to his feet. "Got to have a shower." He tore off the silk shirt and threw it on the floor. "And I've got to have some decent clothes. Something loose and comfortable. I'll be dammed if I'll go around looking like a Harlem pimp."

He stalked towards the bathroom. At the door he turned and glared at David. "I've had all of this shit that I can take. Do you hear? I've had it. You've got your damned bacteria. Now, you get on the phone to your boss and tell him I'm flying home tomorrow unless I hear from my wife and know she is all right."

Just before he slammed the door, he heard David say, "All we've recovered is part of the test bacteria."

When Richard emerged from the shower, some of his irritability had drained away. He shrugged into the terry cloth robe and walked into the bedroom.

Reginald Umbulu was seated at the table, a file in front of him. David was staring out of the window. He turned as Richard came into the room.

"Feeling better?"

"I suppose so."

David crossed to the table and pulled out a chair. "Better sit down then and hear what Umbulu has to say."

Richard looked from one solemn face to the other. With a sinking feeling, he pulled out a chair and sat down.

Umbulu opened the file and cleared his throat. "As Mr. Rubinski requested, we have searched the rooms of the Japanese gentlemen. No other ampoules were found. However, we did find Chinese passports in a hidden compartment in their luggage."

He shifted in his seat. "I must also report that the Arab has escaped."

Anger swept over Richard and he gritted his teeth. "How?"

"Please, sir. My people are not trained agents. They do their best..." He shrugged, his eyes mournful. "The Arab had a knife hidden in his stocking. He stabbed the boy who was holding him and got away in the dark."

Richard choked back his anger. "And the boy?"

"He died." Umbulu looked down at the papers in front of him. His big hands trembled as he shuffled them. "Now, as to the other guests. The Andopoulos couple went first to the bar, had a drink then wandered into the gardens towards the falls. They were not far away when you went over the cliff. They hurried back to the bar and are still there. While they were at the performance, I was able to make a quick search of their rooms. Mrs. Andopoulos is a registered nurse and her specialty is public health."

Umbulu pulled another sheet of paper from the folder and glanced at it. "Mr. Ho Lee also returned to the bar. Mr. Adrian Whitehead went for a stroll in the garden. He spent a considerable time standing in the shadows and staring at the falls. If I judge the time right, shortly after your skirmish, he returned abruptly to the hotel. He went directly to the bar where he ordered a drink. A few moments later, Mr. Ho Lee left his seat at the bar and passed behind Mr. Whitehead. He stumbled and fell against Mr. Whitehead causing him to spill his drink." Umbulu shook his head. "Unfortunately the barman overheard very little of the short conversation. What he did hear seemed to be an exchange of apologies. Mr. Ho then left the bar and took a taxi back to the Elephant Hills Hotel. My man is following him."

"And what about Whitehead?" Richard asked.

"Whitehead went directly to his room."

"The other Arab?"

"Both have disappeared. Habbab was able to elude the boy I had following him after he separated from Abjhan before Abjhan met with the Japanese. We will find them, I promise you."

"Is Bach still in his room?"

"He was still there when I arrived here."

Umbulu pulled another sheet of notepaper from the file. "Perhaps the Italians are not so innocent after all. Mr. Bellegrazia left his hotel by a service door, entered his car and coasted without lights to the bottom of the driveway. He then started his motor and drove away. My man, having no transportation, was unable to follow him so he is continuing to watch his room."

Richard heaved a sigh and forced a smile. "Excellent work, Reginald. Can you continue to keep everyone under surveillance?"

"Certainly."

"Good. David and I have a lot to discuss and then we need to get a few hours sleep. Please wake us if there are any new developments."

Umbulu gathered his notes and left. David stood and walked to the window then turned back to look at Richard. "We've got to stop the exchange of that bacteria."

Richard's head was cradled in his hands, his thumbs massaging his temples. David had to strain to hear his words. "We're too late. The exchange has already been made."

"It can't be. The exchange wasn't to be made until after Barenji had seen the results."

"'And accidents fill the world with woe.'" Richard quoted as he raised his head and looked up at David. "You heard Umbulu. Habbab was watching my act of stupidity. You can bet he was reporting to his boss long before I was dragged off that ledge."

"But Barenji isn't here." He stared down at Richard. "Or is he? Have you spotted him?"

Richard sighed and began to massage his temples again. "David, I wouldn't know Barenji if he walked up and spit in my face."

"Don't start that shit again. Can't you understand this is too serious for you to play these childish games? Our countries, not to mention your wife's safety, depend on you."

Richard's anger exploded. He leaped up, his chair toppling to the floor. He grabbed the front to David's shirt and began shaking him.

"God damn all you bastards to hell! Can't you get it through your stupid heads? You've got the wrong man! *I am*

114

not and never have been a goddamned spy! Jesus H. Christ, if your bumbling idiots are all that is keeping our country safe then it doesn't stand a chance." Richard shoved him away.

David stumbled backwards and landed on his butt on the floor. Richard began to pace the room. David stared up at the angry man. "But you are Zephyr. You have to be. The CIA…"

"…are a bunch of idiots. I am not this Zephyr. I am not a spy. I am quite simply just Richard Royer, once a violinist and now a would-be composer of classical music." He paused in his pacing to look down at the stunned man on the floor. "Oh, for heaven's sake, get up."

David pulled himself up and sat on the edge of the bed, his face red. There was a note of entreaty in his voice as he asked, "You're not serious, are you? You're just saying this to get even for Mayhew's grabbing your wife, right? Right?"

Richard paused. He read the disbelief and fear warring on David's face, met David's gaze squarely, sighed and spoke quietly, "I've never been more serious in my life."

David believed him. Richard read it in the flare of panic in his eyes, the touch of green around his mouth. The blood drained from his face. David swallowed convulsively. "What in the hell are we going to do?"

Richard began to pace again, his thoughts whirling. He felt as stunned as David. The confrontation at the Falls had driven home the fact that what was happening was real. Only too real. The sense of struggling through a nightmare was gone. Only fear and anger remained. There really was a plot. There really was a bacteria and it was now in the hands of terrorists who hated the United States.

He clenched his fists. God, how had he gotten into this mess? More important, how was he going to get out? His legs felt like jelly now and without dialysis, he was only going to get worse. His little caper at the cliff had shown him how little physical strength he had left. How could he hope to go up against a ring of international terrorists?

Should he tell David about his health problem? No, not yet. Where exactly did David fit in? Until he knew that, he'd not risk it. Perhaps he could test him. Watching him closely, Richard said, "Well, I guess this throws it right into your lap."

"Me?" He squeaked the word. "I'm not an agent. I wouldn't know where to begin."

"Then what the hell are you doing here?"

"I'm beginning to wonder about that myself. My orders from the president were simply to stay with you and report back to him directly when you had recovered the bacteria."

"You don't work for the CIA?"

"Good God, no. I'm an administrative assistant to the president. Just a junior one at that. I have no idea why the President picked me for this unless it was because I happen to speak several languages."

"You're not a field agent?"

"No way. I'm just a paper shuffler at the White House."

Richard returned to pacing. Was David telling the truth? If so, what the devil were they going to do? Two babes in the woods. The blind leading the blind.

He stopped pacing and began to rub his temples. *Think, man! You've still got a brain. Use it.*

He turned to David. "Surely the CIA has agents in this area that can take over."

David shook his head. "You met their resident agent."

"Reginald?" He rolled his eyes. "But what were you supposed to do if we had obtained the bacteria?"

"My instructions were to take the next flight to London. I was given a number to call."

"London. Damn. The bacteria will be long gone before anyone could get here from London."

Richard resumed his pacing. It was all in their laps. They would have to do something, but what? He slapped the heel of his hand against his head. Think, damn it. What would Barenji do next? Who the hell was Barenji? The two young Arabs were just soldiers. Where did the Andopoulos couple fit in? Or did they? Bellegrazia had slipped out of his hotel room. Was he Barenji? Was Whitehead? Was Bach? Or was Barenji waiting elsewhere, waiting for the bacteria to be delivered to him?

Richard crossed the room in swift strides, picked up the phone and asked for Umbulu. When the bellman came on the line, Richard snapped, "Find out when each of our suspects are due to check out and where they are going next."

He hung up and stood staring at the carpet. Something nagged at the back of his mind. A wave of nausea swept over him, leaving him weak and sweating. He moved across the room and stretched out on the bed.

Depression settled over him. He wasn't up to this. He would need a dialysis treatment soon. He tried to calculate the time difference between the west coast and central Africa. How long had it been since he'd had his last treatment? Forty-eight hours? More? His mind kept wandering. Then the thought that had been tickling the back of his brain burst through and he sat up.

Thirteen

Russia! That was what he had forgotten. David had mentioned some of the bacteria was to be released in Russia. Before he could consider its importance, he drifted into sleep. It was barely breaking daylight when Umbulu returned. His face was solemn but there was a glint in his eyes. He pulled the inevitable folder from under his coat and placed it on the table. He seated himself and opened it.

"Mr. Bellegrazia has returned to his hotel room. My wife's cousin's boy, whom I had stationed in the shrubbery outside this room, informs me that Mr. Bellegrazia spent nearly half an hour watching your window before searching the room of Habbab and Abjhan. He then followed Mr. Ho back to Elephant Hills."

He turned a page. "The Greek couple is leaving this morning for a three day photo safari of Wankie Animal Preserve. The reservations were made several months ago by a travel agent in Athens.

"The Japanese gentlemen are booked out this morning to Johannesburg with a connecting flight to Bangkok.

"Mr. Adrian Whitehead is leaving this afternoon for London."

He cleared his throat and the glitter in his eyes became more pronounced. "Herr Bach is departing at this moment. He has reservations for a connecting flight to Frankfurt, Germany."

He paused and gave each man a significant look. "When he returned to his room last night, your waiter Luke, just happened to be delivering a room service order. Unfortunately, he misread the room number and delivered it to Herr Bach's room by mistake. While he was apologizing, he happened to notice a baggage check on the floor. Being the good servant that he is, he picked it up and handed it to the man."

Richard sat forward. "And?"

"Herr Bach seemed a little upset."

"Reginald!"

The big man's face broke into a grin. "Luke has an excellent memory for numbers."

Excitement coursed through Richard's body. He struggled against the urge to shake the man. Instead he grinned and cocked an eyebrow. "And?"

"My brother works at the airport. He went to work a little early and examined the article. Of course, he couldn't open it but it is listed as a shipment of equine encephalitis vaccine. It arrived on the same flight as Mr. Ho."

"Bingo," David shouted.

"So damned simple," Richard said. "And I'll bet there is an actual outbreak of the disease in Germany." He turned back to Umbulu. "We've got to get that package. Can your brother get his hands on it for us?"

The smile vanished from Umbulu's face. Slowly he shook his head. "There are now too many other persons about and it is not possible for my brother to leave his desk. Also, the package is forwarded on to Frankfurt. On the same flight as Herr Bach."

"Then get us booked on that same flight," Richard said.

Umbulu looked doubtful. "The plane leaves in less than an hour."

"Just do it and find someone to drive us to the airport." David shoved a wad of bills at him. "Get us checked out. Then have your contact arrange for someone to meet us in Frankfort."

Reginald Umbulu ignored to proffered money and backed out the door. "Your bill has been taken care of. I will call the airport and take care of all the arrangements but you must be in the lobby in ten minutes."

Richard grabbed the first clothes that came to hand—a pair of bright green pants and a yellow silk shirt. He climbed into them, threw the rest of the clothes in his suitcase then stopped. With a sour look at David, he gathered the flashy garments that had been provided for him and threw them in a pile on the floor. Only his own sweat stained garments and his shaving kit went into the suitcase before he closed it. Minutes later they boarded the airport van.

"Why the devil is the bacteria being shipped to Frankfurt? There are direct flights from Johannesburg to South America. It seems to me it would be easier to smuggle it into the country from there. I wish to hell my call had gotten through to London. Who is Bach? Do you think he is Barenji? If not, where is Barenji? It doesn't make sense."

"Yes, it does," Richard answered. "It makes perfect sense."

"Well, I sure as hell don't see it."

"You read the report. Barenji hasn't remained a mystery all these years by taking any risks that can be avoided. Bach is a cutout. If the transfer had been a trap, it would have been sprung on those two we grabbed or on Bach. Barenji was here all right, but he was staying out of the picture. From now on, he'll be doubly careful."

"Shipping the bacteria to Frankfurt is to throw us off the track." David nodded then shook his head. "Maybe not. At least not entirely. Germany has a huge Arab population. Its long been a way station for terrorists. They have a lot of support there. Remember the Baader Meinhof gang?"

Richard agreed. "Don't forget Russia. What better place than Germany to divide the bacteria for shipment to the United States and Russia."

Eyes wide with horror, David gripped Richard's arm. Richard understood. He closed his eyes, trying to shut out the picture of the thousands, millions that might die if they failed.

Weakness swept over him, leaving his muscles with all the starch of wet spaghetti. He licked his lips. His throat was so dry he could barely force the words out. "You've got to make your contacts understand I can't handle this. They've got to send in someone who knows what they're doing."

Fourteen

Washington, DC

Mayhew heard the door open. Out of the corner of his eye he watched Calvin Brooks enter without knocking. Hiding his irritation, he did not look up until Brooks paused and coughed. "Well, Cal?"

"Bad news. Spears's flight to London was delayed due to mechanical problems and he missed his connecting flight to Zimbabwe. He's trying to make other arrangements but he'll arrive at least twenty four hours after Royer."

Mayhew pinched his lower lip between his fingers. Surely the exchange would have been attempted long before Spears got to Zimbabwe. Bergdorf had instructions to call London as soon as they had the bacteria. Dealing with Bergdorf and Royer in London was a complication. Still, that was all it was, a complication. Not a catastrophe. It could be handled. He looked up at Brooks. "Is he still in London?"

"Yes."

"Tell him to wait in London until you contact him again."

"Okay." Brooks shifted, obviously uncomfortably. "There's something else. Whitney and the woman have disappeared."

Mayhew tensed. "What the hell do you mean, disappeared?"

"Just that. Watts was watching the front of the Royer house when Whitney drove up and ran into the house. A few minutes later the woman backed out of the garage and drove off. Apparently, she'd entered from the rear. Before Watts could get to the house, Whitney jumped in his car and chased after her. Neither has been seem since."

Brooks ran a hand through his hair and eyed his boss warily. "That's not all. The FBI is sniffing around. They showed up at the Royer house not long after Whitney and the woman took off. They've got a team in the house and are questioning the neighbors. Watts tried to stay out of sight but thinks he may have been spotted. He cut out and went to the safe house. He found a few drops of blood in the bathroom and the window had been shot out. He's waiting at the house for instructions."

Anger surged in Mayhew. Morons. He was surrounded by morons. He barked, "Why does Watts think he was spotted?"

"He remembered meeting one of the FBI agents a couple of years ago here in Washington. He's pretty sure the man remembered him, too."

"Tell him to clean up the safe house and catch the next flight back to Washington. Tell him to be damned sure he's not spotted again. The last thing we need is the FBI getting into the act." The pencil he was holding snapped in his fingers. He tossed it aside. "Get Bryce on the next flight to Seattle. You can brief him on the way to the airport. We've got to find the woman and find her before the FBI."

"Do we still need her? Royer should get the bacteria within the next few hours if he doesn't already have it."

"And if something goes wrong? Use your head, man. Besides, I have further plans for Royer. Without the woman, we won't have any hold over him. Find her." He bent again to the papers on his desk.

Brooks ran a nervous hand through his hair, but made no move to leave. Mayhew glanced up. "Was there something else?"

Brooks swallowed. "Well, sir, you said... I mean, you indicated..."

"Yes?"

"Well, sir, I was wondering exactly what you have in mind."

Mayhew leaned back, eyes narrowed. He studied Brooks in silence for several minutes then slowly nodded and said, "I want that bacteria."

"Sir?"

"I said I want that bacteria. Cal, this is the opportunity we've been looking for, waiting for. That bacteria is going to save this country, maybe the world."

~ * ~

Rachel stared through the plane's window at the barren Kalahari Desert. In the pale early morning light, the land seemed as hostile and alien as the surface of the moon. As empty and tormented as her life would be without Richard.

The banker in the next seat woke up, grunted a good morning, fumbled his way out of the seat and disappeared in the direction of the bathroom. Others on the plane began to stir. The stewardess brought her a complementary toiletry kit. When her seatmate returned, Rachel went into the bathroom. When she returned, face washed, teeth brushed, hair combed, the stewardess was beginning to serve breakfast.

Rachel ate without being aware of what she was eating, barely tasting the food. When the tray had been removed and the table stored, she turned back to stare out the window. She watched, without really seeing the changing landscape, as the plane approached Johannesburg. Richard would need dialysis soon. Would she be in time?

His rapidly poisoning blood was not his only danger. Barenji. Just thinking the name made her shudder. She had to find Richard before he found Barenji. Or Barenji found him.

Fear lay like a rock in an empty hollow under her heart. Richard. Barenji. Richard. Barenji. The names ran through her tired mind with the cadence of a dirge.

Disembarking at Jan Smuts Airport, she found herself breathing heavily as her lungs struggled to adjust to the five-thousand-foot elevation. Going through customs, she ran into her first problem with the dialysis machine. The customs agent called two security guards who took one look at the machine and blanched, roughly handcuffed her and hustled her into an office. She mentally ground her teeth in frustration as she waited under the grim eyes of a guard.

She was ready to scream by the time a senior officer finally appeared and began to question her. The dialysis machine was finally brought in, encased in a bomb disposal container. The big Afrikaner made several calls to medical experts. She was asked to demonstrate how it worked to a doctor who was whisked to the airport in an official vehicle. She was finally released two hours later, nerves frazzled, without apology.

At the Air Zimbabwe counter, she booked a seat on the next flight to Victoria Falls. Two hours. She was going to be too late. She knew it, could feel it deep in her bones. She glanced blankly around the terminal for a moment. Feeling as disjointed as a marionette with its strings broken, she moved across the room and sank into a seat. Her life was shattering, splintering like glass, shards of pain and despair piercing her very being.

From deep within her body a scream began to build, sweeping through her like a tidal wave. She gripped the armrests, clung to them. No. No. No. She couldn't give way now. She had to do something. Anything. Action. Don't think, do.

She jumped up, staring wildly around. Outside, she saw a line of taxis and stumbled towards them. Johannesburg. Food. She needed a good meal. And clothes. Something cooler and more comfortable. Wasn't shopping supposed to be the panacea for all feminine ills? She found a taxi and asked to be taken to the closest boutique and had him wait while she selected a couple of outfits.

Back at Jan Smuts Airport, her emotions under a fragile control, she changed into a cool cotton pants suit. At the gift shop, she purchased a couple of magazines. Less than half an hour now until her plane was called. She could manage that. She leafed through the books without taking in any of the contents. Time was running out. She could feel it like an ache in her bones. Richard. Barenji. Richard. The cadence started again.

Fifteen

Victoria Falls

The Air Zimbabwe flight trundled slowly along the taxiway and stopped. Rachel glanced impatiently out the window at the line of passengers boarding another plane. Her gaze lighted for a moment on two garishly dressed men and passed on then returned. It couldn't be! She gasped and pressed her forehead against the window. It was!

Richard!

With shaking fingers, she unfastened her seat belt and scrambled across the man in the aisle seat. She had only taken a couple of steps down the aisle when the stewardess blocked her way.

"Madam, please return to your seat until the plane has taxied to the gate. We are sorry for the delay but the plane ahead of us was late. We must wait until it has left the gate."

"I have to get off now."

"That's impossible."

"I have to. My husband is boarding that other flight and I have to catch him."

"I'm sorry but you will have to wait until we move into the gate. Now, please return to your seat." She must have read the desperation in Rachel's face for her voice softened. "I will

127

arrange for you to be the first off the plane. It is the best I can do."

When at last Rachel was able to deplane, Richard's flight was only a dot on the horizon. On trembling legs, she entered the terminal and sank into the nearest seat. So close. So damned close. Tears burned behind her eyelids. She blinked them away. Tears wouldn't help. Richard was still alive. Concentrate on that. He was alive and going somewhere. Where? Think.

She closed her eyes to recapture the brief scene. Those awful clothes! Another man behind him dressed with similar atrocious taste. A disguise, of course. Her lips curved in an unconscious smile. Not even the clothes could diminish his good looks.

She opened her eyes and looked around the terminal. Pulling herself together, she approached the ticket counter. "Can you tell me where the plane that just left is going?"

"Nairobi, Kenya, with a stop in Harare."

"I think I recognized one of the man boarding that flight. He was dressed in green pants and a bright yellow shirt. Is he stopping in Harare? Perhaps you didn't notice him?"

The girl laughed. "I certainly noticed the silk shirt. I would love to have a blouse like it."

"Was the gentleman about 6 feet tall with brown curly hair and hazel eyes?"

"He sure was. Is he your friend?"

Rachel thought fast. Until she knew what was going on, it would be better not to claim a too close relationship. "Well, he's not exactly a close friend. He's the brother of my college roommate. Is he going to Harare? Perhaps I will see him there."

"Oh, no, I don't think so. Let me check." She riffled through a batch of flight coupons. "No, Mr. Rossiter and Mr. Rubinski are booked through to Nairobi with a connecting flight to Frankfurt, Germany."

Why was Richard using the name Rossiter? Or was he the one calling himself Rubinski? "Well, how extraordinary. I'm going to Frankfurt, too. By the way, when is the next flight?"

"But, Madam, you just arrived."

Damn. The shock of actually seeing Richard only to lose him had scattered her wits. Now the girl was suspicious. She forced a blithe smile. "Yes, I know. I only planned to stop here long enough to see the falls. Is there a tour I can take and still get to Harare tonight?"

"I thought you wanted to go to Frankfurt?"

"Oh, yes. I mean, no. I mean, I'm going to Frankfurt after I see the falls and Harare and Nairobi." Damn, she was blowing this. She kept the smile pasted on her face. "Is it far to the Falls? Won't I be able to see it in a few hours and still get to Harare tonight?"

"Yes, Ma'am. There is a flight leaving at 5:10 this evening. Do you wish me to book you a seat?"

"Yes, please, and can you recommend a tour of the Falls?"

The young woman frowned then her face cleared. "I believe there is someone at the airport now who can help you. I'll be happy to check."

As Rachel left the counter, the girl stared after her thoughtfully then picked up the telephone.

~ * ~

Reginald Umbulu breathed a sigh of relief as the plane left the runway. He turned, moving heavily back into the terminal and went in search of his brother. Perhaps being an international spy was not such a great thing after all. Death in the movies was not at all like real life. No one mourned in the movies. He wasn't looking forward to facing the dead boy's mother. He had said they would find the Arab, but did he really want to? Another killing wouldn't bring the boy back to life.

His brother was busy, so Reginald wandered out onto the tarmac. He stood, frowning, pinching his lower lip between his fingers.

Why were the Arabs and the CIA and the Chinese playing their games in his country? He didn't want to be responsible for another death. Let them take their deadly games somewhere else. What was in the ampoules that the CIA was so anxious to recover? A chill crept over his body as he remembered the one that had been thrown into the river.

His brother ran up, eyes bright. "Betty Mbimi called from the front counter. A woman who arrived on the flight from Bulawayo is asking questions about those two men that just left."

A few minutes later, after a hurried conference with Betty, Reginald approached Rachel. "You are interested in a tour to the Falls?"

"Yes. But it will have to be a short one."

"That was explained to me. If you will come this way?"

"Are you a tour guide?"

"Oh, no, Madam. I am the head bellman at the Victoria Falls Hotel. I will take you to the hotel. We can arrange a tour for you from there."

He saw refusal on her face and smiled. "Perhaps you did not realize that it is fourteen miles to the Falls or that the Victoria Falls Hotel is built at the edge of the falls." His smile broadened at her look of surprise. "Yes, indeed, Madam, our gardens go right to the edge. Please come with me. The hotel van is parked right outside."

He settled her in the first row of seats where he could see her in the mirror, started the van and pulled out onto the road. Without thinking, he turned on the radio to a program of local music, keeping the volume low.

"It is to be regretted that you do not have the opportunity to stay in our hotel. It is a most attractive example of colonial English architecture. Also, we have an interesting exhibition each evening of native music and dancing. You are from America?"

Rachel answered with a sharp yes. She wished he would shut up. She needed to think. She stared blindly out the window, her thoughts racing. Why was Richard going to Germany? Why was he dressed in those outlandish clothes? Who was the man accompanying him? Where was Barenji?

"We have had two of your countrymen staying with us. That is why I was so opportunely at the airport. They left just now on the flight to Harare."

He saw her head jerk around and their eyes met in the mirror. He looked quickly away. Oh, yes, the lady was definitely interested.

"What did you say?" Rachel asked.

"They were very important men in your entertainment industry. They came to see our dancers. Maybe they will take them to America to perform on television. Yes, they were very important men. Very beautiful clothes." He gave a sigh of envy. "And of such beautiful colors."

"Really? Perhaps I saw them at the airport. Was one wearing a yellow shirt?"

"Yes, madam. And of the finest silk."

"You say they were talent agents? Do you know from which agency?"

"Ah, that, Madam, I cannot say."

"I thought I recognized one of them. The brother of one of my college friends. Were they here long?"

He shook his head. "No. They were called away suddenly. I, myself, had to rush them to the airport."

"Do you know where they were going?"

"But, of course. It was I who made their reservations."

"Where did they go?"

"Oh, my. I think somewhere in Europe. Yes, Germany, I think."

"Did they have your make hotel reservations, too?"

"No, only their airline seats."

Disappointed, Rachel turned back to the window. Could Mossad act in time to have an agent meet their flight and follow them? She must get to a telephone. She could only pray that the number she remembered had not been changed.

Umbulu hit the brakes so hard that she was thrown against the front seat. Angrily, she righted herself and glared at him. The anger faded as she saw his face turn a chalky gray. He turned up the volume of the radio and the deep plummy accents of the newscaster filled the van. Rachel's heart dropped as she listened.

"...of epidemic proportions. Sixteen of the dead are children. Health officials are sending emergency teams to Deka. Word has just been received that four people are also reported dead in Msuna and another twenty are ill.

"In other news..."

Sweat popped out on Umbulu's forehead as he turned off the radio and pulled back onto the road. Whatever was in the ampoule had done this. He knew it is his gut. Should he report this to the authorities? But what would he say? He didn't know what was in the ampoule. And they would ask questions to which he had no answers. Admit to being a spy for the Americans? No. No. His hands began to shake. What then?

He drove by instinct, his thoughts racing, completely forgetting his passenger. He parked the van and dashed into the hotel.

Rachel climbed out and followed him, interrupting his whispered conversation with the switchboard operator.

"Excuse me, but is there a telephone? I need to make a long distance call."

Her voice was like a slap in the face. He whirled on her. She was one of them, one of the fiends that had brought this death to his people.

"You! You know about this. Come with me."

He clutched her arm, pulling her down the hall and into his office. He slammed the door and glared at her. "What was in the ampoule?"

"What are you talking about? What ampoule? I need a telephone."

"No telephone until you answer me. What was in the ampoule?"

Rachel took a step backward and stared up at him, her thoughts racing. What the hell was going on? "I don't understand you. What ampoule? What are you talking about?"

"The one the Arab threw in the river. What was in it that is killing my people? The ampoules your friends were so anxious to recover."

"My friends?"

"The ones that just left. The ones you were asking about. The agents of your CIA. I was helping them to catch terrorists." He looked at her suspiciously. "Are you an agent of the CIA, too?"

"No, of course not. I don't know what you are talking about." What the hell was Richard involved in? Would it help to claim to be an agent? No. She couldn't risk being questioned, delayed. Damn. "Look, I'm short on time. I shouldn't even be here, but I couldn't resist a quick stopover when I was this close to Victoria Falls." She dug her passport out and waved it at him. "I'm not really an American, I'm Swedish but I went to college in Massachusetts. I thought the man I saw at the airport was my roommate's brother, Richard Rossiter. I may have been mistaken. I haven't seen him in years."

He glared at her. "It was Mr. Rossiter. And now you arrive. You were planning to meet him here. Don't deny. It is obvious."

Rachel shifted her glance guiltily around the room, looking everywhere but at Umbulu. "How did you know?" she whispered, twisting her hands.

"Madam, it is obvious."

"Oh, dear. I'm so embarrassed." She looked up at him, forcing a tear. "I... I didn't realize I was so obvious. Oh, please don't tell anyone."

"Why were you meeting Mr. Rossiter. Was it because of the ampoules?"

"Please. I don't know what you're talking about." Her hands fluttered in a helpless gesture. "His sister told me Richard was coming here. I was in Johannesburg and... and... it was just an impulse. I mean, I thought... meeting again in such a romantic spot... maybe, well, maybe Richard would see me as... as more than just... his sister's school friend. Oh, this is so embarrassing. And now, if I don't call my office, I'll probably lose my job."

She rummaged in her purse for a handkerchief and dabbed at her eyes. "Oh, why did he have to leave so soon and spoil everything?"

"They were in a hurry to catch the same flight as Dr. Bach," Reginald said without thinking. "Are you sure that you know nothing of what was in the ampoules?"

She shook her head and walked over to the open window. "No. I don't know anything about any ampoules. Why do you keep asking me that? Please, I must make a telephone call. Oh, I feel like such an idiot."

Knuckles pounded imperatively on the door. Umbulu whirled and jerked it open. The man in the hall spoke rapidly. "The Arab. We found him. Tsuni's brother was there. We couldn't stop him—"

"Quiet," Reginald snapped, shoving the man into the hall. Over his shoulder, he growled at Rachel, "Use that phone. I will arrange for someone to take you back to the airport." He left the room, shaking his head.

Women. With everything else, he didn't need a hysterical, love-sick woman on his hands. If the Arab was dead, so much the better. They could dispose of the body where it would never be found. Tonight he would make his last report to his contact. He would wash his hands of the whole matter. Being a spy in a book or a movie was one thing; real death was something else. He would tell the person not to come to his country with their killing.

In the office, Rachel grabbed the telephone and placed a call to Frankfurt. The timing was too critical, she couldn't depend on her personal code to generate action fast enough. It was time to come out of hiding. Richard's life could well depend on the help she could receive from Mossad. It was time to reactivate Zephyr. She stared out the window, drumming her fingers on the table as she waited for the call to go through. Her skin crawled as somewhere down the river a hyena laughed, and then another and another.

Sixteen

Jerusalem

Itzak Dann put down the memo and glanced out the window. The buildings across the road wavered and danced in the heat that was blanketing Jerusalem. He ran a hand over his bald, freckled scalp. Adjusting his wire framed glasses, he picked up the memo again. It was a routine report except for one small item. A retired agent, Ellia Davidian, had contacted the London office using out of date codes and one of those codes had indicated extreme emergency. Just seeing the name was like having a white hot poker stabbed in his gut.

He was the only one left alive who knew that Ellia Davidian was Zephyr. Zephyr—the almost mythical super agent—his creation. The only one who knew why she had left the Mossad, left Israel. He had personally created her new identity. A cover so deep that even the CIA would never be able to penetrate it. It had been the least he could do for her. Once she had left Israel, he had forced all thought of her from his mind.

If Zephyr was active, was calling on Mossad for assistance, something big was going down. More than big, something crucial. Given her antipathy towards all covert organizations and Mossad in particular, she must be desperate.

136

He pushed a button and summoned his aide then stood up and moved to the window, thinking about Zephyr.

He had learned to accept the pain when an agent was lost, reject any sense of guilt. Every Mossad agent knew the danger, knew the risks. Except Zephyr. What he had done to Zephyr still burned like acid in his soul.

He spoke without turning as the door opened. "Notify all chiefs of station immediately. Any requests from Zephyr or Ellia Davidian are to be treated as direct orders from me. Reactive both codes so that there will no delay in response. Also, have them report any contact and any action taken directly to me immediately."

He turned then and moved back to the desk. "I want a complete report on the London contact."

His aide nodded and retreated only to reappear a few minutes later with another memo. "I've notified our station chiefs. This just came in from Frankfurt. They have received a telephone contact from Zephyr requesting surveillance of two passengers arriving from Zimbabwe. Zephyr used the old code for highest priority."

~ * ~

Seattle

James Eberle knocked on the door then entered without waiting for a response. Walter McPherson motioned him to a seat. "What have you found out?"

"There's no question that both the Royers have been kidnapped, or at least taken away. McGregor was at Green Lake early, questioning everyone that was in the park at the approximate time Mrs. Royer was last seen. Two other joggers witnessed Mrs. Royer getting in the car. Both agreed that the car was gray. At least one of the descriptions of the men corresponds with that given by the two ladies who came to my office. The others vary in only minor details. Both new witnesses agree that there was some kind of confrontation. They didn't report it because neither wanted to get involved."

He flipped a page in his notebook. "The car is a rental. The agency just got back to us. The reservation was made through the agency's Washington DC office. It was delivered to Boeing Field. I talked to the driver that delivered the car. The four men came in on a private jet. He only got a good look at one of the men."

"They didn't take the driver back to the rental agency?"

"No. They slipped him two twenties and told him to take a cab."

"What have you found out about the Royers?"

"Nothing. Actually, quite a lot but nothing that would throw any light on their kidnapping. They are comfortably situated but not rich by any means. They don't have enough liquid assets to be able to pay a large enough ransom to make it worthwhile. Royer is considered to be a talented composer, but isn't known outside the classical music field."

"Political?" McPherson asked.

Eberle shook his head. "Royer is a registered Republican, Mrs. is a Democrat. They have voted in every election in the past six years but neither of them is active in any political party. They support the Seattle Symphony and the Pacific Northwest Ballet. No affiliation with any special interest group or cause.

"We swept their house. It's squeaky clean. We did come across one interesting fact. Royer is suffering from kidney failure. Requires dialysis on a regular basis."

"Have you checked with his doctor? When is he due for another treatment?"

"He isn't. It seems he has his own portable machine. We didn't find it in the house." He closed his notebook and looked at his supervisor. "Walter, I'm sure the CIA is involved. Did you find out anything from Washington?"

"No. At least, not directly. I think you're right. Those bastards at the CIA are stonewalling. However, I did pick up hints that something is going on over there and I've got some feelers out."

McPherson leaned back in his chair. "If we don't know why they were taken, let's see if we can find out where."

"I've got Ken Bennett searching property records and MacGregor coordinating with the police to trace the movements of the gray car.

"There is one other thing. Could be coincidence but I don't like coincidences. A stolen pickup truck was found a block away from the Royer house. It was stolen in Bothell yesterday morning. The owner only got a quick glance at the thief but he's sure it was a woman."

"Mrs. Royer?"

Eberle shrugged. "I think we should check out that area. If they took her to a safe house, I'd like to find it. Like I say, I don't like coincidences."

Walter McPherson nodded. "Keep me informed. I want enough to pin this on those bastards. They've no authority to operate within the United States. I'm sure as hell not going to let them get away with kidnapping citizens off the street in my bailiwick."

Seventeen

Frankfurt

The call from Zephyr followed by the message from Itzak Dann had thrown the Frankfurt office into full alert status. Obviously something big was going down. Zephyr was active again! The words were whispered from ear to ear, churning excitement in some, anxiety in others. No one spoke the name aloud. Two agents rushed to the airport. Aaron Ben Judah and Sol Brenner watched the passengers from Lufthansa flight five eighty one progress through Immigration control. Aaron had already spotted the bright yellow shirt, when the immigration agent gave them the sign. Whoever they were, they must be important to bring Zephyr out of retirement and to have Itzak Dann is such an uproar.

~ * ~

Richard moved a few steps away from the Immigration booth, his eyes following the back of Herman Bach as he waited impatiently for David.

"It's okay," David said as he caught up. "He'll have to pick up his luggage the same as we do."

They dashed down the corridor then moderated their pace as they approached the baggage area. Bach was nowhere to be seen. They pushed their way though the crowd but their quarry had disappeared.

"The rest room," David said.

"No—wait, there he is. Outside. Shit. Here, get the luggage and check us into a hotel." Richard shoved his claim check into David's hand.

"What hotel?"

"The Frankfurterhof," he cried over his shoulder. It would be damned expensive but it was the only hotel he could think of on the spur of the moment.

He burst through the doors just as Bach's cab was pulling away. Without a thought, Richard shoved in front of a family of tourists and crawled into the next cab. Thank God, David had given him some money on the plane. Pulling a wad of bills from his pocket, he waved them in front of the driver's face.

"Hurry. Follow that cab."

The man's stolid face took on a mulish look. "Where did you wish to go, sir?"

"Just follow that cab."

"And why should I do that, sir?"

Bach's cab was almost out of sight around the concourse. Damn. It didn't happen like this in the movies. Richard thought fast. "Because I've forgotten the address. Hurry or you will lose Herr Bach and I won't know where to go."

Richard sighed with relief as the driver finally pulled away. He sat perched on the edge of his seat, willing the driver to go faster. He paid no attention to the black BMW that fell in behind them a moment later.

As the taxi sped towards the city, Richard finally settled back in the seat. He was completely lost by the time the cab pulled up in front of a brick building. He glanced hastily around. The buildings appeared to house small businesses with apartments above. Some of the businesses were beginning to open. He spotted a cafe on the next corner.

"Drop me off at the cafe," he told the driver.

Out on the sidewalk, he felt suddenly very conspicuous, as well as chilly, in his rumpled shirt and creased pants. He scurried into the cafe and took a seat in the window where he could watch Herr Bach's building.

Half an hour and three cups of bad coffee later, Herr Bach had not appeared, but a haberdashery across the street was opening. Paying for his coffee, he crossed the street and entered the shop. Minutes later, he was back on the street attired in heavy wool pants, tan turtleneck sweater and tweed jacket. In his pocket was a tweed cap.

He strolled slowly up the street, pausing to glance in the shop windows until he reached the building into which Bach had disappeared. Women's lingerie was exhibited in the window of the shop occupying the ground floor and Richard shifted his gaze up the steps to the three bronze plates beside the door. Herman Bach's name leapt out at him from the second plate. In the shallow alcove, three letterboxes were arranged and below each box was a button and a speaker.

He moved past the doorway. The sign over the next shop read, H. Strauss, Buchhandler and he entered. A stooped figure with receding white hair and goatee was dusting a rack of books. Richard wandered to a table at the front of shop and casually began to shift through the pile of books, keeping one eye peeled outside.

"*Guten Morgan. Interessiert sie geflugel?*"

Startled, Richard glanced at the book in his hand. Smiling, he laid the book back on the table. "I'm sorry. I don't speak German."

The old man's brown eyes twinkled merrily. "Then I do not think a German text on poultry raising would be of much interest to you," he said. Although heavily accented, his English was good. "You are an American? I have only a few English books."

"Yes. Actually, I wanted a book in German. It is a gift for a friend."

"Ah. A woman friend?"

Richard's interest was caught by a swarthy young man crossing the street. "Yes. Yes, a woman friend." Dressed in western clothing, the man was definitely Middle Eastern.

"Does she like poetry?"

"What? Oh. Yes." The man passed in front of the bookstore and started up the steps. Richard grabbed a book from the table, moved quickly to the door and stepped outside, pretending to examine the binding in the light. The young man pressed the center button then spoke softly into the speaker. Moments later he disappeared through the door. "A very uninteresting and inexpensive binding, I'm afraid. Is your friend a mathematician?"

"No—of course not."

"Then I really do not think she would be interested in a differential calculus text book, either," the old man said, gently taking the book from Richard's hands and turning back into the shop.

Over his shoulder, he said, "I have a very fine edition of Goethe that might be of more interest. Even more interesting are some of Dr. Bach's patients."

"What?" Richard followed him but stopped just inside the door.

"I said some of Dr. Bach's patients are very... ah... unusual. That young man, for example. Definitely not a patient. A husband, perhaps? But one never sees an Arab woman visiting the doctor. In fact, one rarely sees any young women visiting the good doctor. Only a few old crones."

"I don't follow you."

"Oh, was it not Dr. Bach who interests you? Your new clothes are much less noticeable than the yellow shirt and green pants you arrived in." He laughed at the rueful expression on Richard's face. "An old man needs little sleep and a childless widower like myself has plenty of time to observe the neighborhood. I saw Herr Doktor Bach arrive and then the taxi drop you at the cafe. I hope Meyer did not... uh, what is the American expression?... take you to the laundry?"

"Take you to the cleaners. How do you know that man wasn't one of Dr. Bach's patients?"

"Because, my dear sir, Herr Dr. Bach is a gynecologist."

Richard grinned, liking the keen old man. "Does the doctor have many Arab visitors?"

"Not a lot. They come and go." He moved to a rack of books and began running his fingers over the bindings. "Sometimes several in a few days and then none for several weeks. Always men, never women. An odd clientele for a gynecologist, wouldn't you say?"

"Very. Do you know where the doctor lives?"

"But of course. On the second floor. He has an apartment behind his consulting rooms." He took down a small beautifully bound book.

Richard attention switched to the upstairs door as it opened and the young Arab came down the steps. Richard moved farther back into the shadows as the Arab passed the shop and stepped off the curb.

"Thanks for the information. I have to go," Richard said and moved to the door.

"Wait. You have forgotten the book for your friend."

Richard reached impatiently in his pocket.

"No. No. Take it as a gift. Consider it as payment for a very interesting morning, for bringing a little excitement into an old man's life."

"Thank you." Stuffing the little book into his pocket, he smiled again. "Thank you very much."

Stepping out briskly as though intent on some errand, Richard walked to the corner; then crossed the street and followed the young man down a side street.

Half a block down the street, David groaned, as realization struck him. Herr Dr. Bach hadn't been carrying anything when he left airport. Neither was the young Arab ahead of him. *Where is the goddamned bacteria?* He hesitated then shrugged and continued to follow the Arab. He could only pray that David would have better luck at the airport.

~ * ~

Aaron Ben Judah watched Richard climb out of the taxi and enter the cafe. He parked the BMW and waited. When Richard left the clothing store, Aaron left the car and strolled leisurely down the street. When Richard seemed settled in the bookstore, Aaron Ben Judah risked a call from the kiosk outside the cafe.

"Rossiter and Rubinski are following someone and they are obviously amateurs. They split up at the airport. Sol is covering Rubinski. I followed Rossiter. He followed a man to a house here on Tannerstrasse. Right now he is in a bookstore, H. Strauss, Bookseller. Now the interesting part is the man he was following, Dr. Herman Bach."

He waited until the voice on the other end of the wire stopped sputtering. "I thought that name would interest you. Why would Rossiter be interested in that old Nazi? Wait. Someone has just gone into the building. I didn't get a good look at him.

"I think it might be a good idea to keep an eye on the good doctor for a while. Can you get someone over here right away? If I'm still around, I'll be in the cafe on the corner."

"Wait. The man just came out. An Arab. Rossiter is following him. I'll call when I can."

~ * ~

David watched Richard jump into the taxi. With a shrug, he turned his attention to the arriving luggage. His case arrived. He retrieved it and waited impatiently for Richard's. A few minutes later, a frisson of excitement raced up his spine as he spotted the case of vaccine.

Forgetting the other suitcase, he concentrated on the vaccine. It had to be the one. There wasn't another like it on the carousel. Why hadn't Bach claimed it? His gut tightened. Could it be a decoy?

Moments later a hand reached through the crowd and grasped the case. David began pushing his way through the milling passengers, stretching to catch a glimpse of the claimant. He reached the edge of the crowd in time to see a young man, hair spiked and painted in an absurd shade of orange carrying the case towards the passage to the departure lounge.

David pulled his ticket jacket from his pocket and pretended to be studying it as he followed. The young man went straight to the coffee bar. David headed for the newsstand and purchased a map of the city, a guidebook, and as an afterthought, a couple of candy bars.

Leaning against a wall, he watched the boy over the top of the guidebook. He almost missed the pickup. A family group was clustered around the coffee bar blocking his view. David shifted his position. Seconds later the boy crossed to the men's room and it was a moment before David realized he was no longer carrying the case.

David glanced quickly around the room. It was only by chance that he noticed the two countermen in an argument. His interest quickened as one took off his white jacket and threw in on the floor. David moved towards the door as the irate counterman left the coffee bar carrying the case.

Abandoning his own luggage with barely a thought, David followed him out of the terminal. Out of the corner of his eye, he saw someone pick up his discarded suitcase and smiled wryly. He hoped the thief liked gaudy clothes.

~ * ~

Richard was beginning to feel as though he had walked halfway across Germany by the time they reached the Altstadt. His legs ached and his lungs felt on fire. Where the hell was the bastard going? Several blocks, or was it miles, earlier, when his quarry had been held up by a traffic light, Richard had purchased a pair of sunglasses and a couple of candy bars. What he really wanted was water. Gallons of water. His mind conjured up pictures of great silver water pitchers, beaded with condensation, rows of crystal glasses filled with water. He could almost hear the ice cubes tinkling.

They turned into Grosser Hirshgraben. He regretted buying such heavy clothes. He could feel the sweat running down his ribs and back. Richard was considering crossing to follow on the opposite side of the street when the Arab suddenly went into a house. He felt his pulse begin to race. Was this where the bacteria was to be delivered? What should he do now? Would David be at the hotel? He slowed, glancing quickly along the street for a telephone.

Two young women, obviously tourists, approaching from the opposite direction, went into the house. Puzzled, Richard moved closer then stopped. Number 23. Goethe's house. Depression washed over him. The man was sightseeing.

Then it hit him. The man wasn't sightseeing. He knew he was being followed. Unsure of what to do, Richard walked slowly on down the street. Would the Arab come out soon or was there another exit? He turned the corner and stopped. Now what? He needed to change his appearance, but how? Damn it, this spy stuff was completely out of his ken.

The first thing was to get rid of the coat. As he took it off, the cap fell out of his pocket. He picked it up with a grin. He'd forgotten buying it. Putting it on, he added the sunglasses. Now, what else? His height, his walk. He tugged a button from the sleeve of the coat and slipped it in his shoe. He took a few steps. He definitely now had a limp. One that might become permanent, if he had to walk very much farther, he thought with a grimace. He dropped the coat against the wall of the building, in the shadow of some steps, relieved to be rid of its weight.

Stepping back around the corner, he pulled the book from his pocket, and leaning against a building, began to peruse it while munching on candy. Half an hour later, his man came out of the museum. This time he strolled slowly, giving every impression of being an interested sightseer. By the time they left the Carmelite Monastery, Richard was ready to collapse from fatigue and hunger.

He staggered slightly as he reached the sidewalk. He looked at his watch but his vision blurred. Ahead, his quarry turned the corner and for a moment, Richard was tempted to call it quits. He desperately needed water. Doggedly he began to follow. The sidewalk wavered before his eyes. Each step became an effort, as if climbing a hill. He began to stagger. Somewhere behind him a motor roared. He never saw the motorbike speeding up behind him, only heard the whine as the rider changed gears. A woman's scream blended with the motor's roar as he was knocked to the pavement.

He stared up at the cloudless sky. The bike had only grazed him. He knew he wasn't hurt, but he didn't have the strength to get up. Slowly the buildings, the sky above him began to spin and turn dim.

Eighteen

Richard was first conscious of a burning thirst. Someone was wiping his face with a very wet cloth. Except for the foul odor, it felt good but he wished someone would bring him a drink. A hair tickled his nose. He sneezed, opened his eyes and quickly closed them as the dog's tongue made another pass over his face.

"Liebchen, nein, nein."

He opened one eye and squinted up into the gravely benign face of a huge St. Bernard. The chattering of voices impinged on his consciousness. He looked up into a mass of faces peering down at him. Most were speaking in German and he understood none of it.

"English," he croaked. "Speak English."

A few scattered phrases in heavily accepted English followed.

"Ah, he awakens."

"The police should be called."

"Young people have no respect, no manners."

"No. No. Call an ambulance."

The big dog was pulled away and replaced by a man's face. An arm moved to support his shoulders as Richard struggled to a sitting position, and murmured, "…okay."

He could hardly force the words through his dry throat. "Taxi. Hotel." The chattering faces withdrew.

"Which hotel?" the man asked in excellent if slightly accented English.

"Frankfurterhof. What…what happened?"

"You were hit by a motorcycle. Can you stand?"

"I think so."

The man helped him to his feet then held him as a wave of dizziness swept over him. He fought down the urge to vomit.

"Shouldn't you go to the hospital?" the good Samaritan asked.

"No. No." The dizziness receded and he straightened up. He looked around, trying to get his bearings. Memory rushed back. Where was the Arab? Gone. He had to find David. "I must get to my hotel."

A taxi, summoned by one of the onlookers pulled to the curb. The Samaritan helped him into the back seat then climbed in the front and spoke to the driver in German. Richard closed his eyes, fighting down a return of nausea. A few minutes later the taxi came to a stop in front of the hotel. Still dazed and shaky, Richard allowed himself to be helped to the desk.

Aaron Ben Judah explained the accident to the desk clerk then turned to Richard. "Are you registered here?"

"Yes. At least I think so. Richard Rossiter. David… my friend David Rubinski was bringing our luggage."

"You will have to complete the registration form," the desk clerk said.

"Yes, of course."

By the time the formalities were completed, Richard was more in command of his facilities. As the bellman took the key, he turned to thank his deliverer but the man was gone. Wearily he followed the bellman to the elevator.

David sprang up from a chair as Richard entered the room. "My God! What happened to you?"

"I got hit by a motorcycle. I'll tell you everything in a minute, but first I've got to have a drink then a shower. And food. Call room service and order whatever they can deliver fast."

Ten minutes later, wrapped in the large terry robe provided by the hotel, Richard stretched out on the bed. "Have you been able to reach your number in London?"

"Yes. We should have some assistance shortly. Tell me what happened."

"I followed Bach into town. He lives behind his office. By the way, he's a gynecologist but only has a few elderly patients. He also has Arab visitors from time to time. Men, never women. Shortly after he got home an Arab showed up. He didn't stay long. I thought he might be more likely to lead me to the bacteria so I followed him. On foot, for hours. He led me on a walking tour of the city. Obviously he spotted me. Just after we left the Carmelite Monastery, I was run down by a motorcycle."

"Could it have been an accident?"

"No. The cyclist came up onto the sidewalk. So I'm afraid we've lost our best lead. Did you bring the luggage?"

David grinned. "I'm afraid not." He explained the incident at the terminal. "So your suitcase is probably still at the airport and mine is probably being peddled at some used clothing store."

"It looks like we've struck out all the way around."

David's grin widened. "Nope. I followed the attendant to a house in a working class neighborhood. I couldn't stay because I stood out like a sore thumb in those pimp clothes so I beat it back here to the hotel and called London. I picked up this outfit and have been waiting for you. I—"

A knock on the door startled them both. Cautiously, David opened it and admitted the room service waiter. As soon as the man was gone, Richard sat up.

"David, what about my wife?"

David reached for his jacket. "We'll talk when I get back. I've got to get back and watch that house. I'll be in a rented brown Citroen." He motioned towards a note pad on the dresser. "I've written down the address. You eat and then rest. As soon as our contact arrives, get us both some clothes. There's money on the dresser." He bolted out the door.

Richard didn't care for heavy German food, but when he lifted the covers, the spicy aroma started his glands salivating and his stomach rumbling. He was soon shoveling forkfuls of *rippchen mitt sauerkraut* and *gurkensalat* into his mouth and following it with hunks of black bread.

Finally sated, Richard shoved the cart into the hall, turned out the lights and stretched out on the bed. The food had helped but he was still weak. What worried him more than the physical weakness was his increasing mental deterioration. It was becoming more and more difficult to concentrate, to think clearly.

Staring at the ceiling, he tried to sort out his thoughts but he kept thinking of Rachel. Would he ever see her again? Hold her in his arms? Or would he die in some hotel, alone and afraid? Did it matter? If they didn't recover the bacteria there was going to be a lot of deaths. He was dying anyway, wasn't he? He brushed a hand over his face, trying to wipe away his thoughts, and found he was crying.

He sat up. What the hell was he doing? Lying in bed wallowing in self-pity. Shit. If he was going to die then, damn it, he ought to make his death count for something.

He turned on the lights, grabbed the packet of stationery and settled himself at the table. Perhaps, if he wrote his thoughts down, he'd be better able to concentrate. An hour later, he threw the pen down and stood up. He crumbled the notes in a ball, pitched them towards the wastebasket from where they bounced and lodged behind the dresser. He headed for the bathroom.

Minutes later, after another shower, he dressed, pocketed the money and the address and left. He found a department store and purchased a camera case, cheap camera and a couple of rolls of film, an electric shaver and in the men's department, fresh underwear and a couple of loose, comfortable outfits.

~ * ~

From the end of the hall, Aaron Ben Judah watched Richard leave. Moments later, he had the door open and was in the room. It didn't take him long to find Richard's notes. He glanced at them briefly then pocketed them. Holding the note pad to the light he read the address David had left. A faint scratching at the door alerted him. He dropped the note pad and moved silently across the room.

He was behind the door as it opened and a man stepped into the room, a Walther PPK gripped in his hand. Aaron moved swiftly. A judo chop to the external anterior thoracic nerve with his right hand, followed by a rabbit punch with his left and the man collapsed at his feet.

Aaron glanced quickly up and down the empty hall and shut the door. He pocketed the Walther, made a quick body search, found the CIA identification and replaced it in the man's pocket. He placed the gun back on the floor and slipped out the door.

In the lobby, he found a phone.

"Rossiter has left the hotel. I searched the room and found some notes. This is bigger than we suspected. Get someone to watch this house, right away." He gave the address. "I'm coming in. I'll need a secure line to Itzak Dann."

~ * ~

Richard left the elevator and walked slowly down the hall. He paused half way to his hotel room and leaned against the wall. His shopping expedition had left him weak and sweating. His throat felt as dry as parchment. Water. Then he had to rest. Thank God his part would soon be over. He just had to hang on until the CIA arrived. Then he would check himself into a hospital.

He walked the rest of the way down the hall. The knob turned under his hand and Richard took a step back. His heart began to race. He distinctly remembered locking the door. He put his parcels down and rubbed sweaty palms on his trousers. Stepping to the side, he pushed the door open with his toe. Nothing.

Cautiously, he peered through the opening and his eyes widened. He stepped inside and closed the door. He quickly bent and picked up the gun as the prone man groaned. Backing across the room, he sank into a chair, keeping the gun trained on the intruder.

The man sat up, blinked several times and finally focused his eyes on Richard. He gazed narrowly at the gun in Richard's hand. "You didn't have to hit me so hard. Are you Bergdorf or Royer?"

"Royer, and I didn't hit you. Who are you? How did you know my name? I found you stretched out on the floor."

"Kelly, CIA." He quickly produced his ID. "Someone must have been searching your room. Anything missing?"

"I don't know, I just got here. But I doubt it. There's nothing here to steal."

"Then you don't have the package?"

Package? Richard's eyes narrowed. "Can you describe this package?"

Kelly gave him a baleful look. "No, I can't. My orders were simply to pick up a package and deliver it to Washington on the next flight. Are you telling me you don't have it?"

"Not the whole thing. David has the partial shipment we took off the Chinese in Zimbabwe."

"Sure your burglar didn't get it?"

"Yes. David has it with him. His instructions were not to let it out of sight until someone collected it." His lips twisted into a weak grin. "I don't think your boss had a lot of confidence in Umbulu's ability to deliver it. He'd probably have sent it through the mail carefully labeled MOST UTTERLY TOP SECRET."

Kelly ignored Richard's feeble attempt at humor. "Where the hell is Bergdorf?"

Richard filled him in on their activities. "David is watching the house, now."

"Let's get out there. My orders are to pick up the package and get it to Washington on the next plane."

"But what about the rest of the... ah... shipment?"

Kelly shrugged. "I guess that's your worry. Let's go."

Nineteen

Seattle

It hadn't taken the FBI long to locate the Royer cabin in the Cascades. Agent Ken Bennett whistled when he saw the gun rack in the cabin. "Would you look at this collection?" He lifted a shotgun from the cabinet and stroked it lovingly. "An old Fox rabbit ears."

Eberle frowned. It was quite a collection of guns. Still, they were all hunting rifles and shotguns. A lot of them antiques. No assault rifles, no handguns. Nothing any normal gun collector wouldn't have. It was definitely a private collection, not an arsenal. "Just check to see if any of them have been fired recently. I'm going to look at the bedrooms."

He was carefully searching through drawers in a dresser when he heard the shout from outside. He laid the pile of sweaters down and hurried to the back door as Michaels rushed in, his eyes like saucers in his round, youthful face. Peter Michaels was only two weeks out of the academy, an accountant by training. Now, his freckles glistened like traffic lights on his pale, green tinged face. He looked about fifteen.

"In the outhouse." he gasped. "You've never seen anything like it."

Eberle left him leaning against the wall of the cabin and followed the path to the outhouse. One look in the hole and he felt his own stomach churn. He backed out and sucked in deep breaths of the cold mountain air. What was going on? What in the hell was going on? He began to sweat.

Half an hour later, the body had been retrieved and Eberle stared down at the CIA identification with dismay. Obviously this was more than a run-of-the-mill kidnapping. McPherson needed to know about this right away. Within hours they would be inundated with Company men, tripping over them every time they turned around. They wouldn't be able to keep the Royer kidnapping or the murder of the CIA man quiet. All hell was going to break loose.

~ * ~

London

Sir Edmund Mortimer glanced up from under shaggy brows as Merton Chadwick entered the office quietly and slid a folder onto the desk. "Well, Merton, spit it out."

Chadwick flashed a rueful smile. "Am I really that obvious, sir?"

"After ten years—yes. What have you got?"

"I don't know, sir, but whatever it is, it's not good. Our agent traveled from Johannesburg with a female agent and checked into the Elephant Hills Hotel. The two American agents that Bottoms spotted in the Azores arrived by private jet, were picked up and taken to the Victoria Falls Hotel. He believes their contact was the concierge, Reginald Umbulu. Two Chinese, one known to be an agent, went to the Victoria for dinner."

He paused and the smile slipped away. "Also in the dining room was Mussa Abjhan, a known terrorist. He was with another Arab who we can only assume is also a terrorist."

"Were the Americans meeting with either of them?"

"It would appear so from Bellegrazia's report. At least they seemed to be keeping an eye on them. There was some kind of contretemps and the two Arabs have disappeared."

"Were the Americans involved?"

"Bellegrazia believes so. Rossiter returned to the hotel in pretty bad shape. Their primary interest seems to have been a German, Dr. Herman Bach. They left on the same flight as he did."

"To where?"

"Frankfurt."

"That's it?"

"No, that's just the teaser, you might say. Shortly after they left, a woman showed up inquiring after them. Bellegrazia identified her as a former Israeli agent. She also departed for Frankfurt on a later flight."

"Well, well. So we have a known Arab terrorist, a known Chinese agent, two Americans, a German and an Israeli. As you say, quite a gathering."

"Add one more player. Bellegrazia says our old friend, Ho Lee, was also on the scene."

"Curiouser and curiouser."

"Indeed, sir. As a footnote, Bellegrazia reports that he heard a news broadcast on the way to the airport. It seems that any number of people down river from the Falls are dying of some unknown disease."

Sir Mortimer stared across the room at the picture of the queen for several minutes. His eyes were cold as he looked back at Chadwick. There was steel beneath the velvet tone as he said, "Alert Frankfurt. Let's keep an eye on these people."

~ * ~

Washington, DC

Mayhew glowered at Brooks. "What do you mean, the FBI found Whitney? Where? Does he have the woman? What the hell has Bryce been doing, sitting on his ass out there?"

"Bryce couldn't move in too close. The FBI was already on the woman's track." He hesitated then continued. "Whitney is dead. It seems the Royers had a mountain cabin. Apparently, Whitney followed her there and she killed him."

Brooks jumped as Mayhew slammed his fist on the desk. "Find her. Find the bitch."

"Bryce has traced her car to Sea-Tac airport, but hasn't been able to track her from there. She could be anywhere."

"Spears has reported. Apparently the president's little boy called in from Frankfurt."

"Frankfurt? What the hell are they doing in Germany? Their orders were to bring the bacteria to London."

"They didn't get it all, only a couple of ampoules, but they were able to locate and identify the rest of the shipment and followed it to Frankfurt. Bergdorf was calling for help." Brooks eyed Mayhew warily. "He also says that Royer is not Zephyr."

"Bullshit. Of course, he's Zephyr. That dammed Royer is trying to pull something. Get onto Frankfurt. I want them covered like a second skin. Tell Frankfurt I want hourly reports. And Brooks, I don't want that bacteria headed for Russia stopped. No, wait. Let me think."

Mayhew swung his chair around and stared out the window. It would have been a hell of a lot simpler to have handled things in Africa. Frankfurt could be tricky. London would be better. He swung back. "Let's not get Frankfurt involved except for courier duty. Have Frankfurt pick up the two ampoules and bring them here. Use the diplomatic pouch. Tell them nothing."

He leaned back in his chair, tenting his fingers over his potbelly. "Send Watts up. As soon as I brief him, I want him on the next flight to London. He's not to contact anyone in the London station. His orders will come directly from me. Have Spears meet his plane. Get back to Bergdorf. Once they have the bacteria, they are to go to London." He looked Brooks in the eye. "As soon as we have the bacteria intended for this country in our possession, I want Bergdorf and Royer taken out."

Brooks blanched, his skin taking on a greenish hue. "Bergdorf is the president's man. There will be hell to pay. Gossard won't let it rest."

"So. We'll make it look like either the Arabs or the Israelis are responsible." He leaned forward. "Neither Royer or Bergdorf must leave London alive." He sat back. "And, Calvin..."

"Yes, sir?"

"Find the woman."

Twenty

Frankfurt

Richard and Kelly had the taxi stop around the corner from the address David had given Richard. Instructing the driver to wait, they strolled around the corner and found David with his head under the raised hood of the rental car, pretending to tinker with the engine. He straightened as Richard stepped off the curb, shooting a quick look at the CIA man. "I see help arrived. Man, are we glad to see you."

"Sorry. My orders are simply to pick up a package from you and get it to Washington by pouch. You do have it?" Kelly asked.

"Yes, in my coat."

"Want to get it?"

"How about showing me some ID first," David said, wiping his hands on his handkerchief. Kelly brought out his identification and David took his time studying it, ignoring Kelly's impatience. At last he handed it back and picked up a wrench. "Are they sending someone to help us?"

"I have no idea. I'm just to act as courier. Are you going to give me the package so I can get out of here?"

162

"I suppose so." David put down the wrench and walked around the car. Reaching in the window, he pulled out his coat and removed the box from the inside pocket.

"Here you go. What are we supposed to do about the rest of the bacteria?"

"Bacteria? Is that what is in this package? Is it dangerous?"

"You could say that. I'd be damned careful with it. What about the help we asked for?"

"I don't know anything about that. I'm just a courier. My instructions were simply to pick up a package from you and deliver it to Mr. Mayhew at Langley." He turned away. "Good luck with whatever you're after."

"For God's sake, we can't break into that house alone," David complained to Kelly's back as he moved towards the waiting taxi.

Richard waved his hand. "Listen, I think I have part of this figured out. Remember what you said about half of the bacteria going to Russia? Well, I think that's what they're doing now. Splitting it up."

David turned back from watching the departing taxi. "So?"

"So, I suppose we'll have to split up, too."

"No way. My orders are to stick with you."

"Orders. Everybody's got orders. What do you suggest?" Richard leaned against the car, his legs quivering.

"Shit, I don't know. I guess we'll just have to follow whoever leaves first."

"Oh, great. And suppose that person is going to Russia?"

David blanched then shrugged. "What I really need to do is get on the phone to the president. This is getting all together too complicated. Where the hell is the CIA? Why haven't they sent the help I requested?"

"Maybe they know something they're not telling us," Richard said.

David shrugged again. "And maybe they don't know a damned thing."

"Yeah. I haven't been impressed by the bastards I've seen so far. Slimy sons-of-bitches." The anger that burned in his belly flared up. He kicked the front tire then stomped around the car struggling to get his temper back under control.

Half way around the car the second time, he stopped and strode back to David. "Did it ever occur to you that maybe they are playing some game of their own? Does it really make sense to you that with all their trained field agents, they would send a broken-down violinist to pull their chestnuts out of the fire?"

"But they thought you were Zephyr."

"Did they? Just who is this Zephyr? Have you ever heard of him?"

"The CIA has a file on him—"

"The CIA. Did you actually see this so-called file?"

"No, but—"

"Given there is or was some super-agent called Zephyr, it still doesn't stand to reason that the CIA would call on a Mossad agent. Shit, I'm about the most non-political person you're ever likely to meet, and even I've heard about the inter-agency rivalries. Even if they truly believed I was this Zephyr, why would they go to the trouble of kidnapping my wife to force me to work for them?"

"Because Zephyr is the only one who could recognize Barenji."

"Bull shit! You and I, a couple of babes-in-the woods, located the bacteria. You can't tell me the CIA, with all their trained, experienced field agents, couldn't have done as well or better."

David's face had paled. "What are you saying?"

Richard shrugged and leaned against the car. "I'm not sure. Something about this whole setup is beginning to smell worse than a wet polecat. I think we'd better stay alert and watch our backs."

"Jesus."

"Yeah. Oh, oh, someone's coming out. What's he carrying?" Richard straightened, rubbing his gritty eyes.

"Looks like one of those black bags my uncle used to carry."

"Your uncle, the doctor?" Richard asked with a grin.

"Yeah." David grabbed the wrench and slammed the hood down. He made a production of trying to start the car as the man paused on the sidewalk then moved away from them down the street.

Richard leaned in the window. "I'll follow on foot. It will be less conspicuous. If he gets in a car, you can pick me up."

Richard moved off down the street, hands in his pockets, feeling about as inconspicuous as a boil on a Las Vegas showgirl's butt. He tried to whistle but his mouth was too dry. The man he mentally dubbed as Black Bag walked three blocks then joined half a dozen women and a couple of men at a bus stop.

Richard joined the queue and, within a minute, entered the bus a few passengers behind Black Bag. He worked his way to the back of the bus and took an aisle seat where he could watch his quarry. As the bus made a turn a few minutes later, Richard spotted David's car half a block behind. A black BMW also made the turn behind the bus.

Black Bag got off on Neue Mainzerstrasse. Fortunately several other passengers got off at the same stop and Richard stepped out after them. He pretended to study an advertisement and watched out of the corner of his eye as Black Bag walked on down the street. He had just turned to follow when the man signaled a taxi. Richard moved to the curb and a moment later, David pulled up beside him.

Richard clambered into the car. "He's in that taxi."

David followed, allowing only a couple of cars between the taxi and the Citroen. After a few blocks, David said, "Damn, he's headed for the airport."

"There goes the new clothes I bought. At least I had sense enough to stick a change of underwear and shaver in here," Richard said, patting the camera bag.

"Follow him and try to get us seats on the same flight while I check this car in," David said pulling into the spot vacated by Black Bag's taxi and tossing his passport to Richard.

A while later, David found Richard leaning against a pillar, reading a paper back novel. He looked up and said, "We're on a British Airways flight to London leaving in just over an hour."

"Oh, great. Why the hell is he going to London? Why not straight to the States? Look, keep an eye on him. I've got to make a couple of phone calls."

An hour and a half later Richard settled into his seat on the plane with an audible sigh.

David buckled his seat belt and leaned back. "I've been thinking about what you said. Something has been bothering me. How could the CIA have made such a mistake?"

"What do you mean?" He turned to stare at David.

"The CIA was positive that Zephyr was living in the Seattle area under the name R. Royer. If you aren't Zephyr, who is?"

Richard began to shake his head then stopped, his eyes widening. A million disjoined memories flashed through his mind. It couldn't be! The blood drained from his face. He began to sweat. "No. Oh, no," he whispered, "Rachel. Rachel is

Zephyr." Then he began to chuckle. The chuckle turned to hysterical laughter. Sweat and tears ran down his cheeks. Abruptly the laughter stopped. Pulling out a handkerchief, he wiped his face. From the corner of his eye he saw the concerned look on David's face and his anger flared as David asked, "Are you okay?"

"No, goddamn it, I'm not okay. We've got to end this thing soon so I can get back on dialysis. I'm way past due."

"Dialysis? You're on dialysis. Jesus! Why didn't you say something. Is that what that thing in your ankle is for? How often...er...how long....Oh, shit. I thought you were a junkie. Why the devil didn't you say something?"

"And risk you bastards killing Rachel? You fucking, screwed-up assholes! Just shut up and leave me alone."

"But—"

"Shut up and leave me alone. Just shut your mouth."

He leaned back and closed his eyes. Rachel. Oh, God, Rachel, what have they done to you? He'd always suspected, no, known, that there was something in her past that she had kept hidden. He pictured her again as he had first seen her, clutching the dead baby in the Lebanese ruins, her eyes blank with terror.

Could his wife really have been an Israeli agent? He pictured her body, so firm and strong. Remembered her almost fanatical obsession with fitness and the inner hardness he had never been able to penetrate, even during her breakdown in Lebanon. Yes, a lot of things about her that he hadn't understood now made sense. Rachel had been an Israeli agent.

Whatever had happened to her in Lebanon had nearly destroyed her. Only a tough iron-will had held her together, enabled her begin reconstructing her life. But there were cracks, tiny fractures deep within her psyche. He had felt them and loved and respected her enough to leave them undisturbed until she was ready to reveal them on her own.

Where was she now? What had they done to her? Would that inner core of steel be enough? He shuddered. Even steel could break if subjected to enough strain.

Rachel. Rachel, where are you?

~ * ~

Washington, DC

Satterfield, a sinking feeling in his gut, entered the Oval office in response to his friend's call. President Gossard shifted in his chair and looked up. "Arthur, I've just heard from David Bergdorf. They were not able to intercept the transfer of bacteria in Zimbabwe. But they were able to follow it to Germany where Royer believes the shipment was split up. Bergdorf called from the airport in Frankfurt. They are on their way to London following what they believe to be the consignment headed for the United States."

"Good God, it could be in the country within the next twenty-four hours."

The president nodded. "Arthur, I think it's time to call in the FBI."

Satterfield tensed then forced himself to relax, silently admitting that not even he was immune to the rivalry between the two agencies. But there was simply too much at stake to pander to petty jealousies. It went against the grain but he nodded, "Very well, Will. Do you want to brief the director or shall I?"

Wilton Gossard smiled for the first time since he'd received Bergdorf's call. "You do it, Arthur. It will sound better coming from you. I know I can count on your diplomacy. By the way, Bergdorf said they were able to obtain two ampoules of the bacteria and had turned it over to your man, Kelly, to bring to Washington. I want those ampoules sent down to the Center for Disease Control in Atlanta as soon as they arrives."

"Thank God. Perhaps they'll be able to come up with an antidote, if not a vaccine."

If not …The two men stared at each other. Satterfield saw his own fear and horror reflected in the president's face.

Satterfield broke the silence that lay heavy between them. "What about the Russians?"

"I'll have to tell them."

"Do you think they'll believe you?"

Gossard shrugged. "God help them if they don't."

Twenty-one

London

Two Mossad agents watched the passengers from British Airways flight 915 as they moved through passport control. It didn't take them long to spot the two Americans and their quarry. They also spotted something else that made them change their method of surveillance as they moved out to the busses for the ride to Victoria Station. They split up, one moving in to find a seat on the bus, the other ducking back into the terminal then running for their car.

The bus was crowded and the Israeli had to push his way to the back. His glance met that of another man and they both quickly looked away, ignoring each other as they rode into London. As soon as they reached Victoria Station, the other man hurried to a phone and the Israeli leaned against a wall pulling out a newspaper.

Harry Weiss glanced around as his partner arrived, panting. "What the hell do you make of this?"

Joshua Cornblatt shrugged. "Damned if I know, but first chance we get, I'm calling Dani Urazi. If we're to keep a loose cover on those two Americans and that Arab they're following, we're going to need more help. Did you spot Andrews?"

"The CIA man? Yeah, also the SIS boy. By the way, he recognized me. Quite a gathering of the clan, wouldn't you say, old chap? Whatever this is, it must be big to have both the CIA and SIS involved. What do you make of the other two Arabs?"

"I think they're just here to protect their boy and checking to see who else is interested in him."

"My thought, too. And there's no way they can miss this parade. Hey, looks like we're getting a break. The bastard's settled down for a cup of tea. There goes Andrews, probably calling for more backup. Go call Dani. Tell him to get some more bodies here fast."

~ * ~

Chadwick popped his head in the door and smiled at Sir Edmund. "Update. Seems the next act of our little drama is to be played out here in London, Sir. The two Americans arrived a couple of hours ago following an Arab with an Egyptian passport in the name of Dr. Fava Faroush. Two other Arabs began to follow the good doctor when he left the airport. The Americans are being followed by two Israeli agents. When they left Heathrow, the Americans were also being followed by Andrews, a CIA chap from the embassy."

"Heavens, it's a wonder they aren't tripping over each other's toes. How many agents did we have there?"

"Only one, Sir Edmund, Frank Carruthers," Chadwick said, laughing. "I wouldn't have minded seeing it. Rather like a Monty Python movie, wouldn't you say?"

Twenty-two

Frankfurt

Aaron Ben Judah was at the airport when Rachel arrived. He rushed her out of the terminal and into a waiting car without doing more than identifying himself.

He thought he had never seen anyone, outside of a battle line, look so tired and haggard. The intensity in her eyes shocked him as she asked, "Were you in time to pick them up? How did Rossiter look? Where is he now?"

"We picked them up all right and we're still on them. Now, we need to know what is going on."

"Tell me first how Rossiter looked?"

Aaron shrugged. "What do you want to know? They were doing a pretty good job, for amateurs. We weren't sure at first whether their interest was in an old Nazi, Dr. Herman Bach, or in a package that came in on their same flight. We have both covered."

"But how did he look?"

Aaron eyed her so strangely she knew she would have to tell him the truth. "Rossiter is my husband. The CIA kidnapped me to force him into doing a job for them." Her lips quirked. "They think he is Zephyr."

Aaron sighed. "So you called on us to help you find your husband."

"Not entirely. I don't know what is going on, but whatever it is, you can believe it will be bad for Israel. They wanted Zephyr to identify Barenji."

"Barenji!"

"Yes. And there's no way my husband can stop him. Richard is a violinist, not an agent."

"Well, I wouldn't say he was doing too bad a job." Aaron pulled Richard's notes from his pocket and tossed them in her lap. "Better read those."

Rachel felt the blood draining from her face as she read. So this was what Whitney had meant, what he had been trying to tell her even as he died. "Dear God in heaven," she said, smoothing the papers on her knee then handing then back to Aaron. "They have to be stopped. Barenji is sure to hold out some to use against Israel. Where is Richard now?"

"On his way to London."

All thoughts of Barenji and the bacteria fled. "London!" Richard wasn't here. She wanted to scream, to pound her heels, throw a tantrum like a child. Anything to ease her frustration. Instead, she said, "Take me back to the airport. I'll catch the next plane. I've got to reach him."

"He's being followed. When we get to the house, I'll call London and see that he is protected. What *we* have to do is locate and hijack the bacteria headed for Russia and identify Barenji."

"No. No, you don't understand. I have to get to Richard. He's been without dialysis too long all ready. If I don't get this machine to him, he'll die."

"How many Jews will die in Leningrad alone, if we don't stop that shipment?"

Rachel slumped in the seat, torn by the decision she was being asked to make. Not that she really had a choice. It had been made for her, long ago, before she was born, and by people she had never known. No matter what had been done to her, she was still an Israeli, a sabra. No matter how much she resented it, Israel came first.

Aaron pulled up in front of a two-story house. "The house beyond the back yard is occupied by the terrorists," he explained, guiding her through the front door. The smell of freshly brewed coffee was overwhelming. It made Rachel lightheaded and she gripped the back of a chair. How long had it been since she'd eaten? She hadn't been able to touch the food on the plane.

"Wait here," Aaron said and disappeared into the hall.

Rachel glanced around the kitchen and spotted the coffee pot. A large package of Styrofoam cups stood beside it. Taking one, she poured herself a cup and sipped it slowly, savoring each swallow.

Aaron called to her from the doorway, "We've set up our surveillance headquarters in the back bedroom."

She followed him down the hall and into the room. The original furniture was piled against one wall to make room for three tables, an assortment of chairs and a variety of electronic equipment.

She was overcome with a sense of deja vu. How many hours, days, had she spent in rooms just like this? Intense moments of concentration followed by hours of boredom. Claustrophobic at times. A prisoner held, not by chains or bars, but by electronic beeps and telephoto lenses.

There were three other men in the room. All greeted her warmly. The feeling of camaraderie, the sense of purpose swept her up, embraced her. For this she had been trained, this had been her life for more years than she cared to remember.

She stuffed her cosmetic case and purse out of the way and crossed the room. On a table against one wall, dozens of photographs had been laid out. Rachel began to study them as Aaron held a whispered conversation with one of the men.

When she had gone through all of the photos, she turned to Aaron. "I assume these are the occupants of the house?"

"Occupants and visitors. Is Barenji there?"

"No."

"Would you recognize his voice?"

"I think so."

"Come over here and listen."

She took the proffered headphones, leaned against the wall and closed her eyes, concentrating on the voices being picked up by the parabolic mike. Twenty minutes later, she pulled off the headphones and handed them back. "He's not there, or if he is, he's not speaking. How many people are in the house?"

"Seven."

"Then he's not there. I heard seven different voices."

"You're sure?"

"Yes."

Aaron sighed. "Okay. I'll make reservations for you on the next flight to London. In the meantime, why don't you catch a nap in the other room? Someone will wake you and take you to the airport. I'll contact Urazi to meet you at Heathrow and take you to your husband."

Rachel stretched out on the bed and stared at the ceiling. So close. So soon. Almost over. In a few hours she would be with Richard. Pray God she would be in time.

Twenty-three

Rachel was aroused from restless sleep by the sounds of scurrying and whispered voices. For a moment as she struggled with the vestiges of a dream in which Richard had died while she ran through a quagmire in slow motion. She glanced around the room, confused, unable to recall where she was. Then memory returned and she sat up, wiping tears from her eyes. A dimly lit figure loomed over her. Her heart jumped then settled as she recognized Aaron. "Plane time?"

"No. We've had to change your flight. Their courier has arrived and they are getting ready to move out the bacteria headed for Russia."

"What about the shipment for the United States?"

"It's already gone. At least as far as London. That's why your husband is there."

"Then that's where Barenji is."

"If you say so. We're going in now. I thought you'd like to be in on this."

"I want to get to my husband."

Aaron sighed. "I can't spare anyone at the moment. As soon as we have the house secured, I'll release someone to take you to the airport."

She followed Aaron into the kitchen where half a dozen agents were gathered. The window was open and she crossed the room to peer out. It was nearly dark but she could make out two men stringing lights in the trees. While she'd been asleep, reinforcements had arrived.

Another man was working at a table set up in the middle of the yard. It grew darker. The men outside called back and forth to each other in perfect German, discussing the attributes of the young ladies expected to attend the party.

She went down the hall, picked up a pair of infrared glasses and climbed the stairs. Positioning herself far enough back in the darkened bedroom that she couldn't be seen, she studied the target house. A face appeared in one of the lighted windows. A few minutes later the back door opened and a man came out. He strolled the backyard. One of the Israelis stringing lights called down to invite him to the party.

As she watched, someone came out of the kitchen carrying a tape player. A minute later, rock and roll music blared from speakers set around the yard. The Arab watched a minute longer then went back in the house.

The other agents filtered out, and using the cover of the trees and shrubs, squatted against the back fence. She put down the glasses and hurried downstairs. Aaron Ben Judah was at her elbow, shoving an Uzi machine pistol into her hand. "Let's go."

Checking the loads, she followed him into the yard. Running bent over, they raced to the fence and bounded over the top. The others leapt the fence and dashed ahead.

Aaron pushed her down behind a wooden bench as the back door was kicked in. Gunfire erupted. With the first shot, a string of firecrackers blasted from the yard behind her and a millisecond later, both yards were lit up as the floodlights went on and a series of roman candles exploded in the night sky. The music swelled to an ear splitting pitch and taped laughter boomed through the night.

She scrambled to her feet and followed Aaron into the house, nearly tripping over a body on the kitchen floor. In the living room were two more bodies and one cowering terrorist hugged the wall.

She whirled, dropping into a shooting stance then straightened as an Israeli shoved two more terrorists, from the hall into the room. "This is all of them. The rest put up a fight."

"Good. Tie them up." He spoke into a radio then turned to the others. "The van will be here in a minute to pick up these bastards. Let's get this place cleaned up."

He led Rachel back to the fence. "Wait in the house. I'll be with you as soon as I can."

As she climbed the fence and crossed the yard, she was startled to see most of the lights in the house were on. Dancing couples were silhouetted against the drawn curtains. The man at the table grinned as she passed and set off another series of fireworks. As she opened the kitchen door, the telephone was ringing. She listened to the one-sided conversation; apparently someone complaining about the noise; and watched mannequins being trundled around the floor by sour-faced Israelis. The music dropped to a reasonable decibel level and the remaining fireworks were carried inside and packed away.

An hour later, Rachel saw the ampoules of bacteria for the first time. "Can you get a couple of these to Washington? The Center for Disease Control should get to work on them right away."

"We've got a courier coming now to take them to Israel on the next flight. We'll send some to Washington by special diplomatic courier."

"Don't give them to the CIA. If we have a reliable contact in the FBI, give it to him."

"Why?"

"I don't trust the CIA."

"I'll need a better reason than that."

Rachel shrugged then reiterated the events in Seattle, including the killing of Whitney. "I think they're playing some kind of game. Until we know what's going on, we need to play it safe. Don't even let them know we've stopped the shipment to Russia. Keep Mossad involvement as low key as possible. I think we're being set up to take the fall for whatever they're planning. Now, get me to the airport."

Twenty-four

London

Watts didn't bother to greet Spears as he emerged from passport control. He simply grabbed the man's arm and led him towards the doors. "You've got a car here?"

"Yeah. What's this all about?"

"Later."

Seated behind the wheel, Spears turned in the seat and asked impatiently, "Well?"

"Is this car clean?"

"Sure. I checked it out this morning."

"Well, check it again."

"Now?"

"Hell, yes, now. Someone could have planted a bug while you were in the terminal."

Watts drummed his fingers impatiently on his knee while Spears swept the car. Spears smile was more than a little sardonic as he climbed back in. "Clorox clean. Where to?"

"Where are Bergdorf and Royer?"

"I don't know. Andrews is tailing them. He'll call the flat when they roost long enough."

"Your instructions were not to involve anyone from this station."

Spears started the motor and threw the car in gear. "I can't be in two places at once, for Pete's sake. Andrews is just tailing them for us. Besides, Royer might have recognized me."

"Okay, okay. Let's get to the flat. As soon as Andrews calls in, we'll take over."

"What's this all about?"

In as few words as possible, Watts explained. "As soon as they locate the bacteria, we move in and take Bergdorf and Royer out. Then we dispose of the Arabs and grab the bacteria."

Spears slammed a fist against the steering wheel. "This is going to be dirty. Scotland Yard and MI5 are going to come down on us like a ton of bricks."

"We're to make it look like Bergdorf and Royer were caught in the middle between the Arabs and the Israelis. Let the fucking Mossad take the blame. What have you got for me?"

"It's in the glove compartment. A Beretta 9 mm automatic and an extra 15 round clip. There's also a silencer."

Watts removed the gun and examined it carefully, before sliding it into his waistband and pocketing the extra clip and the silencer then stared silently out of the window as Spears negotiated the increasing traffic. A short time later, they pulled up in front of a block of flats. Upstairs Spears paced the floor as they waited for the phone to ring. From time to time, he glared at Watts.

"What's bugging you," Watts finally asked. "This isn't your first 'wet' job!"

"No, it's not that."

"So what is it? Killing two of your own countrymen bothering you? It has to be done."

"If you say so."

"I don't say so, these are Mayhew's orders. You want to question him?"

Spears shook his head. "It's not that. I just don't like doing it on such short notice, with no time to properly prepare and in London, of all places. This is not some third world country where officials could be intimidated or bribed."

Watts watched Spears through narrowed eyes. "Relax. It will all work out." He pulled an envelope from his pocket and fanned his face with it. "The Company supplied me with a few little *clues* to drop." He put the envelope back in his pocket. "We'll be on a flight back to the States before Scotland Yard even figures out what happened."

It was a little after seven before the phone rang. Spears snatched it up, listened for a few minutes, told the caller they were on their way and hung up.

"That was Andrews. Let's go. I'll tell you on the way."

Spears wove through traffic, headed out Bayswater Road and passed Lancaster Gate before speaking. "The Arab has gone to ground in an apartment. Royer is in a pub on the corner and Bergdorf is watching the apartment from a doorway across the street. How do we handle this?"

"First we get rid of Andrews. We don't want any witnesses. Then we'll see how things go."

Spears swung onto a side street, drove two blocks and parked. They got out and strolled up the sidewalk. As they paused on the corner, Watts glanced casually into the pub then hastily looked away. Royer was sitting at a table just inside the door watching the street. Watts nudged Spears and they crossed to the other side.

"Royer is just inside the door. Where's your man?"

"Coming up the street now."

Andrews passed them without breaking stride and continued halfway up the block then paused as if looking for an address. Spears and Watts followed leisurely. As they came abreast, Andrews stepped forward, holding out a slip of paper as if asking directions.

"The Arab went in the third building down in the next block. I got into a conversation with the mail carrier. The Arabs are in the third floor rear. Bergdorf is in the service area, fifth building down on this side. Royer—"

"Yeah, we spotted Royer. You can take off now. We'll take over."

"One other thing. I spotted two Arabs following your marks. One of them went on up to the apartment, the other is in the pub. He's at the bar in the back."

"Okay."

Andrews hesitated. "I think there may be another watcher."

"What? Where?"

Andrews shrugged and looked nervously around. "I didn't spot anyone but the back of my neck has been itching, if you know what I mean."

"But you didn't spot anyone? See anything suspicious, out of place?"

"No."

"Okay. Off you go."

When Andrews had disappeared around the next corner, Watts asked, "Is Andrews new?"

"Yeah. This is his first assignment. You think it's just his nerves?"

"Probably. Go down and identify yourself to Bergdorf. Tell him we need to confer and bring him up to the pub. I'll take a look around the neighborhood and join you in a few minutes. I just wish to hell it was a little darker."

"Maybe I should take a walk around first, just in case Andrews' nerves weren't wrong."

"Forget it, there isn't time. Those towel heads could move at any moment."

Spears still hesitated. Watts cuffed him lightly on the shoulder. "Hey, I'll keep my eyes peeled while I look for the right spot."

Spears shrugged. "Whatever."

Watts watched him walk away then turned and studied the surroundings. Hands in his pockets, he sauntered up the street. Nothing. He turned at the next corner and walked down to Bayswater Road. He paused on the corner and stared thoughtfully up the road towards Kensington Gardens. Finally, he shook his head. Too far. Too much time lost. The Arabs might make their move before they could get back. He watched a young couple cross the road and enter the park. It would be just his luck that some horny couple would stumble onto the bodies before they could get away.

He turned and walked briskly down Bayswater for two blocks then turned up the side street below the Arab's apartment building. On the corner, he passed two men in work clothes immersed in an amiable argument about soccer. Halfway up the second block he found what he was looking for, a service area extending to the rear of a hotel.

He stopped and lit a cigarette. Over the flame, he glanced back. The two men on the corner were still arguing. He shifted his gaze. From his right, a man was approaching at a leisurely pace. Watts glance sharpened instinctively. The man stood out like a flamingo in a flock of pigeons in his bold checked jacket and bright ascot. Watts was reassured. Although the man's face was obscured by the brim of his Trilby and Watts couldn't see his eyes, there was something so typically English about him, that Watts let him pass without a further glance.

When the checkered jacket disappeared around the corner, Watts flipped the match away and entered the service area, counting the buildings on his left. Part way up the area, he stopped and studied a stack of crates. He turned around slowly, assessing visibility from the few windows overlooking the area, judging the depth of the shadows.

An Arab suddenly entered from the street and Watts broke into a slow smile as he stepped into the shadows behind the crate, pulled out the gun and dexterously attached the silencer. With his right side to the wall, he dropped his arm, hiding the gun alongside his leg. The Arab's footsteps grew closer. He unzipped his fly with his left hand and began to urinate against the wall.

The Arab sprang around the crates, knife in hand. Watts almost laughed as he watched the expressions on the man's face change from suspicion, to surprise, to embarrassment.

Watts allowed his own face to depict first surprise and then fear as he let his gaze focus on the knife. He backed away, moving along the wall farther into the shadows, zipping his fly with shaking fingers. "Oh, I say...what..."

The Arab lowered his knife, uttered what sounded like an apology and turned away. As he turned, Watts brought the gun up and fired twice into the man's back. The Arab was dead before he hit the ground. Watts jammed the gun back in his waistband, grabbed the dead man by his feet and dragged him behind the stack of crates. As an afterthought, he pocketed the Arab's knife. He removed the envelope from his pocket, wiped it with his handkerchief then gripping it with the corner of the handkerchief, shoved it inside the Arab's shirt against his skin.

Making certain he had the alley to himself, he lifted the gun, calmly removed the silencer and dropped it in his pocket. He wiped his hands on his handkerchief, refolded it and slipped it back in his hip pocket then returned the gun to his waistband. He strolled out of the alley and headed for the pub.

Watts had no sooner turned up the sidewalk, than Joshua
Cornblatt darted out of the recessed doorway a few feet away,
quickly examined the body, removed the envelope, crept back
to his hiding spot and began to speak softly into his radio.
Down the street, the two soccer enthusiasts turned and strolled
up the street.

Watts stepped into the pub and swiftly surveyed the murky
interior. The paneled walls and long bar were dark with the
patina of age, the floor uneven and worn with the tread of
thousands of feet. A smoky haze hovered near the soot-stained
ceiling and blackened beams. The fetor of spilled beer, sweat
and centuries old dust tickled his nose.

Spears and Bergdorf were at the table with Royer. He felt
a tiny frisson of alarm as he spotted the man in the plaid coat
and Trilby at the end of the bar. He watched the bartender
deliver a pint and lean on the bar in a friendly conversation
about football pools. Watts dismissed them from his mind as
Royer spotted him and half rose from his chair.

"You! Where's Rachel? Where is my wife?"

Watts moved quickly to the table and laid a restraining
hand on Richard's shoulder. "Calm down. I'll answer all your
questions, but not here and not now."

"Yes, here and now."

Watts ignored Richard, sat down and turned to David.
"Bring me up to date and don't leave anything out."

Richard slammed a fist on the table and glared at David.
"No. Not one word until they tell me about my wife."

David raised a placating hand in Richard's direction while
he stared stonily at Watts. "He has a right to know about his
wife. If you know anything, tell him."

Watts cast an appraising glance at Richard, noting the
sweat on his face, the sallow complexion. Would believing his
wife was dead make him easier to handle? He glanced across

the table at his partner. Shields avoided meeting his eyes, leaning back in his chair as if to distance himself from whatever was coming.

Watts looked back at Richard. No, the bastard might make a scene that would be remembered. "You wife is fine."

"How do I know you're telling me the truth? Where is she?"

"She's still in Seattle, in a safe house we have there. The situation has been explained to her and she is cooperating."

Richard stared at the man. He was lying. If the situation had been explained to Rachel, she would have told the truth. They would know he wasn't Zephyr. They would know about his kidneys. Fearing he knew the truth, Richard slumped down in his chair, motioning David to speak. She's dead. Dead or she wasn't Zephyr. Because if she was a Mossad agent, they couldn't have held her against her will. She would have found a way to get free.

Half an hour later, Watts was satisfied they had told him everything. "Okay. We're going to take that bacteria now." He gave Richard a grimace that Richard supposed was the nearest the man could come to smiling. "You'll be back in the States with your wife before you know it."

David jerked forward, his voice doubtful. "What do you mean, take the bacteria now? Just the four of us? Richard and I aren't even armed."

"Yes, now. And you will be. We're going to leave here, walk to the end of the block and turn the corner. You two go out first, we'll be right behind to cover you. When you turn the corner, you'll see a service area half way down the block. It extends behind the Arab's building. Several other agents will join us there. They're bringing firearms for you. As soon as they arrive, we'll split up and take the apartment from front and back."

Richard threw David a relieved look. The professionals were taking over. They would soon be out of it and he would know the truth. Richard eyed Watts. If Rachel were dead, he'd hunt this man down and kill him.

Okay," David said with a grin, "let's get this show on the road." He stood up and threw an arm around Richard's shoulder. "Hang in there, buddy. The final curtain is about to fall on this melodrama."

As the two men walked out the door Watts slipped the knife to Spears. Keeping his voice too low to be heard by the men ahead, he said, "Knock Bergdorf out then use this on him."

"Where did you get it?"

"Off an Arab that followed me into the alley. Wipe it clean and we'll press the towel head's prints on it."

Richard cast a glance at the two men behind him. Something wasn't right. He tapped David on the arm and whispered, "I don't like this. Stay on your toes. I think we're being set up."

Richard reached the stack of crates a couple of steps ahead of David. He spotted the dead body and yelled a warning to David. Instinctively, he dropped into a crouch. Watts' bullet missed his head by less than an inch. Whirling, he lunged for Watts' legs, but a ton of bricks seemed to descend on his head. As he slipped into a tunnel of darkness, he thought he heard the eerie, raucous sound of hyenas laughing.

Twenty-five

London

Rachel felt like throwing herself into Dani Urazi's arms when she saw him standing in the terminal. She hurried forward, heart racing with hope. "You have him? He's safe? Where is he? Take me to him."

He stared fixedly at her. "You're Zephyr? Little Ellia Davidian? My, God! This is unbelievable. Do you realize that you are a legend in the Mossad?"

Rachel brushed a hand across her face. "Dani, for God's sake. Who cares? That's past history. Is my husband safe?"

"What? Your husband?"

"Yes. Richard Royer or you probably know him as Richard Rossiter. Is he safe?"

Urazi snapped out of his reverie. Taking her luggage, he moved towards the door. "We've got him and his friend, and a dead Arab, we'd like you to look at. It may be Barenji. Also two dead CIA agents."

Rachel heard only the first words. "I want to see Richard."

"But—"

Rachel waved a hand to silence him. "I want to see my husband. Now."

The drive in from the airport seemed to take forever. Rachel stared with unseeing eyes at the passing scenery. Neither spoke until Dani pulled in front of a semi-detached house in Islington. Dani put a hand on her shoulder as Rachel opened the car door. "He's in the first bedroom at the top of the stairs. He took a blow to the head and is still unconscious. We have a doctor with him." Rachel tried to shrug his hand aside. He tightened his grip. "Wait. There are complications. The doctor believes he is also suffering from acute kidney failure."

Rachel tugged loose and jumped out of the car. "I know," she said, pulling the dialysis machine from the back seat. She was hammering at the front door before Dani was out of the car.

As it opened, she pushed her way inside, and avoiding the outstretched hand of the agent who had opened the door, dashed up the stairs and threw open the bedroom door.

A glance at the still, waxen figure on the bed and Rachel doubled over as if by a blow to the solar plexus. Too late. She was too late. Richard was dead. She fought for breath and felt her knees buckle. Dani's arms came around her and she leaned against him for support.

Through a mist of tears, she saw the doctor rise and turn towards her. As if from a great distance, she heard his voice. "He's still alive."

It took a moment for his words to register but then they did and she ran across the room. Kneeling beside the bed, she opened the case, murmuring as she worked. "Richard. Richard, I'm here. We'll have you on dialysis in a minute. Richard. Oh, my darling."

His eyelids fluttered. His cracked lips formed her name. "Rachel? Rachel?" He turned his head and stared at her. "You're alive." Tears filled his eyes and slid down his cheeks. He tried to smile. "I thought they'd killed you." He reached up and ran a shaky finger down her cheek then his hand dropped and his eyes closed.

With trembling fingers and a full heart, she got Richard hooked up to the dialysis machine. The doctor watched with interest. When the treatment was started, the doctor took her place beside the machine.

She sat beside Richard, holding his hand. After a while his eyes fluttered open again and he murmured her name. She leaned down to catch his whispered words. "You're Zephyr?"

She hesitated. Even if it meant that he would turn from her in disgust, there must be no more secrets between them. Reluctantly she nodded.

He squeezed her fingers and tried to raise his head.

"Lie still, darling. We have plenty of time to talk about it later."

"No. I ...understand...so much...more...now. Stop them, Rachel. Stop...the bastards."

"I won't leave you."

"You must. I'll be… okay. Just don't... trust... anyone. Go. Now."

"No!" The word was a cry wrenched from her heart. "No, I won't leave you again."

"You... must. Promise me." He squeezed her hand. "Promise me you'll stop them. Promise."

The waxiness was fading and color was returning to his cheeks. "All right." She ached to hold him, to nurse him back to health, but she really had no choice. Barenji had to be stopped.

"Promise?"

"Promise."

His eyes closed. Rachel looked at the doctor. The doctor nodded. "He'll be all right. I'll take care of him."

Dani led her out into the hall. "We've arranged for him to be taken to a private hospital as soon as the doctor feels he can be transported."

Rachel nodded and would have gone back into the room, but Dani laid a hand on her arm. "We need your help, Ellia."

She shook off his hand. "Don't call me that. My name is Rachel. I'll help you, but you'll have to wait. I need to stay with my husband until he's ready to be moved."

"Ellia... Rachel—"

"No!" She turned away and re-entered the room. Urazi started after her then shrugged and went down the stairs.

Rachel watched from an upstairs window as the doctor helped Richard into his car, her gaze clinging to it until the car disappeared from sight. "I should be with him."

"He'll be okay. He just needs a few days to recuperate and get his strength back. Dr. Eliason's clinic is very private and we'll have plenty of security around the place," Urazi said.

"I know." She turned away from the window, straightened her shoulders and looked up at him. "Let's get down to business. Tell me what happened here."

When he finished, her jaw muscles ached as she whispered through gritted teeth, "The bastards. How is Bergdorf?"

"He's okay. The knife barely grazed his ribs. He's resting in the other room."

"Let's go talk to him."

"Come down to the basement first. I want you to take a look at the bodies before we dispose of them."

Rachel followed him down the stairs, her thoughts still with Richard. She shivered in the dank air. Urazi opened a door, switched on the lights and motioned to the body on the left. "Look at the Arab first. Do you recognize him?"

Rachel had seen a lot of dead bodies. She felt no queasiness at the prospect, but as she glanced the waxen face, recognizing it, she recoiled. The blood drained from her face, leaving her weak and trembling. She turned away and rested her forehead against the damp brick wall.

Her voice cracked. "He's one of Barenji's assassins. The one he sent after me in Beirut." She shuddered. "He likes to use a knife. He was called Ahab."

Dani Urazi lifted a sympathetic hand then dropped it and turned to the other two bodies, giving her time to recover.

After a moment, he asked, "How about these?"

She straightened, took a deep breath and crossed the room. She studied their faces. "I don't know this one, but the other was one of the men that kidnapped me. I believe they are connected with the CIA."

"They are. At least they are both carrying CIA identification. If their documents are forgeries, they're damned good ones. Why would they try to kill your husband?"

"I'd like to know the answer to that question, too. There is something fishy as hell going on."

"Let's talk to Bergdorf."

Urazi led the way back upstairs and into another bedroom. David Bergdorf was stretched out on the bed, but he sat up as they entered. Urazi grinned down at him.

"Meet Zephyr."

David pushed himself off the bed and extended a hand. His lips twitched slightly as he said, "Mrs. Royer, I presume."

Rachel ignored the hand and looked him over coldly. "You fools nearly killed my husband."

David let his hand fall to his side. "I know. I'm sorry."

Rachel glared at him, anger wild inside her. "Being sorry doesn't cut it. I don't want your apologies; I want to know what is going on. Tell me everything."

"I don't think I can. I'll need to talk to the president."

"If you want my help, you'll tell me now. Otherwise I'll walk out that door and leave you to your nasty little games."

"You're really Zephyr?"

"Yes."

David leaned back against the wall and studied her. Finally, he leaned forward and said, "Okay. A CIA local overheard a conversation in Beijing..."

When he had repeated everything he'd been told, Rachel asked, "Where is the bacteria now? Why did the CIA try to kill you?"

David slumped back down on the edge of the bed. "The answer to both questions is, I don't know."

Urazi swung a wooden chair around and straddled it. "By the time we'd cleared up the little contretemps in the alley, the Arabs had flown the coop. They left in a hurry but didn't leave much in the flat. The only thing we found of interest was an airline timetable with a flight to Washington circled. We think someone will be on that flight, possibly with the bacteria, but we don't know what day."

"We have to assume it will be today. What time did that flight leave?"

"It hasn't. It leaves at two-fifteen."

Rachel glanced at her watch then at Dani. "It's eleven thirty. We can still make it. Get us two seats and transportation to the airport."

Urazi headed for the door. "Three seats. I'm going with you."

Twenty-six

London

Sir Edmund Mortimer had lost some, but not much, of his usual aplomb. He finished reading the report and frowned up at Chadwick. "Do I understand this correctly? The CIA attempted to kill two of their own citizens? The Israelis stepped in and killed two CIA agents in Bayswater? Who killed the Arab?"

"That's pretty much the case, Sir Mortimer. We don't know who killed the Arab. Could have been either party."

"I assume we still have someone keeping an eye on the Israelis. What are they doing now?"

"They took the two Americans and the three bodies to a house they have been renting for the past few months. They've also brought in a doctor."

Mortimer tapped a finger angrily on the report. "If the Americans want to kill their citizens, why the devil can't they do it in their own country? Why come to London? This is all just a little too much. I won't have it. Get me their Chief of Station. No, forget Morris, get me Satterfield in Washington." He swiveled his chair to stare out the window. "When I've finished talking with Satterfield, get me Itzak Dann in Jerusalem."

~ * ~

Washington, DC

Elwood Mayhew was also staring out his window. Outwardly he knew he appeared calm, but in his gut a fiery tension raged. He glanced down at his fingers, gripped across his belly so tightly the knuckles were white, and willed them to relax. "No word yet from Watts?"

"No, sir. Should I call Morris in London?"

"Hell, no. We don't want them involved." Mayhew swung back to his desk and glared up at Brooks. "I got a call from the FBI about Whitney. They know we took the Royers and they want to know why." He knew he was spitting saliva with the words and his loss of control further angered him. The uneasiness in Brooks eyes wasn't lost on Mayhew. He struggled for control. It wouldn't do to let Brooks know how angry he was. "They wanted to know about the bacteria. Want to send it to Atlanta. That senile bastard upstairs must have blabbed. Or that fool in the Oval Office. Well, I stalled them. Told them the courier hadn't arrived yet."

"Perhaps we should give them one of the ampoules. Just in case," Brooks said.

Mayhew's head snapped up. "No. I've got plans for it." He forced a smile but Brooks continued to watch him warily. What was wrong with the man? Didn't he realize how important this opportunity was? No, maybe he didn't. How far could he trust Brooks? Could he make him understand without telling him too much? "I've got plans for that bacteria and no one is going to stop me. No one," Mayhew repeated softly.

"Sir, maybe—"

"I want you to contact Soon Wing in Honolulu. Tell him to contact his assets in China and tell them to expect a live shipment. Then have him go to the safe house near Kona and wait."

He studied Cal Brooks' worried face. "I need you with me on this, Cal. I know you love this country as much as I do. If we let them, those weak-kneed, lily-livered bastards that have run this country into chaos, we will give away our last hope. Trust me, Cal. We've going to save this country."

~ * ~

Satterfield watched Wilton Gossard run a hand through his all ready mussed gray hair as he asked, "What the hell is going on, Arthur?"

He ran his hand over his face, trying to wipe away the exhaustion he knew accentuated his hound dog look. He shook his head slowly. "I wish to hell I knew, Will.

"What did the FBI say?"

"Only that one of their agents had *acquired* the three vials of bacteria from a *friendly* Mossad contact. The contact refused to say where or how the bacteria had been obtained, only that he understood we were interested in it."

"Thank God, we got it."

"Will, I also had a call from Sir Edmund Mortimer."

"The head of SIS? What did he want?"

"He was perturbed about the CIA picking London to take out a couple of our citizens. Told me to bloody up our own backyard, not his."

"What the hell?"

"Apparently two of our agents tried to assassinate Royer and Bergdorf."

"My God!" The blood drained from the president's face. "Did they succeed?"

"No. According to Sir Mortimer, the Mossad stepped in and took out our two agents then spirited Bergdorf and Royer out of sight."

Gossard leaned back in his chair, studying his friend. "Arthur, is there a possibility that Mayhew has turned?"

197

Satterfield gnawed on a knuckle, his eyes on the three glass ampoules on Gossard's desk. Finally, he looked up meeting the president's gaze. "I don't have any proof, Will, but I've considered the possibility. Either that or he's cracking up. Whichever, I just don't trust him. I want to pull him off this."

"I'm not sure that's such a good idea." Gossard leaned forward, both elbows on the desk. "Art, I've known you for a long time. I know you won't let personal feelings prevent you from doing what has to be done."

Satterfield's gut tightened. Whatever was coming, he knew he wasn't going to like it. Will never called him Art unless what he was going to say was unpleasant. But the president was right. This was no time for personal feelings. He nodded slowly.

"Art, I want you to get together with Jackson. Tell him everything. I want you to work directly with the FBI, but turn the responsibility over to them. And, I want you to ask the FBI to keep tabs on Mayhew until this thing is cleared up."

"Is that an order, Sir? Have you talked with Jackson?"

"No and no. I thought you would prefer to handle it yourself."

"Thank you." He motioned towards the ampoules. "What about those?"

"I'm having them hand-carried to Atlanta immediately."

Satterfield rose. "I'll contact Jackson and set up a meeting right away."

Gossard stood up, a lopsided grin on his handsome face—his eyes warm with understanding. "Thanks, Arthur. I knew I could count on you."

~ * ~

Cal Brooks opened Mayhew's door without knocking. It was a habit that was starting to annoy Mayhew. "What is it now?"

Brooks flinched but stood his ground. "Boss, we got problems. Spears and Watts are both dead."

"What?" Alarms went off in Mayhew's head.

"Dead. Morris is fuming. He wants to know what's going on. He got a message, in one of our codes, to pick up an important parcel at the safe house Spears was using. The agent he sent found the bodies."

"Who killed them? Where are Royer and Bergdorf? The bacteria?"

"Royer has disappeared. So have the Arabs. Bergdorf is on a flight to Washington that left London half an hour ago."

Mayhew clenched and unclenched his hands. Could nothing go according to plan? Was he surrounded by nothing but incompetents? He fought to control the rage building within him. He couldn't lose control now. He had to think, to revise. He was smarter than they were. Everything could still be salvaged. It wasn't too late. Not if they acted fast. "Get someone we can trust out to the airport and pick up Bergdorf. We have to make damn sure he doesn't get to the president."

"Boss, that's not all."

Mayhew glared up at him, eyes narrowed.

Brooks swallowed. "By the time our agents in Frankfort located the house where the Arabs were staying, they had cleared out."

Mayhew smiled. "That's not bad news. They're on their way to Russia."

"Maybe. Our man asked a few questions. Not enough to alert anyone. One of the neighbors complained of a 'wild party' in the area. Lots of loud music, raised voices and firecrackers a couple of hours before everyone left."

"Celebrating?"

Brooks tone was noncommittal. "Perhaps. Or some other agency took them out."

"Who? We're the only ones who know about the bacteria."

Brooks' look suggested he thought his boss was being deliberately obtuse. "Royer could have contacted the Israelis. But there is worse news. Satterfield has another meeting with the FBI. He's on his way to see Jackson now."

Mayhew swung his chair around, his back to Brooks and stared out the window. Why was Satterfield meeting with Jackson? Had someone is his group talked? No. All the agents involved owed their loyalty to him. Satterfield couldn't have any concrete information, only suspicions. The question was how much did he suspect? There was no way Satterfield could know what was in his mind. No one knew, not even Cal. Still, it would be better not to take any chances on being stopped now. Not when success was so nearly in his hands.

He turned back. "Cal, this is what I want you to do..."

Twenty-seven

London

Dani Urazi entered the terminal first, picked up his ticket, and after a quick but comprehensive look around, removed his sunglasses and began to polish them. David Bergdorf pushed through a tourist group and headed for the ticket counter. A few minutes later, ticket and boarding pass in hand, he walked briskly towards the departure gate.

Rachel watched Dani follow at a more leisurely pace before she picked up her ticket. Wearing a long blond wig and contact lens that made her eyes a vivid blue she walked down the corridor with the poised movements of a model. She paused, her glance sweeping the area as though looking for a seat.

Her glance flicked over the profile of a man standing near the window and she felt the blood draining from her brain. Sheer horror kept her gaze locked on the handsome features as she put a hand on the counter for support. An icy hand gripped her gut and her very bones seemed to freeze as wave after wave of terror swept over her.

"Madam, are you ill?"

The concerned voice of the female counter attendant snapped her out of her trance. Professional training took over although her brain was still whirling.

"No. No." Rachel turned her back on the man at the window and forced a smile. "Where is the WC?"

The attendant pointed, a concerned look still on her face. Rachel thanked her. Fighting down the urge to run, she compelled her body to continue her pose, and moved gracefully away.

In the privacy of a cubicle, her control shattered. She fell to her knees, vomiting into the bowl. Weak and shaky, she pulled herself up and leaned against the door, gathering her strength.

Finally, Rachel left the cubicle. Like a sleepwalker, she moved to the basins. She removed her makeup, scrubbed her face and rinsed her mouth. Gradually the mind-numbing terror eased, although fear remained. Staring into the mirror, she studied her features one by one. Would he recognize her? In Lebanon, her hair had been dark, almost black, she'd worn brown contact lens, and never worn anything but native sandals or combat boots.

Removing the wig and sweeping her hair back with both hands, she scrutinized her ears. Ears were one of the hardest of all human features to alter without surgery and one that all agents were trained to study. She couldn't change she shape of her ears but she could change their relationship to her head.

From her case, she extracted a tube of surgical adhesive. Brushing her hair into a pony tail, she applied a small amount of the adhesive to the back of her left ear and pressed it tightly against her head until the adhesive set. She repeated the same procedure with her right ear. Then she replaced the wig and combed it to fall in waves around them. She added large clip earrings that hid her unusually pointed lobes.

She began to redo her makeup, highlighting the sides of her nostrils to make her nose appear broader then plucking and reshaping her eyebrows to make them thinner and more highly arched. Lastly, she rolled two cotton balls into pads and slipped them between her gums and cheek.

Replacing the cosmetics, she closed the case with a snap. One last glance in the mirror. She hardly recognized herself. Maybe, just maybe he wouldn't recognize her either.

She took a deep breath and moved to the door. Straightening her shoulders, she opened it and walked out with the pelvis forward stride of a runway model.

Mustafa Barenji was still standing by the window.

She turned away, choking back the fear that threatened to swamp her again. She wanted a cigarette. She hadn't smoked in years, but now she craved one. Checking her watch, she walked out to a newspaper stand and purchased a pack of Players. Leaning against the wall, she opened the box with shaking fingers. A couple of puff made her dizzy and she crushed it out. Turning back to the newsstand, she picked up a current best seller and paid for it.

Back in the waiting room, she found a seat, opened the book and tried to read. Half an hour later, when they called her flight, she couldn't remember a word she had read.

As soon as Barenji disappeared down the ramp, she collected her things and followed. She settled into her first class seat, the only seat that had been available, and breathed a prayer of thanks that Barenji was traveling coach as were Dani and David.

When the big plane leveled out on its transatlantic flight plan, Rachel gratefully accepted a gin and tonic from the stewardess. She gazed out the window and saw, below the fluffy white clouds, the blue glistening waters of the Dead Sea.

Memories, long suppressed, rushed back. After all these years, she could still feel sweat trickling down her ribs, smell the hot sand and the salt water. She saw herself sitting alone in the barracks at Ein Geddi, her packed bags at her feet. The other trainees had all left by bus an hour before. At the last minute she had been ordered to stay. Why? Was she being kicked out? It was an absurd thought. This was only a refresher course, after all. She had always been at the top of her class in all phases of the training. Why was she being singled out? What had she done wrong?

The door opened and one of the girls from the kibbutz stuck her head in. "Your car is here," was all she said before ducking back out.

Ellia Davidian, for that had been Rachel's name then, picked up her bags and walked out into the hot desert sun. She climbed into the Army sedan. "Where are we going?"

"Kfar Giladi."

"Why?"

"I wouldn't know. I'm just here to pick you up and drop you off."

The drive was long and hot, the driver surly and uncommunicative. The closer they got to the northern kibbutz, the more nervous she became.

When they arrived at the kibbutz near the Lebanese border, she was taken directly to one of the guest rooms usually kept for tourists and told to wait. She paced the room while a million thoughts ran through her mind. She tried to remember every event in her life, searching for anything that might possibly be cause for Mossad to reject her.

Her father had been killed during the Six Day War and her mother a few years later by a terrorist bomb. At seventeen, she had been alone in the world. Because of her language skills, she'd been recruited into the Mossad soon after she'd done her

204

compulsory national service. She'd been good at her job, but six months ago, she'd been sent for field training. Why?

Hours later the door opened and a man walked in. "Miss Davidian. Please sit down. I am Itzak Dann. I have a very special assignment for you."

Stunned, she had sunk down on the edge of the bed. In her wildest dreams, she had never imagined meeting personally with the head of one of the special sections of Mossad.

Rachel tore her gaze away from the window and the past. It had all been so long ago and she had built a new life for herself. She motioned to the stewardess for another drink. The memories wouldn't go away. The stewardess had no sooner handed her the drink than the memories crowded back. It had been a very special assignment all right. A very special assignment. She was to be given a code name—Zephyr. The west wind. She was to infiltrate a specific band of Palestinian terrorists and identify their leader, Mustafa Barenji.

At least that was what she had been told. Rachel's lips curled in contempt at the remembered naiveté of the young Ellia Davidian. How proud she had felt at being singled out, how stupidly enthusiastic.

Only after she escaped from Lebanon, had she learned the truth. For months, Itzak Dann had collected intelligence from various agents and leaked that information back to the Palestinians as having come from one unique agent: Zephyr. And, as Dann had intended, legend grew around this super agent until the right time came.

Rachel succeeded in her mission. She wormed her way into the group and at last, met Barenji. Then on instructions from Dann, she went to Beirut. Itzak Dann leaked the information that she was Zephyr and the trap closed, not on Barenji, but on her. The tethered goat.

The pain of that betrayal pierced her afresh, tearing at her heart and soul. Then the old rage swept through her. The plastic glass in her hand cracked and she stared down at it. They had almost broken her, too. Grabbing a cocktail napkin, she scrubbed her hand and the tray with short vicious swipes. Well, they hadn't succeeded. Neither of them. Barenji had escaped the trap Dann had set and she had escaped Barenji and his assassin. Damn them. Damn them all. She stuffed the napkin into the remains of the glass and tossed it on the table. And they hadn't broken her.

She leaned back and closed her eyes, struggling to break with the past. The past was done; it couldn't be changed. It was time to forget the hurt, the betrayal. It wasn't the danger. No, at the time she had been young enough, dedicated enough to have willingly given her life for her country. But the way they had used her, lied to her, betrayed her...

Put it behind; think of the future. She was older now. Wiser. This time, she would not be dragged down by them. She'd play their dirty little game this one last time but not for them. For Richard. For their own future, Barenji had to be stopped, but she would play by her own rules, not theirs.

Once this was over, they would leave her alone. If they didn't...if they tried to pull her back...send some one for her again...Wasn't it the Roman emperors who killed the messenger that brought bad news? When in Rome...

Twenty-eight

Washington, DC

The humid capital air hit Special Agent James Eberle in the face like a wet dishcloth as he left the terminal. He hated hot weather and the humidity made the heat almost unbearable. He loosened his tie as he climbed into a cab and told the driver to take him to the FBI building.

The phone call ordering him to Washington on the next available plane had come just as he was leaving for lunch. There had barely been time for him to run by his apartment and throw a clean shirt, a change of underwear and his shaving kit in a bag.

During the flight, he had racked his brain for a reason for his recall. It had to be the Royer incident. Everything else on his desk was routine. Were the CIA creating waves? Were they after his scalp?

He ran a hand over his jaw and felt the beginnings of a five o'clock shadow. Should he have taken time at the airport for a quick shave? He frowned and then shrugged. If he was going to be on the carpet for stepping on CIA toes, what did a shadow on his chin matter? These weren't the good old Hoover days. Not that he'd been with the Bureau back then, but he'd heard tales. Besides, what could they expect, hauling him back here on such short notice. Still… He opened his bag and pulled out his rechargeable shaver.

His nerves were strained to the breaking point and he was sick enough to vomit by the time he was escorted into the director's office. Jesus, to be chewed out by the Old Man himself. He must have really screwed up. He was swallowing bile as he crossed the carpet and was halfway across the room before he noticed the other man seated on the couch.

"James Eberle. You wished to see me, sir?" His voice was as raspy as the rusty hinge of a long unused gate. He felt the heat rising in his face. God, what a stupid thing to say. This man had ordered him to cross the continent. Of course he wanted to see him.

"Sit down, Eberle. I have a copy of your report on the Royer kidnapping here." He tapped a folder on his desk. "I have a few questions."

Eberle sank into a chair with relief. He wasn't sure how long his legs would have supported him. "Yes, sir," he murmured, weakly.

"By the way, this is Arthur Satterfield, Director of the CIA. I'm sure he'll have some questions for you, too."

He felt the heat rising in his neck and face again as he acknowledge the introduction with a nod. God, he was really in for it. Goodbye career.

"Anything that is said in here today is completely confidential. Not one word is to leave this room. Is that understood?" Jackson said.

Eberle nodded, swallowed and croaked, "Yes, sir."

The director's granite face cracked into a hint of a smile. "Relax, son. You're not here to be chewed out. Now, start at the beginning and tell us everything you know then everything you suspect about the Royer kidnapping."

Three hours later, a shocked Eberle left the director's office alternating between euphoria and anxiety. He knew now what was behind the Royer kidnappings, the death of the CIA man in the mountain cabin. He rubbed a hand over his eyes. For a moment, he wished he were back at his desk in Seattle. He wasn't ready for this kind of responsibility. On the other hand, this was the kind of case that could make his career... or break it, if he fouled up.

He walked down the corridor following the secretary to his new, but temporary, office. By the time they reached the elevator, his mind was already focusing on the things that needed to be done, the support personnel he would need.

Twenty-nine

Washington, DC

Rachel stayed in her seat as the plane taxied into the terminal and passengers began to crowd the aisle. Casually she pulled a compact from her bag and began to repair her makeup. The passengers bumped and jostled each other as the door opened and they surged forward. As Dani Urazi moved beside her seat his left hand bumped briefly against hers.

She flipped the compact shut, returned it to her purse and bent down to retrieve her case from under the seat as Barenji shuffled past and disappeared out the door.

Rachel thrust her way into the crowd and out into the accordion ramp, moving with the flow. Inside the concourse, she spotted Urazi. Catching his eye, she moved her head slightly and stared at Barenji's back as he moved into line at passport control.

Urazi ambled over to stand in the same line. Rachel walked over to another line and stepped up behind David Bergdorf. Rachel shifted her case, striking David on the thigh, and under the cover of apologizing, whispered, "Barenji is just being questioned in the second lane to the right."

David took a look and glanced hastily away. "I know him."

"What?"

"He was in Zimbabwe. He's an Englishman. Called himself Adrian Whitehead. Are you sure?"

"Yes."

"We'd better let Urazi know."

"I did. I passed him a note as he was leaving the plane."

"I've got to contact the president. I'll meet you at my apartment later." He gave her his address as he moved up to the immigration agent.

Finally clearing customs, Rachel reached the exit in time to see Barenji move out the doors towards the rank of waiting taxis. She saw Urazi talk briefly with a man standing by the wall, watched the man fold his paper and follow Barenji. She saw Urazi striding away from her. She started after him. Suddenly, he increased his pace and swerved towards the exit. She lost sight of him as a group of Japanese tourists erupted through the doors.

She heard his voice, loud and jovial, "David, old chap. Here I am. Did you think I had forgotten to meet you?"

She shoved her way through the throng and stopped. Two men, one on each side of David, were hustling him towards the door. Urazi clapped a hand on David's shoulder, nudging aside the man griping David's right arm.

Laughing, he slid his arm around David's shoulder, neatly turning him away from the man on his left. "Weren't trying to avoid us, now were you? Come along, mustn't keep the ladies waiting. They have a welcome home party all ready in progress." He cast a benign look at the two men. "Are you friends of David? Come along. The more the merrier."

Urazi continued to chatter as he eased David away. The two men stared angrily after them for a moment then one shrugged and turned away towards a bank of phones. The other hesitated briefly and then followed David and Urazi outside and took the next taxi.

Rachel waited until the other man finished his phone call then followed him into the parking lot. When he climbed into a nondescript Plymouth, she walked on behind the car with only a casual glance at the license plate. She stopped beside a new Lincoln and fumbled in her purse as though searching for her keys. As the car drove away, she hastily scribbled down the license number and turned back to the terminal.

In the ladies lounge, she quickly exchanged the blond wig for a brown one, removed the soggy cotton from her cheeks, and wincing, peeled the adhesive from the backs of her ears.

Removing the suit jacket, turning it so that only the contrasting lining showed and folding it over her arm, she picked up her case and headed for the Avis counter.

An hour later she drove past David's building. The Plymouth was parked at the corner, a man at the wheel. A moment later, she spotted the second man. She cruised around the block again before parking on the side street, and carrying her case, walked casually back to the building. The Plymouth was still parked at the next corner and the other watcher was still in the service area of a building across the street. Without breaking her stride, she mounted the steps and walked into the foyer.

She moved to stand in front of the elevators. Slipping the compact from her purse, she ran a hand over her hair. In the mirror, she watched the man leave his hiding place and start across the street. She snapped the compact shut as the elevator doors opened. Stepping quickly inside, she punched the button for the fourteenth floor.

A few minutes later, after walking down two flights of stairs, she knocked on David's door. Rachel stepped inside when he opened the door and greeted her. Urazi was on the phone.

She turned to David. "You were followed. They have you staked out. One in a brown Plymouth up the block. The other is on foot across the street."

David ran a hand through his curly hair as he turned to pace the room. "Damn it, I've got to get to the president."

Dani Urazi hung up and David grabbed the phone and began dialing. Rachel dropped onto the couch. "Well?"

"Two of my men picked up Barenji as he left the airport and followed him to a warehouse. They have reinforcements arriving soon and will keep him covered. How did you get here?"

"I rented a car. It's parked around the corner. Was it the CIA that tried to grab David at the airport?"

"Probably."

"What the hell is going on? They try to kill them in London and now try to kidnap David here. It's almost as though they want Barenji to succeed."

She rummaged in her purse, brought out the paper with the license number and handed it to Dani. "We can't stay here. They have this place staked out."

"I know."

David hung up and turned to them. "The president wants to see me immediately. Do you two want to stay here?"

"No," Rachel answered.

"Do you have a car?" Dani asked.

"Yes."

Where do you keep it?"

"The building next door has a basement garage. I keep it there."

"Is there a way to get to it without going outside?"

"Yes, there is a connecting door from this basement. It's kept locked but since I rent a parking space, I have a key. Why?"

"What's the license number?" David gave it to him and Dani made another call. When he hung up he scribbled the Plymouth's license number down and gave it to David. "When you see the president, have the FBI check out this plate. It's the car that is following you. Give me your car keys. Rachel, give David the keys to your car." He headed for the door. "Let's get out of here. I'll explain on the way."

In the elevator, Dani pushed the button for the second floor. "We wouldn't want to walk into their arms if the CIA is waiting in the lobby. Rachel and I will take your car. David, you crouch out of sight in the back. I'll drive around the corner to Rachel's car. You jump out and get to the president. If they know your car, they'll follow us."

"But what about you?"

"Don't worry. Before they can do anything, I'll have picked up help."

David led them down the service stairs to the basement and through the connecting door the parking garage. Dani frowned when he saw David's car, an older Ford Escort.

David saw the frown and grimaced. "I know, not something James Bond would drive but it get me around and it's cheap to operate."

"It will have to do. Someone will either return it or notify you where to pick it up. Let's go."

Dani drove out of the garage and around the corner, slowing barely enough to let David jump out before speeding on down the street. Only seconds after David had jerked open the door of the rented Chevrolet and dived in, the Plymouth turned the corner and fell in behind them.

Dani swung onto P Street, crossed Rock Creek and at Dupont Circle, turned onto Massachusetts Avenue. Despite her tension, Rachel felt a tinge of excitement as they passed the cluster of embassies near Scott Circle. This was her first visit to the nation's capital. Washington. District of Columbia. The political capitol of the free world. The most powerful city in the world.

At Mt. Vernon Square, Dani turned south on 7th Street. Rachel's excitement turned to awe as they crossed The Mall and she found herself staring at the Capitol Building. She wanted to spend time here, to explore this fabulous city. Silently she vowed to have Richard bring her back to Washington when this nightmare was over.

The tension swept back. The nightmare wasn't over yet. Dani pulled into L'Enfant Plaza Hotel and handed over the keys for valet parking. Gripping her elbow, he hustled her across the lobby and into an elevator. They were whisked inside room 842 which opened almost before he finished knocking.

There were two men and a woman in the room. They wasted no time on greetings. The woman motioned Rachel into the bathroom and handed her a shopping bag containing fresh lingerie, slacks, blouse, cardigan sweater and a pair of flat-heeled shoes.

When she came out of the bathroom, bathed and refreshed, the woman and one of the men were gone.

Dani grinned at her. "Now you look more like the Ellia Davidian I knew at Ein Gedi."

"Where are my clothes?"

The man turned away from the window. "Sarah is wearing them. She and Mark are decoying your friends away from the hotel."

He turned to Dani. "Don't be fooled by the looks of the car we have for you. The motor is a work of art. It will out run

215

anything outside of Indianapolis. The radio is state of the art and good for up to a hundred miles. If you need them, there are two portable radios under the front seat."

"Any artillery?"

"Under the dash."

"Okay." He turned to Rachel. "Let's go."

~ * ~

Mayhew's blood coursed with anger. "Fools! Idiots! How in the hell could you have let Bergdorf get away? Not once but twice. Get out. Get out!

The man scurried out of the room and Mayhew turned to Brooks. "He'll be with the president by now. Satterfield informed me a few minutes ago that since they can now assume the bacteria is or soon will be in the country, he's turning the whole thing over to the FBI. With Bergdorf's report, they may be able to start piecing things together. At best, we'll be cut out. We've got to move fast."

Noting the worried look in Brooks eyes, he came around the desk. "Relax. I've had plans for just such an eventuality for months. Did you pick up the car and the supplies?"

"Yes."

"Let's go."

"Where?"

Mayhew's lips curled. "I have my own safe house."

~ * ~

London

Sir Edmund Mortimer threw down his pen and glared as his aide entered. "Well, what is it? What have the bloody Yanks been up to now? Not more bodies, I hope.

"They've gone, Sir."

"They?"

"All of them. Dr. Favi departed this morning on a flight to Rome." He smiled. "You have to admire the Israelis' chutzpah."

"They're noted for it. What have they done, now?"

"They hauled the bodies of those CIA agents back to their own flat then used the Yanks own code to call Morris and tell him to pick up a package."

"Nice touch, that. You said they were all gone?"

"Morris has arranged for the bodies to be shipped back to the States tonight."

"The dead Arab?"

"Buried discreetly in the Jewish cemetery. Nice quiet production, complete with aging mother and bereaved widow.

"One of the Americans, David Bergdorf, left on a Delta flight for Washington this afternoon along with a woman and Dani Urazi."

Sir Mortimer's eyebrows shot up. "Urazi? Their Chief of Station?"

"Yes, sir. I've had some judicious inquiries made. The other American is regaining his health at a clinic run by Dr. Eliason and is expected to leave London within a couple of days."

"What about the Arabs in the apartment?"

"They bolted. One went to the airport and is booked on a flight to Athens. The other two are in an apartment off Sloan Square which belongs to an Iraqi couple and their three children."

"Can we get rid of them, too?"

"Taken care of, sir. They are here on student visas. I've arranged for their visas to be revoked and they will be leaving the country tomorrow."

Sir Edmund leaned back in his chair. "At least they've cleaned up their own mess. I suppose we should be thankful for that. Well done, my boy. I suppose Satterfield or Dann will let us know what it was all about." He turned to look out the window. "Someday."

Thirty

Washington, DC

Rachel slid lower in the seat and propped her knees against the dash, her gaze riveted to the door of the warehouse halfway down the block. How many of these stakeouts had she been on over the years? She'd never get over how boring they could be. Hours of doing nothing, trying to maintain at least a minimum level of concentration when there was nothing on which to concentrate. Waiting. Thinking. What was Barenji doing in the warehouse? Was there some secret exit they hadn't found? How many terrorists were inside? What were they planning? How well armed were they? Would the stakeout end in a firefight? She shifted again trying to find a more comfortable position.

"Take a nap. I'll wake you if there is any movement," Dani said.

Rachel shook her head. "How many men do we have covering the warehouse?"

"Four, besides us," Dani Urazi answered.

"Not enough. We don't know how many are inside. I think we should call in the FBI."

"Not yet. We want Barenji."

She nodded in agreement. If the FBI got Barenji, there would be months of legal bickering, even the possibility of bail. Once outside of prison, Barenji would be long gone. Much as she had come to love the United States, to admire the American system of jurisprudence, she was still frequently appalled by the American's naiveté. They were unwilling or unable to accept the fact that there were times when justice must be swift and sure and without mercy. A mad dog can't be left running loose in the hope that a cure will be found for rabies. Mossad had no such inhibitions. She smiled. It was one of the reasons other western clandestine services were so jealous of the Mossad. But it was also one of the reasons the Mossad was so effective.

"Oh, oh." She felt Dani tense.

Rachel dropped her knees and peered through the windshield. A dark van cruised along the cross street, made a U-turn at the corner and came to a stop in front of the warehouse. She counted six men as they climbed out of the van and disappeared inside the building.

Dani and Rachel exchanged glances. Even in the dim light, she could read the worry and indecision on Dani's face. They were now definitely outnumbered. Was it time to call in the FBI?

A few moments later a red sports car turned the corner and parked behind the van. The driver and a passenger also entered the building.

"With Barenji, there are at least nine in there now." Urazi slammed a fist against the steering wheel then reached for the radio. "We'll have to call in the FBI. Shit."

~ * ~

Cal Brooks poured himself a cup of coffee then called over his shoulder, "Coffee's ready. Want a cup?"

Mayhew paused in his pacing. "What? No. No." He clasped his hands behind his back and continued wearing a path in the carpet of the studio apartment.

The telephone's strident ring shattered the night silence. Cal swore as coffee sloped over his hand. Mayhew pounced on the instrument, listened a moment and slammed the receiver back.

He knew his eyes must be glittering from the look on Cal's face. He looked away, trying to get a grip on himself but he couldn't control the excitement in his voice. "Our FBI informant just reported that the Israelis have located Barenji and the bacteria. It will take them a while to get organized. We can beat them there if we hurry. Let's go."

~ * ~

Rachel continued to watch the warehouse door while her thoughts wandered. After the new arrivals had entered the warehouse, there had been no further activity. Idly she ran a finger back and forth over the armrest. The FBI was on the way. It would soon be over. Richard was alive and would be home in a few days. Life would be back to normal. Her hand strayed to her belly. They would have a child. Richard would simply have to agree...

The warehouse door opened. Rachel sat up, heart pounding. She heard Urazi's indrawn breath. Moments later one of the terrorists came out and studied the street. As they watched, he turned back to the door and nodded.

Rachel's gut tightened. Where was the FBI? She cast a desperate glance up and down the street. Out of the corner of her eye, she saw a flicker of movement from the dark recesses under a loading dock down the street. Dani started the car.

Barenji, carrying an attaché case in one hand and a carry-on garment bag in the other, strode to the Nissan Z and slid in.

As the sports car pulled away, the Arab darted back inside the warehouse and slammed the door.

Urazi had their car moving before Barenji reached the corner. Rachel grabbed the radio. "Our pigeon is flying. Heading east. We need alternative cover immediately."

The radio sputtered. Max Cohen, one of the Mossad agents, said, "Stay with him. I'll cut in front of you two blocks down. Then you can cut out and ride shotgun a block over."

A blue Mercury pulled out of a cross street in front of them. They followed two car lengths back behind the Mercury until Max Cohen cut in front of them. Three blocks farther Urazi turned off and increased his speed until they were traveling parallel to the Z one block to the south.

A voice crackled over the radio. "He's heading onto the freeway. North on 270."

Urazi swore. Slamming on the brakes, sliding into a U-turn, he raced back to the cross street, spun around the corner, ran the stop sign at the next corner and swung onto the access ramp. Rachel was thrown against the dash then bounced against the door. She grabbed the armrest with her right hand. Bile rose to the back of her throat, caused not by the motion of the car, but from her fear. They couldn't lose Barenji now. They couldn't!

Grabbing the mike from Rachel, Dani shouted, "We're on 270. Where are you?"

"Still heading north. Better hurry up, I think he's getting antsy."

Minutes later they had Cohen in sight and Urazi visibly relaxed. His voice was calm when he picked up the mike. "Okay. I have you. Have you been close enough for him to read your license?"

"No."

"Good. Cut out at the next exit, wait five minutes and come on back. We'll leap-frog."

Max turned off at the next exit and Dani settled into the right lane two cars back from the Z.

Dawn was breaking as they neared Frederick. Urazi radioed Cohen to move up. When Barenji switched to Interstate 70, Urazi was right behind him.

"Where the hell is he going?" he snapped.

"How the hell do I know," Rachel snapped back.

"This is your country. Where does this road go?"

"Damn it, Dani, I live three thousand miles from here. I've never been in this part of the country."

She opened the glove compartment and pulled out a handful of maps. Leafing through them, she selected one and stuffed the others back. Opening it across her lap, she bent over trying to read in the pale light.

"If we stay on this road, we'll be crossing into Pennsylvania soon. Then west into Ohio."

They crossed out of Maryland. Half an hour later, the Z pulled into a large truck stop. Dani slowed, letting a blue Mercury Monarch pass him. When it, too, turned into the truck stop, he followed. Rachel contacted Cohen and told him where they were stopping.

Barenji drove past the pumps and parked near the restaurant. Dani pulled into a self-service island. "I'll get gas. Why don't you go in and get us something to eat. Better stock up in case he doesn't stop again."

"You forget, Barenji knows me. I'll fill up, you get the food."

Rachel was checking the oil when Cohen pulled up to the other side of the pumps. She slammed down the hood and moved back to the pump.

Cohen got out of the car. Keeping his back to her and his voice low, he said, "I think you have a tail."

"What?"

"Either you or Barenji, probably Barenji. A blue Mercury. Two men. They came onto the freeway behind me in Washington. They've been behind you since we left Frederick. They gassed up at the full service island and now they're parked over by the restaurant."

"Are they FBI?"

"I don't know. Could be FBI or could be CIA."

Rachel shivered. The CIA had tried to kill Richard in London, had tried to kidnap David at the airport. She hoped it wasn't the CIA. "Do you think they've spotted you?"

"No."

"You need a different set of plates."

"No sweat. I've got half a dozen in the trunk. So do you."

"Do you have a hat?"

He turned around then and glared down at her. "What do you think I am, a novice? I got half a dozen of those, too. Also a couple of hair pieces and a bunch of eyeglasses, both plain and colored lenses."

Rachel smiled. "Sorry. When he pulls out, you had better take over and we'll drop back."

Dani sauntered up, his arms full of paper bags. He opened the passenger door and put them on the seat. "Barenji's just finishing his breakfast. I'll go pay for the gas." He strolled toward the kiosk, while Rachel hung up the hose and replaced the gas cap.

Cohen made a production out of sniffing the air and rubbing his stomach. Taking the hint, she reached in the car and pulled out one of the sacks. Inside were half a dozen hamburgers. She pulled out two and handed them to him. He tossed them on the seat of his car and walked away grinning.

Rachel slid behind the wheel and when Dani returned, pulled the car to the side of the restaurant. Dani handed her a container of coffee and a Danish. They watched Barenji come out of the restaurant and pull over to the gas pumps. Rachel gulped down the last of her coffee and started the car. The Z moved into the early morning traffic with Max Cohen close behind, his car now bearing New York plates. A few moments later the blue Mercury drove out.

When they hit the Pennsylvania Turnpike, Rachel appreciated the work done on the motor. Barenji took off like a scalded cat leaving Max Cohen in his stock car behind. Rachel had only a brief glance at the driver of the Mercury as they passed, but knew she would recognize him again anywhere.

"Pittsburgh. He's headed for Pittsburgh," she exclaimed as they flew past the I-70 cutoff. Barenji slowed down and Max soon caught up and passed them. They continued to leapfrog, dropping back when traffic thinned out, closing in when it increased. They ate the now cold hamburgers as they drove, washing them down with cold coffee.

Later, as they followed him onto the Highway 30 off ramp, she said, "He's heading for the airport."

Dani grabbed the radio. "Max, he's headed for the airport. Get up close and follow him inside. Leave the keys in the car and Rachel will park it. If he is taking a flight, get us seats on the same plane."

Another voice broke in. "This is Moab. We're about forty miles behind and have been tracking you. Leave the keys in both cars. We'll take care of them. Leave a message with your destination on the door of the second stall in the men's rest room. We'll try to arrange to have you met."

Max Cohen passed them just after they crossed the Monongahela River at McKeesport and half an hour later they pulled into a long-term parking lot. Rachel considered taking the two portable radios but decided against it. They might cause comment at the security check. Barenji would be looking for just such an incident.

Carrying her case, Rachel entered the terminal, and passing Cohen without acknowledgement, went into the ladies room. She stood at the mirror repairing her makeup until two women left then cracked the door. A few minutes later, she saw Dani run a finger along his nose and walk over to the newsstand.

She walked to the newsstand and began leafing through magazines, working her way towards him until they were side by side. When he replaced a copy of Time Magazine, she picked it up. Slipping the ticket envelope from the magazine to her purse, she carried the magazine to the counter and paid for it then took a seat nearby.

She watched Max Cohen leave the airport. A few minutes later Dani left the newsstand and went in the men's room. She cast a quick, covert glance at Barenji then removed the ticket from her purse and glanced at it. The destination on the ticket was Los Angeles with a plane change in Chicago. She glanced at her watch. The plane would leave in thirty-five minutes.

She slipped the ticket back in her purse, picked up her things and headed for the departure gate. As she walked into the boarding area, the first person she saw was the driver of the blue Mercury.

~ * ~

Washington, DC

James Eberle was one of the first FBI agents to arrive at the warehouse. He, as well as the others, was wearing the standard windbreaker with FBI lettered across the back. A Mossad agent slipped out of his hiding place and crossed the street, approached one of the agents and was immediately brought to Eberle.

When he heard the agent's report, he grabbed the radio and ordered the department helicopter circling in the distance to commence aerial surveillance of the Z car. Swearing under his breath, he ordered his men to move in on the warehouse. He'd have to trust to the Israelis and the helicopter to keep tabs on Barenji.

What worried him was the report on the blue Mercury. It had to be Mayhew. The CIA man had outwitted the FBI agent assigned to follow him and disappeared. Somehow, he had learned of the terrorist's whereabouts. What else would he be doing here? He obviously had his own game plan, but what? Was he working for the Chinese? Or had he just gone bananas?

Half an hour later, Eberle had a dozen Palestinians in custody and a dozen ampoules of the bacteria on their way to Atlanta and the CDC.

Three hours later he was in FBI Director William Jackson's office reporting to Jackson, CIA Director Satterfield and Presidential Aide David Bergdorf.

The lines on Satterfield's face seemed to be carved in granite as he said, "So Mayhew, and I assume the second man in the car was his personal assistant, Calvin Brooks, are following Barenji. Are you sure it is Barenji?"

"Yes, the Israelis positively identified him. We have aerial surveillance in place and he is also being tailed by Mossad."

"Are they working with us on this? Can we trust them?"

"I think so, sir. I have been in touch with their Chief of Station. They will pass all information on to us. Right now it appears that Barenji is headed towards the Pittsburgh area."

Satterfield, pacing the office, stopped in front of a map of the United States. Running a finger over the various highways leaving the Washington area, he asked, "Why Pittsburgh? Why not New York? Philadelphia? Where is he going?"

David Bergdorf joined him at the map. His finger moved farther west. "I think the bacteria we recovered at the warehouse was to be used here on the east coast. What he is carrying is most probably for distribution either in the Midwest or the west coast."

"Yes. But again, why Pittsburgh?"

Bergdorf shrugged. "Perhaps he plans to drive across the country." He looked at the map again. "Or perhaps he thinks security will be lighter there."

The phone rang sending the tension in the room spiraling upward. Jackson answered then handed the receiver to Eberle.

After listening for a few moments, the FBI agent said, "Good. I want agents at both airports. Surveillance only on Barenji. Do not attempt to apprehend him, but if he contacts anyone, move in and arrest them after he leaves."

He hung up and turned to the others in the room. "Barenji is at the Pittsburgh airport. He picked up a ticket to Los Angeles with a change of planes in Chicago. I'd like a military flight to Los Angeles. If I can get out of here in half an hour, I should be able to get to Los Angeles about the same time as Barenji. Can that be arranged, sir?"

Jackson nodded, his hand already reaching for the phone.

Bergdorf turned. "I'm going with you."

Thirty-one

The flight to Chicago's O'Hare Airport was short. Rachel, seated one row behind and across the aisle from the driver of the blue Mercury, spent the time studying him. She mentally named him Pot Belly.

As the passengers crowded into the aisle anxious to disembark, she managed to get directly behind him. He smelled of sweat and Old Spice. That he was CIA she had no doubt. She was also sure that he had no idea who she was therefore he had to be after Barenji. They moved onto the ramp. She saw him discreetly signal a taller man wearing an Italian silk sport coat; saw the infinitesimal nod in response before they were both swallowed up in the crowd as it erupted into the departure lounge.

Inside the terminal, Rachel was at once made aware of the fact that O'Hare was the world's busiest airport. Sweat beaded on her forehead as a momentary rush of claustrophobia swept through her. The noise, the crush of people combined with a lack of sleep disoriented her and left her feeling weak and panicked. Barenji. She mustn't lose Barenji.

Her glance locked on the back of his head and the panic subsided. Pushing her way through the throng of travelers, she struggled to keep him in sight. They moved down the concourse towards another departure gate.

Rachel looked for Dani and finally spotted him in conversations with two men. As she watched they split up and were lost in the crowd.

She was fourth in line behind Barenji when he checked in for the connecting flight to L.A. There was a little more than an hour before their boarding call. Barenji left the desk and took a seat in the first row of chairs. She watched him place the briefcase on his lap and fold his hands on top of it.

While she waited her turn at the check-in counter, she surreptitiously studied the case. At first glance, it appeared no different than a thousand other briefcases. With further concentration, she realized it was slightly larger and deeper than common. Also an unusual row of brass studs decorated the brown leather just below the lid and a deep scratch, less than an inch long marred one corner.

Glancing up from the case, she met Barenji's eyes in reflection in the window. Her mouth went dry. To show recognition or fear would be deadly. It took an immense effort of will to idly hold his gaze for a moment before letting her glance slide casually away. Her heart was pounding so hard she felt it should be audible to the world. She could feel the sweat collecting along her hairline while a chill raced down her spine.

As soon as she checked in for her flight, she crossed the lounge, selected a seat in the last row and took out the Time magazine. Conscientiously turning a page every minute or so, Rachel kept her head bent while peripherally aware of every movement Barenji made. Occasionally she looked up, glanced at her watch or looked casually around the room. Once she saw Barenji was watching her and her throat tightened. *Dear God, don't let him recognize me now!*

Barenji stood and crossed the waiting area, passing so close to her seat that she could smell his aftershave. She watched him from the corner of her eye as he left the area. She rose to follow, saw Dani walking slowly after him, and sat back down.

~ * ~

Dani followed Barenji into the men's rest room. There were several men in the room. Dani crossed to the urinal and unzipped his pants as Barenji hesitated then entered a cubicle. A moment later another Israeli agent entered and joined Dani at the urinal. The cubicles on either side of the one Barenji entered were occupied. Dani crossed to the lavatory, grabbed a couple of paper towels, damped them and bent down, slowly wiping his shoes. He straightened as the door to the left of Barenji opened.

A middle-aged man came out, glanced around and hurried out the door. Dani met the other agent's glance in the mirror. The agent quickly zipped up and hurried out. Dani was crossing the room when the cubicle on the right of Barenji opened and a young man stepped out colliding with Dani. Dani put out a hand, grabbing the man's shoulder in an obvious effort to maintain his balance. He smiled and began to apologize. The young man tried to slap Dani's hand away but Dani tightened his grip.

"Hey, come on, buddy. I said I was sorry."

"Let go of me."

"Sure, sure." Dani let go of the man who darted out of the room. Dani looked around the room and shrugged, saying to the room in general, "Pleasant little son-of-a bitch," as he walked after him.

In the corridor, the young man was standing on tiptoe trying to see through the crowd. There was no sign of the middle-aged man or the Israeli agent. The young man began pushing his way down the corridor. Dani moved to a bank of telephones, stopped at the third from the right and lifted the receiver and dialed a number, watching the men's room door out of the corner of his eye. He saw Barenji come out and head back to the waiting area.

Seconds after an announcement on the public address system requested Mr. Bob Smith to please pick up a white courtesy telephone, a man approached the phone on Dani's right, picked up the receiver and said in a low voice, "Stevens, FBI."

"Barenji just passed a package. One of our agents is following and will be in contact." Dani went on to describe the two men and the radio frequency the agent would be using.

The FBI agent hung up first and jogged towards the exit. Dani waited a few minutes, hung up and went in search of his other agents.

~ * ~

As the first boarding call was announced, Barenji stood again and walked quickly, not towards the loading gate, but back into the terminal. Rachel's gut twisted. He had spotted her and was making a break. She moved to follow then slowed, glancing around quickly. She needed backup. Both the concourse and waiting room were crowded, but no one was paying her the least attention. Dani would have agents here, but she couldn't identify them. She spotted Pot Belly strolling towards the concourse. Dani was nowhere to be seen.

Uneasy, she quickened her steps and followed Barenji down the concourse. Moments later, he disappeared through an unmarked door. Fear rose, choking her. Was he meeting someone? Was the door an unmarked exit? She mustn't lose him now. Where was Dani?

She reached the door, shot a wary look around then gripped the handle. Cautiously, she opened the door and peered in. Barenji had disappeared. With a last glance down the corridor, she slipped inside. Rachel found herself in a short hall with three doors; two on one side and one at the end, all closed.

Releasing a tight breath, Rachel tiptoed to the first door and pressed her ear against the wood. Silence. Slowly she tried the knob. Locked. She moved to the second door. Silence. Again, locked.

She pressed her ear against the door at the end of the corridor. It took a second for her to realize the heavy thumping was not coming from the space beyond but was her own heartbeat. Taking a deep breath, she peered inside the door. Gray light filtered through closed Venetian blinds revealed a small room, which appeared unoccupied. A copy machine on a cabinet stood against the wall on her right. There was a bank of file cabinets on her left. Confused, she pushed the door open and walked in. Where was Barenji? In one of the locked rooms?

Rachel turned to leave. Her gaze swept over the files and she realized they weren't against the wall as she'd first thought. She turned back and edged around the last file cabinet. In the corner was a table with a coffee maker, a package of Styrofoam cups and various paraphernalia. Beside the table was a second door.

She crept to it and listened. Nothing. She turned the knob with icy fingers. Inching the door open, she peeked through the crack. The room was deeply shadowed. Warily she pushed the door farther open. It appeared to be a supply room. Metal racks reaching within inches of the ceiling and filled with boxes and cartons, marched in rows down the long room. Fear clutched at her as she moved down the first aisle.

She was less than a foot from the end of the aisle when a box flew off the rack behind her. Decks of playing cards, displaying an airline logo, scattered across the floor at her feet.

Crushing back a scream, she whirled, took a step backward. An arm came around her from behind, jerking her off her feet, slamming her against the wall. Fingers slid around her throat, imprisoning her.

Instinctively, she brought a knee up. He blocked her attempt with ease. She heard his soft laugh. He whispered, "Infidel bitch, I'm almost glad Ahab failed in Beirut. I shall enjoy killing you myself."

Panic raced through her. She tried a karate chop but he caught her wrist in his free hand. He released her throat. She tried to twist away from the wall. He slammed her back, jamming a knee into her belly, pinning her to the wall with his weight.

She clawed at his face, fingers searching for his eyes, tearing at one eyelid. He slapped her. Her ears rang and the room tilted. Rachel could taste the salty tang of her own blood. Her fingers scrambled against the rack searching for anything she could use for a weapon and found nothing. Her hand locked around the steel frame and she jerked with all her strength. The rack wobbled but didn't tip.

She made a desperate grab for his testicles, squeezed and twisted. His scream echoed in her ears and she squeezed harder. His grip loosened. She twisted free and aimed a karate chop at his throat.

He batted her hand away with a blow that left her arm numb to the elbow. Then he had her wrists in a crushing grip. He jerked both arms above her head, clasping both wrists in his left hand. He shoved her against the wall. The stink of his unwashed body was overpowering as he pressed against her.

Rachel arched her neck and butted her head into his chin. It didn't bother him. She threw her body and head forward, sinking her teeth into the flesh at the base of his throat. She was fighting for her life and knew it. She bit harder and tasted blood.

His right hand curved around her throat, pressing, pressing. She tried again to knee him. A movement near the door caught her eye. Dani? Hope flared. She stared at the door. Had it opened wider? The pressure on her lungs was unbearable. The room began to dim. *Oh, God, Dani, where are you?* A silhouette etched itself on her brain the instant before she spun down into a thick black vortex.

Thirty-two

London

Richard Royer drummed his fingers impatiently against the wall of the phone booth and swore under his breath as his call was transferred a fourth time. This time the voice that answered, the overseas operator, sounded both young and flustered. "An overseas call for David Bergdorf? Gosh, I...he isn't here. I think...I heard he's gone to Los Angeles. What? No, I don't have a number for him there. Let me see...I can transfer you to—"

Richard slammed down the receiver. Los Angeles? What was David doing in Los Angeles? Where was Rachel? Was she with him? She sure as hell wasn't home or she would have answered the phone. He'd been trying to reach her for hours. If David was in Los Angeles, there was no point in going to Washington.

He eased out of the booth and headed for the British Airways ticket counter. Twenty minutes later, having exchanged his ticket, he dashed down the concourse for an immediately departing non-stop flight to Los Angeles.

Thirty-three

Rachel struggled up through a bank of thick gray fog, grappling with the cold, damp tentacles that tried to pull her down. From somewhere above, she heard voices and struggled to understand what was being said. The words were fuzzy, unintelligible. Somewhere in the fog, danger lurked. She opened her mouth to call. The pain in her throat brought her to full consciousness.

Her eyes focused on the face above her, a face she didn't recognize. He smiled, saying, "Don't try to talk."

Rachel nodded. Another face swan into focus. Dani.

"Is she conscious?" Dani asked.

Memory rushed back and she shifted, trying to sit up. "Barenji?" The word was little more than a croak.

"Lie still, young lady." A hand clamped on her shoulder, holding her down. The first face swam back into view. This time she saw that the man was of middle age his brown hair receding and there was a scattering of freckles across his nose. She concentrated on his words. "I'm Dr. Nelson. Your trachea and larynx are badly bruised. Keep that ice pack on your throat and don't try to talk yet."

She relaxed under his hand. Her eyes flicked around the room, taking in the large walnut desk, the paintings on the wall, the coffee table. She was lying on a sofa. The tips of her fingers played over the soft leather. An executive office. Two men stood near the door in whispered conversation across the room.

Her gaze settled on Dani. She mouthed the word water. He smiled and disappeared. She closed her eyes and waited. He returned in a few minutes. Supporting her shoulders, he held a glass to her lips. The ice tinkled like tiny bells as she sipped. When she had finished the whole glass, she gripped Dani's arm and pulled herself into a sitting position. The ice pack slid to her lap and she set it aside.

Though the intense pain in her throat was receding, she found she could only whisper. "Barenji?"

"He's dead," Dani answered.

She stared him, disbelieving. "Dead?"

Dani nodded. "Dead!"

The room shivered, tilted, settled back. Dead. The word rattled through her brain like a marble in a can. Dead. Barenji was dead. It was over. Richard. She could catch the next flight to London.

One of the men at the door crossed the room and murmured something to Dr. Nelson. A moment later the doctor left the room, and the man perched on the edge of the coffee table. Flipping open a wallet, he showed Rachel his identification. "Masters, FBI. Can you answer some questions?"

She nodded.

"Who was the Arab who attacked you?"

"Mustafa Barenji." Just whispering the name sent shivers down her back.

"You're sure?"

She nodded, saving her voice for what she knew was coming. When she had finished telling them all that had happened before she lost consciousness, she asked, "How did you find me?"

"Urazi and I saw you leave the gate area. By the time we reached the concourse, you had disappeared." He nodded towards the other man, still standing by the door. "Agent Parkins was staked out at the next gate. When we learned you hadn't reached there, we started checking all of the rooms off the concourse. We found you unconscious. Barenji was a few feet away. He'd been knifed in the back."

Rachel sought Dani's eyes questioningly. He shook his head. "There is a door from the supply room to a stairwell. The killer must have slipped out that way. Do you have any idea who it was?"

She shook her head. "The bacteria?"

"None was found on him. He'd passed a package in the men's room. The FBI is rounding up that crew now."

Rachel sighed. "Then it's over."

"No. We think that was just the supply for the Midwest. Barenji was booked through to Los Angeles. We think he still had the supply destined for the west coast."

"Where is it?"

"We don't know. It's disappeared."

Defeat washed over her. She sank back, leaning her head against the cushion. Feeling drained and weak, she let her eyes close. So he had been meeting a contact, someone he trusted. The trail was cold. The bacteria would be dispersed. She was still alive. That, at the very least, was a miracle. She could feel again Barenji's hand closing about her throat, smell the stink of him, see the unholy glitter in his eyes as the door at the other end of the room opened. Saw again the figure silhouetted in the doorway. She sat up, her eyes flying open.

"Pot Belly!"

"What."

"Pot Belly. The blue Mercury. He was following Barenji when we left Washington. I saw him silhouetted in the door just before I lost consciousness."

Agent Masters leaned forward. "Can you describe him?"

Rachel nodded. "Short, about five-six, thin arms, small hands. A round face, fair complexion, freckles or liver spots on his forehead. Blue eyes. Thinning reddish brown hair. Crooked, yellowish teeth. He was wearing a navy blue pinstripe three-piece suit. White shirt. Maroon tie. Cordovan loafers. No hat. Oh, and he uses Old Spice."

"You didn't see all of that in the dark."

"No. He was on the plane from Pittsburgh, seated just ahead of me. I had plenty of time to study him. I was close behind when he deplaned." She hesitated then said, "I thought he was CIA."

Masters jumped up and dashed out the door. Dani leaned over and patted her cheek. She clutched his hand. "Dani, the bacteria is in the briefcase. I'm sure of it." She described the case in detail.

"I'll tell Masters. Try to get some sleep. I'll be back as soon as we learn anything. Agent Parkins will be just outside the door if you need anything."

He helped her to lie down and covered her with an airline blanket before leaving. She retrieved the ice pack and wrapped it around her throat. She felt some of the tension draining away. Her part was over. The FBI would take it from here.

She was drifting on the edge of sleep when Dani and Agent Masters returned. She sat up and tossed the now melted ice pack on the coffee table. Dani settled himself on the sofa beside her. Masters dragged the chair from behind the desk and straddled it. He handed her a fax photo.

She needed only a glance. Looking back at the FBI agent, she said, "It's Pot Belly. You've identified him?"

He nodded and handed her a second fax. "Did you, at any time, see this man?"

Rachel studied this picture a little longer before nodding. "It's Sport Coat. Pot Belly passed some kind of signal to him as they were leaving the plane. Who are they?"

"The one you call Pot Belly is Elwood Mayhew. The younger man is his personal assistant, Calvin Brooks. They're CIA."

Rachel felt the rest of the tension that had gripped her for so long begin to melt away. She released a heartfelt sigh and relaxed against the back of the sofa. "Thank God. It's over at last."

Masters cleared his throat. "I'm afraid not. Mayhew and Brooks continued on the flight to Los Angeles."

"Do they have the briefcase?"

"We don't know."

Rachel sighed again and smiled. "Well, now that the FBI has taken over, I can go to my husband."

"I'm afraid not. My instructions are to put you on a military flight to Los Angeles immediately."

The smile faded and her glance flicked to Urazi. "Dani?"

"I'm flying to Tel Aviv. I have to report to Itzak Dann as soon as possible."

Rachel nodded and looked back at Masters. "With the FBI and CIA on the job, you don't need me any more. I want to go home. My husband needs me."

"Sorry. Apparently, they have some questions to ask you. About a CIA agent named Homer Whitney."

Thirty-four

El Toro Marine Air Station

Rachel was met at El Toro Marine Air Station in Orange County by an FBI agent. After identifying himself, he swept her into a car and drove her to a safe house. Although she and Richard had been to Los Angeles numerous times, she still had no idea where she was. The area was an older subdivision, the streets lined with half-dead palms and the grass in some of the yards beginning to turn brown. The house itself was nearly indistinguishable from its neighbors; a three bedroom ranch of uninspired design. The garage was a converted carport.

The front door opened directly into the living room with a dining area at one end. Although the temperature outside was barely into the seventies, the air conditioner was running. Rachel shivered.

Her escort placed her makeup case on a credenza and said, "You are to wait here. There is food in the refrigerator, if you're hungry. Sorry, there's no liquor but there's coffee, tea and soft drinks." He waved a hand towards a low bookcase. "There are some books and magazines, mostly out of date, I'm afraid."

She noticed there was neither a television nor a radio. Nor was there a telephone. She was cut off completely from the outside world. "How long am I to stay here?"

"I don't know. Please don't leave the house. Stay inside and away from the windows. Someone will contact you." He walked out, closing the door gently behind him.

Contact her or arrest her? How could she prove she had killed Whitney in self-defense? Would anyone believe that an agent of the CIA, an agent of the government would have tried to kill her? What could she expect? Jail? Deportation? Had they broken her cover?

She wandered through the house, her mind in turmoil. Perhaps she should run now. Walk out the door and disappear. She still had several thousand dollars in her purse. Money and the German passport she had used to enter the United States. There was sure to be a non-stop flight to London from Los Angeles International. She could be with Richard in a matter of hours.

Twitching aside the living room drape, she stared out at the browning grass and the lone palm tree in the yard. If she left, she would be a fugitive, at least in the United States. Where would she go? She could always return to Israel, return to her old identity, but she didn't want to. There were other places in the world where she could start a new life.

The trouble was, she didn't want a new life. She wanted the one she had, or at least had had until a few days ago. And there was Richard to consider. Richard's life was here. Her life was here. She couldn't run away. She'd have to stay and take what came. Sighing, she dropped the drape and headed for the bathroom.

She found a good supply of towels, soap, shampoo and other necessities in the bottom of the vanity. The medicine cabinet was well stocked with over-the-counter remedies for almost anything, as well as a few toiletries, mostly masculine. She did find a half-full box of bath salts, and wondered, briefly, which FBI agent liked his bath water softened.

Besides her still painful throat, Rachel's body was bruised and aching from her battle with Barenji. Stripping, she ran the bath as hot as she could stand it, tossed in the bath salts and soaked. By the time she crawled out of the cooling water, she could barely keep her eyes open.

All three bedrooms were fully furnished. She selected the biggest because of the queen bed, and pulled back the spread. The sheets and blanket looked clean, and anyway, she was too tired to care. She crawled between the sheets and was soon asleep.

She slept fitfully, racked by nightmares. She was running through a long corridor. Heavy footsteps pounded behind her. She knew if she looked around, whatever was chasing her would catch her. From a distance, someone was calling her name. She didn't recognize the voice and ran faster, trying to see through the mist that was filling to corridor. She had to get away from that voice.

She struggled to open her eyes. They felt glued shut. Terror raced through her. Was she still dreaming or... A cold hand grasped her shoulder, shaking her. She sat up and screamed.

"Mrs. Royer. Hey, take it easy. Are you okay?"

The panic ebbed as she came completely awake, her eyes focused on the face above her. David Bergdorf. She ran a hand over her face and swung her legs over the side of the bed. "Fine," she croaked. "Just a nightmare."

"You're entitled."

"What time is it?"

"Two-thirty. Better get up. The FBI has arrived. They want to know everything you can tell them. I'll put on some coffee while you get dressed."

A few minutes later, still feeling sluggish and out of sorts, Rachel walked into the living room of the tract house. James Eberle and David Bergdorf stood up as she entered the room.

Eberle stepped forward and extended a hand. A slight upturn at the corners of his mouth was obviously meant to be a smile as he said, "Mrs. Royer."

She shook his hand. "You are...?" Her voice had returned, although she was still hoarse. At least the pain had lessened.

"James Eberle, FBI. The Misses Beeson and Grimes are going to be relieved to know that you are alive and well."

Rachel stared at him. "The who?"

"Two elderly ladies who saw you forced into a car at Green Lake. I'd say you've made a couple of good friends. They came directly to my office to report the kidnapping and demand that we save you."

Rachel sank into a chair. A mental picture of the two little old ladies on their daily constitutional flashed before her. She saw again their startled faces framed by the car window and smiled. Bless them. There were still people in this country who were not afraid of becoming "involved".

Eberle poured her a cup of coffee and returned to his seat. "Now, we'd better get to work. Tell me everything from the beginning."

Rachel sipped her coffee and gave him an edited account of her experiences, deleting any mention of the Mossad agents involved. When she came to the killing of Whitney, she hesitated, but Eberle made no comment. When she finished, she looked him in the eye. "Now, would you mind telling me just what in the hell is going on?"

Eberle leaned back. "Mrs. Royer, we don't know much more than you do. But it would appear that someone in the CIA has either gone bonkers or is a double agent."

"Mayhew?"

He looked at her in surprise. "How did you know his name?"

"Masters in Chicago told me, when I identified his picture. Double agent for whom?"

"We don't know. We were hoping you could tell us."

Rachel shook her head. "I haven't any idea. Where is Mayhew now?"

"He and Brooks checked into the Bonaventure Hotel. We have them under surveillance."

"Why haven't you arrested them?"

Eberle looked as his watch. "We'll be doing so in less than an hour. Our men are getting into position now. The Bonaventure is packed to the roof with conventioneers. If Mayhew has gone bankers, we don't want to risk his letting that bacteria loose. From what Bergdorf has told us, it was dispensed in water in Zimbabwe but it might also be just as deadly airborne. We don't know. We have to be in position to take him in a way that will prevent him from releasing the bacteria. If he's crazy, he might do just that. We can't take the chance."

Eberle set his coffee cup on the end table and stood up. "We're on our way to the Bonaventure now."

Rachel bounded up. "I'm coming."

Eberle shook his head but before he could speak, David Bergdorf spoke up. "I think she's earned to right to be in on the kill."

"You'll take full responsibility?"

"Yes."

They were only a few blocks from the house in Van Nuys when the radio squawked. Mayhew and Brooks, in disguise, had taken the inside service elevator and nearly deceived the surveillance team. Fortunately, one of the watchers had recognized Brooks by his height and blond hair as they were getting into a cab.

"Did they have the briefcase with them?" Rachel asked.

"They each had a briefcase. We don't know if it's the one containing the bacteria. We need you to identify it. Our man is following in another cab. We got the cab number and contacted the company. They say the cabby reported a fare to Los Angeles International."

"Have the company ask the driver which terminal, but wait until he checks in. We don't want to rattle those two into doing something desperate. We're on our way."

Rachel and David exchanged looks as Eberle cut a U-turn, nearly colliding with a school mini-bus. A few hair-raising minutes later, Eberle raced up onto a southbound ramp of the San Diego Freeway.

They tore through the rapidly building traffic, weaving around slower vehicles, cutting in and out of lanes. Rachel clutched the armrest until her fingers became numb, and for once, was glad to have the seat belt. Ordinarily, she hated wearing them.

The airport exit sign flashed by. Seconds later the radio sprang to life, announcing that the taxi driver had reported dropping Mayhew and Brooks at the United Airlines terminal.

They whipped into the traffic circle and came to a screeching halt, barely avoiding rear-ending a bright pink Cadillac convertible. Rachel gritted her teeth in frustration as the traffic inched its way slowly towards the International Terminal at the top of the U-shaped drive. The United Terminal was on the far side. The radio squawked again informing them that the backup FBI agents were just now exiting the freeway.

David leaned over the seat. "Rachel and I will jump out here. We can run faster than this traffic is moving."

Before he finished speaking, Rachel had her door open and scrambled out. The driver on their right gave her the finger as the edge of the door connected with his front fender. She ignored him and darted between cars. David caught up with her as she gained the walkway. They ran, passing the International Terminal, following the curving walk past the commuter terminal.

Someone called her name, startling her into a misstep. She shook her head and kept running. She was hearing things. It had sounded like Richard's voice, but it couldn't be, he was still in London. No one in Los Angeles knew her.

Rachel and David sprinted in the doors at United and slid to a stop. The terminal was packed. David grabbed her arm and shouted above the din. "You check here, I'll check out the departure lounges."

He was gone before Rachel could reply. She began pushing her way through the crowd, eyeing each ticket line, swiveling her gaze, searching.

A hand clutched her shoulder and she jumped. Whirling, she dropped into a karate stance. Her glance swept up the man's chest, settling on his face. Her mind went blank for a moment as she stared into the smiling eyes. Her heart stopped then raced. She launched herself into his arms. "Richard! Oh, God, Richard. You're here."

His arms came around her waist, clutching her against his body. She clung to him for a moment, oblivious to everything but the feel of his arms around her then pushed her shoulders back. Leaning in his arms, she lifted a hand to stroke his face. "Richard."

His hand slid up her spine, cradled the back of her head. Their lips met and all thought of Mayhew, of the bacteria, faded from her mind. Her whole being was centered on the feel of him; his body pressing against hers; the feel of his fingers in her hair; his mouth devouring hers. Richard, safe and in her arms, was all that mattered.

"Mrs. Royer!"

The shocked voice shattered the spell and Rachel turned to stare at the FBI agent. The world swam back into focus. She wiggled from Richard's embrace and grinned up at the intruder. "Mr. Eberle, this is my husband. Richard, this is Special Agent Eberle of the FBI."

Eberle cast a quick, scowling glance at Richard then ignored him. "What about Mayhew?"

"He isn't down here. David has gone to check the gates."

"Let's go. You can have old home week later," Eberle snapped.

They pushed their way through the crowds and onto the "people mover". As they rode down the long concourse, Rachel quietly attempted to bring Richard up to date.

"Mayhew? That was the CIA agent that shanghaied me. The one that ordered your kidnapping to force me to go after Barenji."

Eberle turned. "You've met Mayhew?"

"Yes."

"Good. You'll have to come with us to help identify him. We only have rather poor fax copies of a photograph." Eberle pulled a copy of the faxed photo from his pocket and shoved it in Richard's hand. "Is this the same man?"

They reached the end of the conveyor and trotted down the corridor and onto the escalator. As they rode up, Richard studied the photo. "Yes. This is the man. But I can't come with you."

Eberle glared at him. "Royer, this isn't a game we're playing. We may need you."

Rachel was the first to spot David Bergdorf hurrying towards them and called, "Here, David."

He was breathing heavily as he reached them. "We're too late. Mayhew's gone. He and Brooks left a few minutes ago on a flight to Honolulu with connections on to Hilo."

Thirty-five

Eberle swore. "Where's a phone?"

"Wait." David laid a hand on his arm. "There is a direct flight to Kahului on Maui. We can get a connecting flight on to Hilo and be there within half an hour of Mayhew."

"Can we get seats?" Eberle asked.

"I don't know but I'll check. How are we going to pay for them?"

Rachel interrupted. "Don't worry about that. I've got enough to get us there." She cast a sidelong glance at Eberle. "I assume the FBI will pay us back."

Eberle grimaced. "Don't count on it. I've got to call Washington. Never mind the connecting flight. I'll arrange to have a private plane waiting in Kahului. We might even beat Mayhew." He headed for the bank of phones.

"I have to call Washington, too," David said. "The president will be glad to know you have recovered." He punched Richard lightly on the arm and dashed after the FBI agent.

Richard slipped an arm around Rachel's shoulders as they headed for the ticket counter. Rachel laid a hand on his back, needing to touch him. Suddenly she stopped.

"Where is the dialysis machine?"

He smiled down at her. "In a locker in the International Terminal. Relax. I had a treatment early this morning. I'm good for a couple of days."

"But what if we're gone longer? Oh, God, Richard. I can't go though any more of this strain. Go and get it."

"Rachel, baby, listen."

The tone of his voice sent a sliver of fear tearing through her. She stopped, staring up at him, waiting.

"Honey, I called the house as soon as the plane landed. I thought there might be a message from you." He paused, gripping both her shoulders. "There was a message... from the hospital. They have a kidney. I have to go into the hospital this afternoon."

Her heart leaped. Tears of joy ran down her cheeks. She buried her face in his chest, both arms circling his waist, crushing him to her. She felt his hand stroking her hair.

The moment was shattered by Eberle's voice. "Did you get the tickets?"

Releasing Richard, she turned, wiping the tears from her cheeks with the back of her hand. "I can't go. Richard is going into the hospital this afternoon for a kidney transplant. I'm going with him."

Eberle looked from one to the other. "That's impossible. You are the only one who can identify the briefcase. You'll have to come to Hawaii."

"No. No."

His eyes were as hard as steel shavings. "You have no choice."

"You have to come with us, Rachel." They all turned to look at David who had walked up unnoticed. His face was white and strained. "According to the reports the president has received, more than two hundred people have died in Zimbabwe. Most of them women and children. About twice that many are still expected to die. Reports are also coming in about unexplained deaths along Lake Kariba in Zambia and down river in Mozambique. You have to come with us, Rachel. We need you."

She recalled the drive from the airport in Victoria Falls. Recalled the radio announcer's voice. His words tumbled through her mind. She closed her eyes. Pictures of children, their little bodies twisted in agony, their eyes filled with pain and terror flashed behind her closed lids.

She jerked her eyes open and gazed up at Richard. Her heart was being torn apart. Tears welled up and spilled unchecked. Richard's hand came up, stroking her cheek, his thumb wiping away the tears.

"You'll have to go," he said.

She nodded. For the second time since their marriage, Richard would have to come second. What Eberle had said was true. She had no choice.

Thirty-six

Just before the plane landed in Maui, Eberle had a quiet talk with the chief stewardess. As a result, they were moved to empty seats in the first class section and were the first off the plane at Kahului.

They were met at the bottom of the ramp, whisked into a waiting sedan and driven to a nine passenger Cessna parked near the end of the runway, its propeller whirling. Minutes later they were in the air, skirting Haleakela crater and heading out to sea.

The trip from Los Angeles had been a nightmare for Rachel. No matter how hard she had tried to concentrate on the job ahead, her mind and heart remained with Richard. Now she could hear Eberle talking over the drone of the engine but couldn't concentrate on his words. All her thoughts were back on the mainland.

Mauna Kea, looming on her right as they followed the coastline, brought her out of her reverie. Clouds, painted lavishly with brilliant reds, yellows and purples by the setting sun, crowned its head. Below, long shadows lay like tiger stripes across the verdant foliage. As they circled Hilo, occasional lights sparkled like tiny diamonds set in dark velvet. The sheer beauty of the scene made her heart yearn; made her longing for Richard throb like a toothache. They both loved Hawaii. They had come here at least twice a year in the early days, before Richard's kidneys had begun to fail. The Mauna Kea Resort on the other side of the island had been one of their favorite vacation spots. Perhaps, after the surgery...

The Cessna touched down, breaking off her thoughts and pulling her back to the present. They taxied across the tarmac to a car waiting at the end of the runway. Moments later, Rachel climbed stiffly from the plane.

The warm, moisture-laden air, redolent with heavy scent of frangipani and pikaki enveloped her. Her stomach roiled. The scent was too sweet, too suffocating. It left her feeling enervated and vaguely disoriented.

She was grateful for Eberle's hand gripping her arm as he steered her to the car and held the door for her. He settled beside her and David climbed in the front street with the driver who made a sharp U-turn and shot down the field and out of the airport.

Tension roughened Eberle's voice as he said, "Report."

The driver spoke over his shoulder. "Mayhew and Brooks arrived forty minutes ago, picked up a rental car and headed west. We have a tail on them. They've gone to roost in a house outside of Glenwood. We have them under surveillance and are tracing ownership of the house. We've set up headquarters in a bungalow near Mountainview. I'm taking you there now. We have reinforcements coming in from the other islands. As soon as I drop you off, I'm coming back to pick them up."

"Have you notified the local authorities?"

"No, sir. Our instructions were to keep them under surveillance but to take no other action until your arrival."

"Is there anyone else in the house with Mayhew and Brooks?"

"I don't know. Here we are."

The driver edged the car into the narrow driveway and pulled up behind two cars and a jeep already parked beside a small bungalow hidden from the road by a high hedge of hibiscus. Night had fallen with typical swiftness. Clouds blotted out any moonlight.

Eberle opened his door and stepped out. Rachel slid across the seat and climbed out after him. No light or sound escaped the house. Only their car's headlights pierced the stygian darkness as they walked along the crushed shell path to the door. Shells crunched beneath their shoes, grating on her nerves, making her teeth ache. She resisted the urge to tiptoe.

Before Eberle could knock, the door opened. Light spilled like a beacon onto the tiny porch. A man in a blue suit hastened them inside. Everything about him shouted FBI. She judged him to be in his middle to late fifties. His dark blue suit marked him as an obvious holdover from the Hoover regime. Although his round, clean shaven face glistened with sweat, he hadn't so much as loosened his tie.

Rachel glanced around. They were in a long narrow room plainly furnished with wicker and bamboo furniture. At the far end of the room an ebony and glass table had been shoved against the wall and was covered with radio equipment. A large map of the island decorated the wall beside the table. The drapes were drawn on all of the windows and blankets taped over them to prevent any light escaping.

Rachel's attention switched back to the man in front of them. He extended a hand to Eberle while casting a suspicious look at Rachel. "Agent Peters. Can you tell me what this is about?"

Eberle shook his hand then nodded towards Rachel and David. "This is Mrs. Royer. She's here to identify Mayhew and the briefcase. David Bergdorf is a special representative of the president." Eberle moved into the room, paused then approached the map. "Are Mayhew and Brooks still in the house near Glenwood?"

"Yes. I have three men keeping them under surveillance. Two more agents are on their way from Honolulu. What's this all about?"

"Got any coffee?"

"I can make some."

"I'll make it while you talk," Rachel said. "Kitchen this way?" At Peter's nod, she walked through the dining area and into the kitchen ell. She could hear Eberle succinctly relating details about the search for the bacteria as she made coffee.

Carrying Styrofoam cups and the pot back into the living room, she heard Eberle ask, "How many people are in the house?" She passed the coffee around then, carrying her cup, studied the map.

"At last report, we believe four. Someone opened the door when Mayhew and Brooks arrived. My agent believes it was a man but can't be positive. The person stayed well back in the room and he only caught a glimpse. About ten minutes later, an elderly Chinese arrived. He walked in without knocking. We are tracing the license plate on his car. We're also trying to trace ownership of the house."

The radio crackled just as they heard the sound of tires on the driveway. Peters ran across the room to the table. The door opened and their driver entered, followed by two men. One glance told Rachel they were more Federal men.

The tallest of the three said, "Which of you is Eberle? I have a message. We received this by radio just before we left."

Eberle stood and extended his hand. "I'm Eberle."

He slit open the envelope and pulled out the sheet of paper. His hand began to tremble and when he looked up, his eyes held a haunted look.

Tension and fear tightened Rachel's throat. Her voice was a mere whisper as she asked, "What is it?"

"It's the report from the Center For Disease Control in Atlanta. The bacteria can be dispensed by air and absorbed through the mucus membranes. It can also be absorbed through the skin, although at a slower rate. As far as their people have been able to discover, it can only be killed by extreme heat. Temperatures in excess of 500 degrees Celsius. They are working on an antidote but estimate it will take several weeks."

Peters turned from the radio, breaking the stunned silence. "Morton says there is a lot of activity going on. Mayhew and his crew may be getting ready to move."

Thirty-seven

Elwood Mayhew, wrapped in his own thoughts, spoke not a word during the flight from Los Angeles to Hilo. His mind skittered from thought to thought, unable to concentrate. He knew he should be making contingency plans, evaluating options but his mind refused to cooperate.

Fragmented memories kept crowding in, disrupting his thoughts. The senior Mayhew had been a big, bruising man with a wicked backhand used frequently to display his contempt for his son. "Sniveling pip-squeak" had been one of his less forceful epitaphs. Unfortunately, they had been in the front yard during one of his father's scathing verbal attacks and Elwood's arch enemy, Andy Moody, his next door neighbor, had heard it and delighted in spreading it. Elwood Mayhew had suffered silently all through grade school and into high school with the nickname Pip.

The fact that he had won a full scholarship to Tulane and later to Georgetown School of Law had done nothing to alleviate his father's contempt. He'd simply switched to calling his son "egghead" and other derogatory names. At least the beatings had stopped.

Mayhew burned under the memories and shifted restlessly in his seat. He'd bought champagne and finished the whole bottle, the day he learned his father had died, drunk, in a barroom brawl. He wondered where Andy Moody was now. The last he'd heard, the ignorant bastard was still working as a grocery clerk. Almost sixty and still a grocery clerk. He'd never even made assistant manager.

Mayhew chuckled. When Cal Brooks looked at him, Mayhew turned to gaze out the window. He'd shown them, he'd shown them all and he'd show them again.

In a few days, weeks at the most, he'd be a hero. Everyone would know his name, know he'd saved the country with his brains and daring. They'd all recognize his genius. He'd do what all those jocks, with their muscles for brains, didn't have the intelligence or the courage to do. He'd show them all. For a brief moment he wished his father were still alive to witness his greatest hour. He came out of his reverie when the plane touched down in Hilo.

Mayhew was aware of Brooks' restlessness as his assistant drove the rental car through the late evening heat. It was time to take Cal into his confidence, explain the whole thing to him.

He began to smile. Not even Cal could have guessed exactly what he planned.

"Cal, what is the biggest threat to world peace?"

Brooks hesitated, not knowing what Mayhew wanted him to say. "Iraq?"

"No, no. If we had leadership with any foresight and the guts to act, those fanatics would soon be put in their place. No, our biggest enemy is still Communism. Russia and China."

"Russia isn't much of threat anymore."

"Of course it is. How long do you really think they will continue to flirt with capitalism? Look at the last elections! No, Russia must be destroyed. That's why I made no effort to stop the bacteria going there."

Mayhew patted the attach case on his lap. "And we're going to give China a taste of its own medicine."

He giggled as Brooks turned his head to stare at him. The car swerved. "Watch what you're doing."

Brooks returned his attention to the road.

Mayhew noticed the sweat poring down his assistant's face. "Not getting cold feet, are you, Cal?"

"N-n-no, no, sir."

"Good. I wouldn't want to think that you weren't with me one hundred percent." The words were said softly but there was no mistaking the threat behind them. Brooks shivered.

Mayhew watched him for a few minutes then continued. "With Russia and China destroyed, Cuba will fall, too. Communism will be destroyed once and for all. We'll be heroes, Cal. Heroes."

Thirty-eight

Rachel's knees felt as mushy as wet bread. Would this nightmare never end? She sank down on the arm of the couch, her gaze locked on Eberle.

Eberle whirled. "Tell them to stay with Mayhew but not to move against them. We're on our way. Do you have more radios?"

Peters waved a hand towards the bedroom as he turned back to his radio. "In there."

Eberle returned with three units, windbreakers and caps. He distributed them, took off his suit coat, threw it on the couch and shrugged into his windbreaker. He handed two of the radios to the two agents and headed for the door. With a glance over his shoulder at Rachel and David, he said, "Wait here. We'll be in touch when we need you."

Rachel and David glanced at each other as the men ran out. Car engines roared to life, followed by the squeal of tires on gravel. In the pregnant silence that followed, they continued to stare at each other. Then the stunned look faded from David's face. "Like hell!" He dashed out the door, Rachel at his heels.

The only vehicle left was the jeep. David climbed in, his fingers searching for the keys. Rachel darted around and crawled in the passenger seat as the engine sputtered and caught. David gunned the engine, crimped the wheel into a tight turn and sped down the driveway and onto the road. Rachel bounced, nearly out of the jeep. She landed back on the seat with a bump and held on, her heart jumping like a grasshopper.

Rachel caught a brief glimpse of red taillights before they disappeared around a curve. She clung to the roll bar as David charged through the gears like a grand prix driver, quartering curves, using the brakes as little as possible. They were only a hundred yards behind the last car when it left the highway and turned up a dirt road. If her memory of the map at the bungalow was correct, Mayhew should be only a few hundred yards away.

She yelled at David, "Pull off here. The house should be just over that ridge."

David slid the jeep to a stop then maneuvered off the road and into the brush, dousing the lights and motor. "Wait here. I'm going to climb up and see what's happening."

He stepped out of the jeep. Rachel climbed out and crossed to him. "I'm coming, too."

"No. Stay here. You'll just be in the way."

"No more than you will."

He stopped and looked down at her. His teeth gleamed in the faint light. "You're right. You've had more training at this than I have. Come on."

They began to inch their way up the hill, pushing through the heavy undergrowth. Rachel was breathing heavily when they reached the top of the ridge, not so much from exhaustion as from the hot, muggy air. She wiggled under a bush and lay still, waiting for her breathing to return to normal. David crawled in beside her as she strained to pierce the darkness. To the west, the clouds glowed pink. The hot air was heavy with the odor of burning wood and a smell she couldn't identify.

Rachel nudged David and whispered, "What's that smell? Is there a forest fire?"

"No. Kilauea Volcano is erupting again." He inched forward. "I can't see a thing. Wait here while I try to find Eberle. No sense in both of us breaking our necks out here. I'll be back as soon as I find out what's happening."

~ * ~

Inside the house, Elwood Mayhew finished outlining his plans to the other three men in the room. He watched shock and disbelief spread over their faces and waited.

Soon Wing was the first to react. His round moon face was expressionless as he said, "What you ask should not be too difficult. But what is in these ampoules? I will not be a party to the wanton killing of innocent civilians."

Mayhew choked back the rage that threatened to choke him. "Nothing deadly," he assured the old man with a bland smile. "Only a nerve compound that will disable everyone long enough for our special team to enter the country and eliminate those of the Old Guard who hold your country hostage."

"But, but—" Calvin Brooks stuttered, his face white, eyes terrified.

At Mayhew's glare, he closed his mouth.

Mayhew returned his attention to the older Chinese. "I assure you, this compound has been thoroughly tested on our own people. It causes only temporary and mild discomfort. The effects wear off in a few hours with no lasting impairment."

He turned to the younger Chinese. "Once the hard-liners are taken out, saner minds will prevail. China can take her place among the democracies of the world. Isn't this what you have been working for?"

264

The younger man nodded and Mayhew looked back at Soon Wing and waited. Slowly the old man nodded.

"You'll have no trouble smuggling it into the country?" Mayhew asked.

The corner of Soon Wing's lips twitched. "Getting something so small into China will be no problem."

"It is vital that this be distributed and that its release be timed precisely. If it's not, the whole mission will fail. It could be years before such an opportunity presents itself again. Years."

The two Chinese exchanged a look then Soon Wing said, "We understand. The timing will be exact."

Mayhew smiled. "Then what are we waiting for?"

~ * ~

David slid off to Rachel's left and was soon out of sight. A few moments later a breeze sprang up, the cloud cover parted, bathing the whole hillside with moonlight. A hundred feet or so below her, a bungalow set in a clearing. A compact car and a mid-size sedan were parked in front.

She searched for some sign of the FBI agents. Nothing. Then, out of the corner of her eye, she caught a flicker of movement. Straining her eyes, she watched a figure creep silently toward the house. An instant later, another figure detached itself from the foliage and snaked towards the sedan.

Suddenly the door of the house opened and three men appeared. Two of them carried briefcases. The bacteria! But which case? Both?

From below and to her right, she heard Eberle's voice. "FBI. You are under arrest. Please raise your hands."

Even before he finished speaking, one of the men drew a gun and began to fire. The FBI returned fire and Rachel saw one figure fall. Like the drawing of a curtain, the clouds rolled together, blotting out the moon, covering everything with its thick mantle of darkness. Only muzzle flashes, like tiny fireflies, split the gloom. The sound of gunfire reverberated over the hills, echoing and re-echoing.

She felt her stomach cramp. *Oh, God, please don't let them get away.* Her nerves twanged like a guitar string. Gunfire continued to shatter the night. *God, don't let them hit the briefcase!*

Rachel scrambled to her feet then stood undecided. Brush crackled to her left. She whirled. "David?"

"Yes." He pushed through the brush towards her. "We'd better get back to the jeep before we get caught in a crossfire."

Together, they eased their way back down the hill. They were within ten feet of the jeep when a figure detached itself from the shadows. Even in the darkness, Rachel could see the gun in his hand. Then her gaze fastened on his other hand, on the briefcase he carried then shifted to his face. His eyes glittered with madness as he waved the gun. He began to giggle.

Thirty-nine

Rachel's gut churned as fear and anger warred within her. How could she have been so stupid? Walking up to the jeep like some rank amateur. Her glance settled on the briefcase clutched in his hand.

"Get in the jeep." He pointed the gun at David. "You first. Keep your hands where I can see them or your lady friend gets shot. No. Get in the passenger seat and grip the roll bar with both hands. You!"

Rachel pulled her gaze away from the briefcase and swept over the man as he moved towards her. Pot Belly. Mayhew. He was shouting at her. "Get in and start the motor. Keep your hands on the wheel where I can see them."

Rachel climbed in and turned the keys with shaking fingers. When the motor was running and she was gripping the wheel with both hands, Mayhew climbed into the back seat. Rachel turned her head slightly, just enough to watch him out of the corner of her eye. He wedged the briefcase on the floor between his feet.

Her gaze locked on the case, on the row of brass studs, the scar on the corner. Where was the FBI? Where was Eberle? Bile rose, burning her throat.

Mayhew's voice seemed to come from a great distance. Her mind barely registered his words as she fought the hysteria that threatened.

"Back out of here slowly. Leave the lights off. Wait!"

From the highway came a squeal of tires as two of the FBI cars charged out of the side road and raced towards Hilo. Seconds later another car came out and turned to the west. When they were out of sight, Mayhew ordered her to back out and turn west. In the darkness, it was almost impossible to see the road. When she nearly missed a curve and struggled to keep from going in the ditch, Mayhew told her to turn on headlights but to keep them on the low beam. With relief she complied.

Rachel drove automatically, her mind racing like a hamster in a cage. They had to stop Mayhew, had to retrieve the bacteria. How? She glanced out of the corner of her eye at David then back at the road. If they acted together... She spotted a car blocking the road ahead and her heart leapt.

Mayhew spotted it at the same time. "Stop. Pull over and turn off your lights."

Rachel obeyed. The tropical darkness closed in like a wet blanket. Had they been seen? Surely they had. She could hear Mayhew's ragged breathing, and a moment later the rustle of paper. A match flared. She risked turning her head. He was studying a road map.

"Okay. Turn on your parking lights. Back up. That's it. Now turn down between those trees. We're going to cut across country a couple of miles."

Rachel followed his directions, driving through the brush at a snail's pace, her heart in her mouth. It would have been bad in good daylight. In the darkness, it was pure hell.

Sweat poured off her face, ran in rivulets down her back and only partly from the humid heat. Her fingers ached from gripping the wheel, her shoulders and neck stiff from tension.

Twice they nearly tipped over when the rank humus slid out from under the weight of the downhill tires.

The jeep plowed up a steep rise covered with low vegetation. Suddenly, the tires lost traction on the damp foliage, spun impotently; then the jeep slid backwards and came to a jarring halt.

Rachel downshifted but the jeep refused to move. She threw it into reverse but the rear wheels continued to spin. Mayhew leaned forward and cuffed the back of her head. "Bitch. Stop playing games. Get us out of here."

David spoke, his voice calm. "I think we're hung up. Want me to take a look?"

"You stay where you are." He tapped Rachel on the shoulder. "Get out and see what's wrong. If you're playing games, your boyfriend gets his head blown off."

Rachel climbed out of the jeep, and pushing a tangle of creepers aside, knelt and peered under the jeep. The rear differential was balanced on a rock.

Crawling to the back of the jeep, she dropped to her belly, slithered under and tore the vines away. The soil underneath was fairly soft. She called to Mayhew, "We're hung on a rock. Is there a jack, a shovel?"

The jeep rocked as he moved and she heard him swear. His feet appeared within inches of her hand. Before she could react, he had backed out of reach.

"No. Dig it out with your hands."

"What about a tree limb or something?" David asked.

"No," snarled Mayhew. "This soil's loose enough to just dig with your hands and get that rock out."

She clawed at the ground until her arms ached and her fingers began to bleed. Crawling out, she leaned against the bole of a tree. Mayhew raised the gun. She stared at it indifferently. "Got to rest," she panted.

269

He glanced from her to David. "You. Get under there and keep digging."

David climbed out of the jeep, rolling his shoulders and shaking his arms. Mayhew backed away as David moved around the jeep and squirmed underneath. Twenty minutes later, she heard him grunt. A screech of metal followed and the jeep tottered and settled onto its tires. As soon as David crawled out, Mayhew motioned them back inside.

Now. It had to be now. She had to make a move.

She whirled and kicked. The side of her foot connected with his arm and the gun went flying into the brush. He scrambled for it and David leaped on his back. Mayhew bucked David off. Rachel aimed another karate kick, this time at his head, but Mayhew was surprisingly fast. He threw himself to the side, did a backwards somersault and came to his feet, too far away for another kick.

David threw himself at Mayhew's legs, toppling the little man into the brush. Rachel advanced as the two men struggled. Before she was in position, a shot rang out and she felt a stinging along her right arm.

Mayhew kicked David in the groin and as he double over in pain, Mayhew slid from beneath him, the gun clenched in his fist. He scrambled to his feet, breathing heavily. He glared down at David then at her. "Back in the jeep," he screamed.

And the nightmare continued. They climbed back into the jeep. Rachel tore a strip of cloth off the bottom of her blouse and wrapped it around her arm. The wound was little more than a scratch. Mayhew tapped her lightly on the shoulder with the barrel of the gun and she started driving.

Suddenly they burst free of the vegetation and onto a paved road. Mayhew ordered her to stop while he studied the map again. Rachel wiped the sweat from her face then casually reached up and adjusted the rear view mirror. In the moment that it reflected Mayhew's bent head, she noticed the map was old and ragged. The intent expression on his face told her that he was unfamiliar with the island.

The flame of the match reached his fingers and he flipped it away with a curse. Wadding the map, he told her to drive. Risking a glance at David, she saw his lips pulled back in a grotesque grin over clenched teeth. He nodded slightly.

She turned on the parking lights then threw the jeep in gear and drove slowly down the road. Minutes, which seemed like hours, later they came to a T. Both roads were barricaded. ROAD CLOSED signs glared at them.

Mayhew beat a hand on his thigh, his voice rising shrilly as he cursed. Rachel risked another glance at David. He was no longer grinning. His lips were pressed into a thin white line. A chill raced up her spine.

"Right. Turn right." Mayhew's voice was tight with tension.

Rachel risked commenting, "But the road is closed."

"Probably just a wash out. Nothing this jeep can't maneuver. Go!"

Still Rachel hesitated. A nasty little worm was crawling in her stomach and something was tickling her brain. Mayhew leaned forward and backhanded her.

"Drive, damn it."

She let out the clutch and inched around the barricade. She started to reach for the light switch then stopped when she saw David give a slight shake of the head. The hairs on the back of her neck rose.

The parking lights barely lit the road directly in front of the wheels. Rachel leaned forward, straining to see. Gradually she became conscious of a change in the air. It was hotter but the air seemed drier. The red glow that lit the underside of the clouds seemed lower, brighter. The air was heavy with the stench of burning wood and...and...sulfur?

The shoulder of a hill towered on her right, its edges tipped with an unholy glow. She drove around the shoulder and stared into the brink of hell.

Forty

Molten lava, glowing red and yellow, streamed across the road a few hundred yards ahead. The heat slapped her face with scorching intensity.

As though from a great distance, she heard David yell, "Jump. Rachel, jump."

She saw him arch his back and dive over the seat, grasping for Mayhew. Eberle's words, "Temperatures exceeding 500 degrees Celsius" echoed in her ears.

She risked a glance in the back. A muffled shot sounded. She saw David's body jerk then collapse, pinning Mayhew to the seat.

Her head swiveled back. The glowing inferno was only yards away. The heat was unbearable. She could feel her skin drying, burning. She could hear Mayhew trying to struggle out from beneath David's body. If he escaped...

Richard's face floated before her. She sobbed.

Rachel stomped on the accelerator, felt the tires spin then grab and the jeep charged ahead.

She threw herself out, hit the macadam and rolled onto the gravel. She lifted her head. The jeep plowed into the stream of molten lava. For a split second it was outlined in the red light. Rachel could see Mayhew bucking beneath David's body.

A high-pitched sound filled the air, like a wounded or dying animal. She hid her face in her hands. Then the screaming stopped. Turned to laughter. She looked up. Mayhew was standing in the jeep, holding the attaché case above his head and laughing, laughing like a hyena. Despite the blazing heat from the lava, chills lifted Rachel's flesh into goose bumps. As she watched, Mayhew tottered, dropped the case into lava.

There was a flash, an ear-shattering boom. The jeep exploded in a fiery mass.

The laughter followed her as she sank into a sea of darkness.

Epilogue

Rachel stood in front of the window watching the gentle rain wash the night air. Through its curtain, she could see the glow of a streetlight, haloed in the mist. She absently watched a car pull into the parking lot. Something about the driver's movements as he dashed toward the front door struck a chord. She dismissed the idea and returned to her thoughts.

The horror of the past weeks had begun to take on the surreal texture of a nightmare. She ran her fingers over the scabs on her dry, papery face where the gravel had scraped her skin. The doctor said her injuries would heal without scars, but she knew she would always carry scars inside where they didn't show.

Movement in the waiting room behind her was reflected in the glass. She lifted her gaze from the darkened scene below and turned.

James Eberle walked towards her. He stopped a few feet away. "How is he?"

"The transplant was a success. I'll be able to take him home in a few more days."

He nodded towards the sling holding her left arm. "And how is your gunshot wound and dislocated shoulder?"

"Healing. The bruises are almost all gone, too."

She could see some of the tension leave his face. Slowly, his lips curved into a smile. "Is your husband allowed visitors?"

"Yes. The nurse is with him now, but we can go in as soon as she is finished. It shouldn't be long."

"I have some news but I thought I would give it to you both at once."

She nodded and turned back to the window. She didn't want to hear his news. In the days since she'd been home, she had tried to block out all thoughts of Hawaii, to lock them away in the special room in her mind. It hadn't worked. She frequently awoke in the night, screaming David's name.

A few minutes later, the nurse came out and touched Rachel on the arm. "He's doing fine, Mrs. Royer. He's awake and asking for you. You can go in now."

Richard was sitting up in bed. His eyes lit up as Rachel crossed the room and bent to kiss him. As she settled on the side of the bed, he looked questioningly at Eberle.

"James Eberle, FBI. We met briefly in Los Angeles. I'm here at the personal behest of President Gossard. He felt you had earned the right to know everything that has happened. I'm to answer any questions you have."

Richard shifted himself higher on the bed. "The bacteria?"

"It was completely destroyed. The Center for Disease control has found an antidote and the Israelis have come up with a vaccine."

Rachel leaned forward. "Do you know what Mayhew was planning to do with the bacteria?"

"Oh, yes. As you may know, Calvin Brooks was only wounded. He made a full confession. Actually, he bragged about it. Seemed to think they deserved a medal." He shook his head. "Mayhew thought our last few presidents were too soft. He thought the changes taking place throughout Eastern Europe were simply a plot to make us lower our guard while the communists rebuilt their economies. He saw the Chinese scheme as the perfect way to wipe out all our enemies. He wanted the shipment destined for Russia to be dispensed as planned. The bacteria he hijacked was to be returned to China and dispersed in their own water system."

Richard gasped, "My God, the man was mad! Surely he couldn't have gotten away with it?"

"I'm afraid he almost did. The old Chinese that met him in Hawaii was one of the biggest smugglers in the Orient. With a dozen or more routes into and out of China." He shook his head. "In a way, we've benefited from this. Word of their close escape has filtered back to Beijing. It isn't common knowledge, yet, but a number of heads have fallen and there has been quite a shakeup in their top brass. I think we'll see a more moderate stance taken by China in the near future. Gossard talked with the Russian President. We've let the Russians know, in no uncertain terms, that they owe us and the Israelis."

"What about the CIA agent Rachel killed?"

"Your wife acted in self defense. No charges will be brought. The matter has been closed. By the way, Rachel, you have been granted full American citizenship and all records of your identity as Zephyr have been destroyed. Our Witness Protection program has built your complete history into the records. Birth certificate, school records, medical records, a complete, verifiable identity. It has been done is such a way that no agency will ever be able to penetrate it again." He grinned. "Not even the Mossad. Any more questions?"

Rachel and Richard both shook their heads.

Eberle smiled. "Then I'd better get on to the rest. As soon as you are well enough, Richard, the president has invited both of you to be his guests at the White House. You are both to receive a Presidential Citation."

Rachel stood and began to pace the room, her face rigid. "No. I don't want any award. I just want us to be left in peace. If there are any awards, they should go to David Bergdorf's family."

"I agree with my wife," Richard said.

Eberle's smile faded. "David is being awarded the Medal of Freedom. It will be presented to his parents next week."

Rachel resumed her seat on the edge of the bed. She picked up Richard's hand and squeezed it. Looking up at Eberle, she said, "Then it's finally over."

"Yes. Well, I have to get back to Washington."

When the door closed behind the FBI man, Richard reached up and stroked Rachel's cheek. He traced the line of her jaw, cupped her chin in his hand, his eyes dancing.

"I'll be out of here next week. When does that sling come off?"

"Friday. Why?"

His voice was soft and she leaned forward to catch his words. "What would you say to starting a family next week?"

Meet Judith R. Parker

Judith R. Parker is a retired corporate CFO who resides in the Cascade Mountains of central Washington state with her husband, two dogs and six cats. She is a member of Western Writers of America, Women Writing the West, Sisters-in-Crime, and is a former board member of the Northwest Chapter of Mystery Writers of America.